DRAGON SHADOW

RECLAIMING THE FIRE #1

ALICIA WOLFE

Cover by Clarissa Yeo

CHAPTER 1

I shivered as I sensed new magic. The taste of it spilled over my tongue, rich and coppery, and I could feel the almost electric tingle along my arms. The mage was doing another one of his displays. I wished I could see it from my perch behind the penthouse bar, but he was in another room.

"Nice stems, angel."

I tried—and failed—not to roll my eyes. The man who ran the catering company had all the girls dress in what amounted to formal-wear hot pants, so I was bare-legged all the way to my heels. Heels *and* hot pants, and I was handing the guy who'd spoken two glasses of champagne. Glasses with long stems... Yeah, hence the eye roll.

Instead of biting the jerk's head off, though, I smiled and said, "I hope you enjoy the drinks." I probably should have added *sir* to the end of that, but I just couldn't make myself.

Rather than leaving the bar, he lingered, leaning on the bar itself and letting his gaze travel down my bare legs again. He was a good-looking guy, dressed in a tuxedo like every other man here, and he filled his out well. But he was a class-A creep just the same, I could tell from his leer.

"You know," he said, gesturing with one of his new champagne glasses—which sloshed a bit—he'd better not ask me to refill it—toward the dance floor, "I could talk to your supervisor. Maybe get you some time off. I'd love to take you for a twirl on the floor."

His eyes said he'd like to do more than take me for a *twirl*. Still, it was kind of tempting. I'd never been to a fancy ball in a penthouse atop a skyscraper in the post-Fae New York—or any other New York, for that matter. Magical glowing balls hovered above the dance floor, casting shifting waves of golden light. In the center, a magical fountain jetted scented pink water high into the air, where the droplets seemed to fizz and flicker. *Like a dream,* I thought.

But this guy was an ass, and I had a job to do. And I don't mean bartending. That was just a cover.

I put on my sweetest smile. "What would *she* say about that?"

"She?"

I nodded at the second champagne glass. "The lady who's going to drink that."

His expression soured, and so did his tone. Not even bothering to deny that I'd caught him out, he said, "Your loss, hon."

I'd been demoted from *angel* to *hon.*

"I can live with that," I said.

He grunted and moved off through the crowd, knocking past two people coming the other way and cursing at them.

"Nice," said Lydia, and I turned to see my fellow hot-pants-wearing bartender. She, too, wore a black bow-tie over what amounted to a formal-wear halter top with sequins and a cute black top hat. I had to admit, the hats *were* kind of precious. "You're never going to get tips that way," she added.

I could've told her that soon I wouldn't need any tips. *Once Ruby gets in position.*

"I'll be nicer to the next one," I promised.

"I hope so. I don't want Frank to get mad at you."

Frank was the guy who ran the catering company. The one

who put us in these outfits to be ogled at and propositioned by the rich folk of the city. A real winner.

"I've handled guys worse than him," I said.

Lydia raised her eyebrows. "You just joined the company today, right?" When I nodded, she said, "Well, don't say I told you this, but Frank is on edge tonight. I think it has something to do with the Fae Lord."

I glanced up as a woman approached the bar. Damn. She wore a dress that flowed like quicksilver—I mean, it *moved,* rippling like liquid silver. Metallic silver glints showed in her hair, too, and silver fringed her lashes. But that dress…I couldn't resist a swell of jealousy at seeing it. It had been made with the help of a magic-user and must have cost a fortune. And it was *gorgeous.*

"One vodka, please," she said. "In a chilled glass."

Swallowing down my comeback—*Of course, Frosty*—I poured her the drink, collected a small tip, and sent her on her way.

I turned back to Lydia. "What about a Fae Lord?"

She gestured toward the festivities around us—all the nobs talking, dancing, and generally partying while a fancy orchestra made music on a stage to the right and the mage, having returned to the main room, created magical displays overhead: glittering rainbows, vistas of enchanted cities, alien skies. The host, Walther Hawthorne, my mark, had to be damn rich to afford all this. It shouldn't surprise me he was connected to the Fae.

"One of them is coming here," Lydia said, sounding breathless, and no wonder. Ever since the Fae Lords crossed over into our world from the Fae Lands ten years ago, society had transformed around them. Now one of the actual Fae Lords was due to show up at the party? I had to admit, I was torn. I'd never seen a Fae Lord before—at least in person; they were all over the news—and I was more than curious. I absolutely yearned to lay my eyes on one of the enchanted beings. But I couldn't linger. As soon as Ruby was in position…

"That's amazing," I made myself say.

"Isn't it?" She grinned from ear to ear, her excitement obvious. "I hope he orders a drink! I would love to…to…" She was so eager she couldn't even get the words out.

"To speak with him?" I finished, and she did a little dance.

"That would be badass," she agreed and turned to help the next guest.

I laughed and took a new order, then another. Just as I was pouring a drink, a voice in my head sounded. I nearly jumped.

"I'm ready," the voice said.

Get it together, Jade. It was only my sister Ruby, talking via a magic earbud. The earbud looked just like part of my right earring. Fortunately, Frank hadn't legislated *those,* as well. Ruby spoke so softly I probably wouldn't have been able to hear her at all if I hadn't been a shifter—well, half shifter, anyway.

Somehow, I managed not to spill the drink I'd just poured. Handing it to the guest, I told Lydia, "I need to step out for a moment."

"No worries." She scanned the crowd, face eager for the arrival of the Fae Lord.

I grabbed my little backpack. After excusing myself, I ducked out of the main ballroom and into the more silent corridors of the rest of the penthouse. I passed the hangar where some of the guests had arrived in their enchanted flying steeds, airships, and cars, and I have to admit I *oooh*ed at seeing a floating, cherry-red Jaguar hovering off the ground by magic. These rich folks sure knew how to live.

I pushed even deeper into the penthouse, pausing when I saw two guards ahead. They would prevent guests from going into the personal, off-limits areas of the home. Not a problem. I retraced my steps to the restroom I'd just passed. Going in, I locked it behind me, then quickly shucked off my hot-pants outfit, even my cute hat, and opened my backpack.

Right on cue, Ruby said, "Everything okay?"

"Everything's fine," I said, stepping into my sleek black

leggings, then pulling the shadowy, slinky top down over my head. After that, I strapped on my thin utility belt—think a sexier version of Batman's belt—and shoved my feet into my slippers. A glance in the mirror showed a badass, magically assisted cat burglar dressed in slinky black. Purple highlights glimmered in my raven-black hair, and my eyes burned green out of a half-smiling and, I like to think, not bad-looking face.

"I'm ready," I said. "Game face on. You still in position?"

"Yeah, but it's damn cold out here, sis, so hurry this up."

I nodded, picturing Ruby on her flying broomstick—cloaked with very expensive and hard-to-come-by magic—shivering in the high-altitude winds outside the east wing of the penthouse. She had a magical stone to keep her warm, but it could only do so much. She must be freezing.

"I'll hurry," I promised.

Smiling in anticipation, as this was always my favorite part, I stood on the bathroom sink, only tottering a little, and used my screwdriver to unscrew the bolts around the air vent. Then I went back to the door, listened hard to make sure no one was coming, unlocked it so as not to arouse suspicion, and climbed back onto the sink. With some effort—that burrito at lunch had been a bad idea—I slithered into the duct. I've always been small and light, but Walter Hawthorne had ducts in proportion to the rest of his home, and I could fit by only holding my breath a little.

Using a spell I had perfected over the years, I summoned the vent grate back to the opening, sealing it behind me.

I inched forward slowly, not wanting to make too much noise. The object I needed was in Hawthorne's study. The only problem was that, in examining the duct system diagrams, I'd realized that to go all the way to the study this way would take me an hour, and I didn't have an hour. Ruby sure didn't.

I merely shimmied through that tight, moldy tube until I'd passed where the two guards had been lurking, then, taking care to be even more silent than before, pried open the vent and dropped stealthily onto the carpeted floor. *Take that, Houdini.*

Now to get what I'd come for.

I crept through the halls, careful to be as silent as possible. Swearing under my breath—Ruby said I swore too much, and she was probably right—I passed through a doorway and into a massive mahogany study: gleaming wood everywhere, with a large draped window behind the grand desk. Objects cluttered the room: Egyptian statues, little obelisks, and an ornate gong in one corner.

I stood still, listening hard. The wind against the window, a subtle creak of wood off to my left. Was someone there? No, it was just settling.

I surveyed the surroundings with a critical eye, then crossed to the desk, moving around to the other side, alert to possible booby traps of the magical kind. Sure enough, I felt an energy barrier. The fine hairs lifted along my arms.

Thinking quickly, I scooped a certain leaf from a pouch hanging from my belt—I carried several—and said under my breath, *"Lu'gan'ai, guth'gan'ai, ruthe-vain!"*

The energy barrier dissolved, my hairs relaxed, and I knelt before the safe, which was built into the drawers on one side of the desk.

I studied the black metal door. My half-shifter blood enabled me to see well in the dark, so that was no problem. It also made me a little faster and stronger than normal humans, but that was all. I'd lost the ability to actually shift a long time ago. Well, technically, it had been stolen from me. But I didn't have time to think about that now.

I reached for the dial. *Shit,* I thought, feeling another magical hum. A *second* barrier. Hawthorne was really cautious. Just what was he keeping in this damned thing? I'd come for something, but that item didn't warrant this level of protection.

I'm asking the client for a raise. I wasn't getting paid enough for this crap.

The next barrier proved trickier to overcome. I dug through the small pouches on my belt and plucked out a root of the tash tree and a sprinkle of hellhound-bone dust. Lathering the root in the dust, I closed my eyes and pictured a sun shining over a mountain. Holding that image firmly in my head, I said, "Open, you sonofabitch."

The barrier dissolved, and the safe door swung outward.

Darkness gaped where it had been.

I sucked in a breath and leaned forward, having to peer hard into the gloom. It was resisting even my shifter sight. At last, though, I saw two metal shelves, some paper money, coins, a few contracts...and there!

I grinned and reached inside, plucking out the little enspelled mirror the bastard had been using to spy on my client with.

"Like to watch young women with their clothes off, do you?" I said. "Well, it'll serve you right if other people watch *you* with this."

I snickered and reached behind my back, shoving the mirror inside my pack, right into the cushioned depression I'd created for it. I was just about to rise and go when another object caught my attention. It rested on the top shelf of the safe, behind where the mirror had perched...way in the back. Without my shifter senses, it would have been impossible to see, but I did, if only vaguely. What was it?

Somehow, I just knew. *This* was the object Hawthorne had wanted protected. *This* was the thing he'd spent so much time and money building magical barriers to safeguard.

I paused.

Just go, I thought. *You've got the mirror, girl. Just bug the hell out. Change, go back to the party, and no one will ever know who broke in here.*

But I couldn't. Some impish part of me just had to twist the knife a little deeper into the perverted, pompous assbag. Taking the mirror didn't seem like enough punishment. That just prevented him from being more of an asshole. It didn't really punish him for having *already* been an asshole.

Also, well—I was curious. And we all know where curiosity led the cat. Or, in this case, the cat burglar.

Nowhere good.

Holding back a laugh, very pleased with myself, I reached deep into the safe...deeper...almost there... My fingers brushed the object—what *was* it?—grabbed hold, and yanked it out.

"Ha!"

Balanced on the palm of my hand was a golden antler, as if from a deer, curved gently and sporting a dozen points. It glittered faintly in the dim room.

I felt a huge smile split my face. The thing was *gorgeous.*

"Ooh," I whispered. "You're something special, aren't you?"

I slipped it inside a net dangling from my hips—just in case I saw something I couldn't resist and that didn't fit in my pouches, like now—and let it fall against my thigh. I couldn't wait to get it to Jason's and begin studying it with Ruby. Just what had I caught, anyway?

I rose and retraced my steps, leaving the study and making my way back down the hall. Ruby was supposed to meet me on the east terrace, collect the mirror (and anything else) and go, while I returned to Lydia and the—

Movement. Directly ahead.

I'd been passing through an intersection of two hallways, and I had barely noticed the gargoyles that perched in the shadowed corners of the crossing. Now the gargoyles' eyes sprang open, burning with magical fire.

"Shit!"

I leapt back on instinct, my legs coiling and my hand darting to the crossbow at my hip. It had saved my ass more than once, and it didn't make as much noise as a gun.

The gargoyles shifted on their perches. When they spun slowly around, all four stared at me, eerie life shining in their eyes, their own bodies tensing for action. These things *lived.*

"Holy jeez, Ruby," I said. "I think there might be a change in plan."

"Like what?"

"Like—"

Two of the gargoyles shook themselves and sprang down from their perches. Their batwings opened and caught the air, even though the little bastards couldn't have weighed less than a hundred pounds each. One flew right at my head. I dodged aside, feeling the wind from the thing—creature?—as it flew past.

I lifted my right hand to shoot it with my crossbow, as if that would have done any good against a stone demon, and the second one slammed into my hand, sending the weapon spinning. Pain flared up my arm, but I didn't think anything had been broken. It had been aiming at the weapon, not my flesh. I wouldn't be that lucky a second time.

The other two gargoyles jumped down and took wing.

"Damn," I said.

One zoomed toward my head. I ducked under it and pelted down the corridor I'd just come down, going back toward the study. A gargoyle came at me; I heard it. Twisting my head, I saw it flying straight at my back. If that thing hit me going full speed, it would snap my spine.

"Shit shit shit," I muttered, then flung myself to the ground. The gargoyle blasted through the air right over me, then flew on.

"Jade," Ruby said in my ear, and I nearly had a heart attack. "Are you okay?"

"I—" I swallowed. "I'm fine. New plan. Pick me up at the study. South side, same floor."

"But—"

"Just do it!"

I pushed myself to all fours, then ran toward the study again.

Glancing over my shoulder, I saw all four of the damned things racing straight at me.

Breathless, I crossed the threshold of the study, grabbed its sturdy oak door, and slammed it closed. Bang! The impact of the gargoyles nearly knocked the door off its hinges. Feeling sweat sting my eyes, I watched the door to see if it would explode inward. Instead, I heard the buzzing of the gargoyles' wings and realized they must be drawing back for another strike. I hoped the door had some magical reinforcement, but I knew I couldn't count on that.

I moved to the window behind the desk and ripped open the drapes. Sure enough, Ruby was just pulling her flying broomstick into position on the other side of the glass. Her red hair streamed out behind her pretty, pale young face, and I could see how cold she was, but also how fearless.

I hadn't wanted to enter the penthouse this way because I knew there would be some hellacious wards on that window, but tripping a magical alarm didn't matter anymore. Without hesitation, I picked up the desk lamp and smashed it against the window with all my strength.

Green sparks flashed. A magical blast flung me backward over the desk. I crashed against the door—which bucked against me. Hard. The gargoyles had hit it again.

Stumbling forward, I glared backward to see that cracks had formed in the door, then looked at the window. Through it, Ruby gave me a look and tapped her watch.

Gritting my teeth, I returned to the window.

"Bastard better not do that again," I said and laid my palm flat against the glass. I'd have to use more magic. That both thrilled and terrified me.

"*Cru'nom'shundra,*" I intoned, holding an image in my head of two spears flying.

The protective energy suffusing the window dispersed; I could see the green glow ripple outward. After that, it was easy. I reached out, unlocked the window, and swung it open. Frigid air gusted in, flapping the papers on the desk and making my hair stream behind me. I ignored it as I climbed onto the windowsill.

Boom!

The doors crashed open.

Without looking back, I jumped onto the broomstick behind Ruby, and she took off into the night. Only when I was settled did I glance back. I saw a strange dark figure standing on the roof of the penthouse building, wind whipping his cloak around him. A shiver ran through me.

Just who was that guy and what the hell was he doing lurking on the roof? Was he another thief? He certainly wasn't one of Hawthorne's guards. But somehow he didn't look like a thief either. I sensed powerful magic about him.

I didn't have time to think about it for long, though. The four gargoyles had knocked the door off its hinges, and I'd stupidly left the window open. If I'd been thinking straight, I would have closed it and ensorcelled it to resist them. If I could have come up with such a spell, anyway—something I doubted. Those things were strong.

The gargoyles flew out of the window and blasted right for us. Their eyes shone like death.

CHAPTER 2

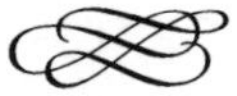

"Did you get it?" Ruby shouted over the wind.

"Focus on your driving!"

"I'm not driving, I'm flying," she said.

"Good, because you're a terrible driver!"

"If those gargoyles don't get us, I'm going to kill you."

"Just make sure they don't."

I glanced over my shoulder. The little buggers were right on our heels like a cloud of angry bees, but unlike bees, they didn't sting. They didn't need to. One good strike from one could cave in our heads, and I'd spent way too much time on my head over the years to see it bashed in by a lump of ugly stone.

"Go faster!" I screamed.

"I'm trying!"

The broom rocketed forward, and I had to grab tight around Ruby's waist or be thrown off. My stomach flipped.

"Watch it," I said.

Ruby's laugh carried over the wind, and I resisted the urge to curse. Her sense of humor sucked.

She'd built leather seats onto the back of the broom, so it wasn't as uncomfortable as her Salem ancestors' brooms probably had been, but that didn't help the sensation of vertigo that sucked at me when I glanced down to see fifty stories plunging straight to the street. Damn, I hated heights. Especially when I wasn't in control of the situation. Ironic that once, long ago, I could fly under my own power.

Ruby turned sharply at the next intersection, and I gritted my teeth as my stomach lurched. I glanced back.

"They still back there?" Ruby shouted over her shoulder.

"Yep."

I didn't tell her how close they were. That would only distract her. But they *were* close, and it was certainly distracting *me*. I could almost reach out and touch them.

I racked my brain for some spell that would slow them down, but my mind was blank. Ruby was the real spellcaster, anyway, not me. I knew just enough magic to help steal things. Because of my half-shifter abilities, I got to do the actual burgling while all Ruby had to do was cast a few spells and hang out on her broom. Not a bad gig, really.

Except for times like now.

"Lose them in traffic," I suggested.

"What traffic?"

She was right, damn it. The upper reaches of the city were reserved only for the vehicles of the wealthy, and though a few enchanted cars, animals and dirigibles tore through the canyons of steel and stone, there weren't many at this hour, certainly not enough to be called traffic.

"How are they even seeing us?" Ruby said.

She had used a spell to cloak her broom; otherwise, we would've been set upon by the cops' aerial division, mounted on their griffons. They kept a close watch on the upper levels. The gargoyles' eyes could see through her spell, though, just like I could.

"Hawthorne's got some powerful magic," I told her. "Magical

barriers and everything. I'm glad we spent the money on those extra spellgredients."

"Better be worth it."

I thought of the golden antler. "I think it will be."

She swerved a hard right at the next intersection, then ducked down an alley. She took one cross-alley, then another. Before long, I was dizzy with the twists and turns, only half convinced I knew what direction we faced. Finally, I swiveled my head to see the gargoyles streak by the alleyway Ruby had just turned down. They hadn't seen us enter.

"I think we lost them," I panted.

"Are you sure?"

"I'm sure I *think* we lost them."

Ruby slowed the broom and wiped her forehead. "Man, that was tense. Are they really gone?"

"We'll find out in a moment."

My heart thumped rapidly in my chest as we waited to see whether the gargoyles would return and set after us again, but the little stone bastards didn't come back and no cry of alarm went up from the aerial police division. I slumped in relief, and I could see Ruby begin to relax, too.

"I don't get it," she said. "Magical flying gargoyles that have enough autonomy to pursue a flying target through a crowded city—that's some major mojo right there. A lot more than necessary to protect a scrying mirror."

"Don't forget the magical barriers and alarms, too."

"What gives? None if it makes sense."

I patted the golden antler against my thigh, but she was half turned around on the broom and probably couldn't see it very well. Noticing the puzzled expression on her face, I said, "I'll tell you later. But there's more to this than the mirror, although I'm not sure what. We might have stumbled onto something big. Let's just get the meeting with the client over with. Then we'll discuss what's what at Jason's."

"Deal—hey, look."

Ruby pointed to something above us. Craning my head, I saw a great skyscraper in the distance framed between the walls of the alley. An elaborate and beautiful palace jutted from the top of the building, its slender white towers blazing with lights. There were a dozen castles atop a dozen buildings in Fae New York these days, but that was *the* castle—or Palace, as it was called. The home of the Fae Queen herself.

Magic had always existed, but in the shadows, hidden from most of humankind. As a half-shifter, I'd known about it, even been part of it, but I couldn't have revealed myself to the average person because we weren't supposed to exist. When the Fae had come, though, they brought a great deal of magic with them, more than could be hidden, and they didn't even try to conceal it. Their magic had changed the world.

"Lot of activity going on there," I said, noting the specs that must be winged horses and other flying steeds of the Fae nobility swarming about the Palace.

"Wonder what the Queen's up to?" Ruby said.

"Yeah. Interesting that it's happening tonight."

"What do you mean?"

"One of the Fae Lords was supposed to be at the party at Hawthorne's."

"Huh." She tapped her chin and seemed to mull on it, then shook the thought away. "Well, whatever it is, it can't have anything to do with us."

I thought of the figure crouched on the roof of Hawthorne's penthouse. "Yeah," I said. "Nothing to do with us. Let's get a move on. This broom's killing me. Seriously, sis, you need to invest in better cushions."

Half an hour later, we sat at the breakfast table of our client, Dorrie Weisman, who lived in an apartment across town. She laughed and clapped her hands when we showed her the scrying mirror.

"You did it," she said. "You really did it!"

She hugged me, then Ruby, and we tried not to look embarrassed.

"All in a day's work, ma'am," I said, tipping an imaginary cowboy hat and speaking in what I thought was a Southern drawl.

Dorrie beamed. She was a pretty young woman, and she'd recently been a maid at Hawthorne's penthouse until he developed an unhealthy fixation on her. She'd quit, but had been plagued by nightmares about him spying on her. After consulting with a psychic—who were totally legit these days; at least a lot of them—she discovered the reason she'd been having the nightmares was because Hawthorne, the creep-fest, was magically spying on her.

Luckily, the psychic knew about Ruby and me, and she'd recommended our services to the maid. Stealing magical items from assholes was what we did for a living.

"I'm so happy it's all over," Dorrie said. Quickly, she wrote a check and passed it to Ruby, who made the check disappear—probably the first magic trick she'd ever learned.

"Don't go," Dorrie said. "I want to celebrate. Care for a bottle of wine?"

"I would love s—" Ruby said, but I shook my head and she fell silent.

"We really can't," I told Dorrie. "And Ruby's only twenty."

"Only till next month," Ruby protested. I swear, she was only four years younger than I was, but sometimes she acted much younger.

"We've got to make tracks," I said, ignoring her. "Hawthorne might still be looking for us."

Dorrie sighed. "Can I see it?"

I fished out the scrying mirror from my backpack and let her hold it.

"This is what he was spying on me with?" she said, and we nodded.

"He's a turd sandwich," Ruby said, and I was impressed. Still, maybe she'd been spending too much time around her big sis.

"Last chance," I told Dorrie. "We'll still let you have it if you want."

Rudy and I offered two pricing structures to our clients: our fee for furnishing the item to them and the price for just making sure the asshat who was using it against them couldn't do it anymore. That cost a lot less, but we offset the loss by selling the stolen item to a fence.

"Tempting," Dorrie said. "I'd like to see how *he* feels waking up in the middle of the night, knowing someone was watching him. But nah, I wouldn't want to." She studied us. "I just want to make sure that you're not reselling it to some jerk who'll do the same thing Walter was."

"Don't worry," Ruby assured her. "We would never do that. Most scrying mirrors are used in magical rites to commune with other dimensions and things, not playing Peeping Tom. We'll make sure it winds up with a mage or someone who will use it properly."

Dorrie nodded and hugged us again. Tears of relief glimmered in her eyes. At seeing her emotion, my own throat closed, and my voice was a little raw as I said goodbye. Ruby gave me a knowing look as we bundled onto her broom—leaving from the fire escape, where the broom had been tied off—and headed into the madness of the city.

"She was nice," Ruby said, leading.

"Yeah." My throat was still a bit closed, and I didn't trust myself to say anything more. Seeing Dorrie had triggered something in me—a vulnerable young woman trying to overcome being abused by a magic-user. Yeah, that hit a little too close to home. Trying to hide my emotion, I cleared my throat and said, "Let's go see Jason."

Ruby half-turned, a grin on her face. "You big softie."

I punched her shoulder. "Just drive, Ginger Witch."

She laughed, flipped me the bird, and gunned the metaphorical motor. The broom shot forward, bound for Jason's.

Our main fence for the past two years, Jason Mattox specialized in finding homes for stolen magical items. I'd picked him because, unlike a lot of fences, he didn't just resell the item to the highest bidder. He made sure the item wouldn't be misused by the buyer first, which was something I respected—and required. Like Ruby told Dorrie, we weren't just in this for the money. We were trying to make a difference. Magic had brought a lot of wonder to the world, but it had given unfair advantage to some assholes who really didn't deserve it, too. Ruby and I liked to think of ourselves as doing the world a tidy service. While making a tidy profit, of course.

We found Jason at his cluttered shop in Queens. New York had changed a lot since the coming of the Fae—the Arrival, people called it, or sometimes the Fae-rival—but Queens was still Queens. Jason operated out of a pawnshop, and Ruby and I didn't bother entering from the front. Ruby parked on the roof and tied the broom off, just like cowboys used to tie off horses, only with less tobacco spitting, and we entered from the rooftop entrance. We knew the secret code.

Trundling down the narrow stairs, we found Jason hunched over a bench in the large storeroom in back of his shop. Strange objects on benches and shelves cluttered the dingy space—weird gears, things with too many limbs in jars, a doll pacing back and forth under its own power—and many of them emitted a magical crackle of energy. One of Jason's underlings must be minding the store up front.

Jason rose and smiled at us when he heard our footsteps; well, mainly, he smiled at Ruby. Sweat shone on his dark-skinned face and glistened on his firm biceps.

"Whatcha working on?" Ruby asked with deceptive casualness, sauntering up to him and peering down at what he'd been studying. She made sure to do it slowly, letting him get a good look at her cleavage as she bent over. I tried not to laugh.

She had bumped him lightly as she passed him—very deliberately—and he seemed momentarily tongue-tied.

"Well—I—I, mean—" He swallowed. Obviously trying not to look at Ruby, who was partly bent over right next to him while she pretended to examine the item he'd been working on, he said, "It's an enchanted clock. Ancient, like three hundred years old. Long before the Fae arrived, but it still possesses magic. At first, I thought it was very cunning clockwork, but after looking at it, I can now positively say it's magic."

"What's magic?" I said, drawing closer and looking at the beautiful old cuckoo clock.

"This," he said, touching something on the side of the device.

Instantly, the cuckoo door popped open and tiny figures burst out on a little dais. Dressed like old-timey Europeans, they danced in a circle, men and women, and I gasped at how intricate and graceful their dance was, almost as if the figures were alive, the dresses swooping and swishing, the men smiling and nodding. Music accompanied the dancing, too, waltzy old orchestral music. At last, the dancers quit dancing, bowed to each other, and vanished inside the clock. As soon as they were gone, the music stopped.

"Magic did that?" Ruby asked, wonder on her face.

Jason smiled at her appreciation. His chest sticking out a little, he said, "Isn't that wild? I didn't think an animation spell could last this long, not in a simple clock, but the proof is right there. I've done some tests. No one has renewed the spell in at least two hundred years."

Tapping her chin, Ruby squinted at the clock, then moved around the bench to examine it more. She moved her hips just slightly more than necessary, and I had to resist a grin. Jason noticed her hip-swaying, too, though I didn't think *he* realized it was intentional. Ruby, I realized, was beginning to be a total slut.

I approved.

"I think it's the wood," she said.

His Adam's apple bobbed up and down. "The...wood?"

Her cheeks flushed. Tapping the clock, she said, "The *wood*, you idiot."

"Oh. Right."

"It's some sort of oak, but I don't recognize the kind. Maybe if—"

I cleared my throat, and Ruby frowned at me.

Sighing, she said, "I think what my *very rude sister* means is that we should do business first, *then* examine the clock." To me, she rather pointedly said, "Maybe Jason and I can examine it in *private* while you go do broody loner half-shifter burglar things."

I rolled my eyes. "Whatever. Jason, are you ready for some business?"

Reluctantly, he nodded, switching his attention from Ruby—this clearly took some effort—to me. "Whatcha got?"

I showed him the mirror, and he quickly examined it, seeming only somewhat impressed, and named a dollar figure. It proved higher than I was expecting, but I tried to raise it anyway.

"That was my final offer," he said firmly, not going for it.

I opened my mouth to argue, then caught Ruby's narrow-eyed look. I huffed. "Fine. Accepted."

Why was she sticking up for *Jason?* She should be using her hold over him to exert a higher price for *us*. Someday, I would have to teach her better.

He gave me the money, and then set the mirror down on another workbench so he could examine it more thoroughly before he sold it. He liked to know exactly what he had before letting it go. He was more of a collector than a seller and part of him hated to let go of the items, I knew, but business was business, and he did it briskly.

Normally, this would have concluded things, and Ruby and I

would have gone on our way—or maybe she would have stayed, the scamp—but today wasn't a normal day.

My hand strayed to the golden antler, still in its netting on my hip.

Jason seemed to recognize my distraction. Frowning, probably eager to begin his alone time with Ruby so they could, ah, *study the clock*, he gazed down to the antler.

"What's that?"

Strangely, part of me was hesitant to give it up. Shaking off the weird notion—*money was money, honey*—I removed the antler from its netting and held it up to the light.

"We found this in the same safe the…"

I stopped when his eyes went wide. Jason was black, but in that moment, his skin turned ashen.

"What?" Ruby asked, sounding breathless. Her hand darted toward his, as if to reassure him, but at the last moment she drew it back.

Jason visibly shook it off, whatever it was. Color returned to his face. "That," he said, speaking slowly and dramatically, "is the antler of a Golden Hind."

"Why did I have to get the hind part?" I said. "I should've gone for the front."

Jason leveled a sour look at me. "That's not funny."

"I thought it was pretty funny," Ruby said, hiding a snicker behind her hand.

"Let me take a closer look at it," Jason said.

We gathered around his great table. He examined the antler with a range of instruments, all magical, from enhanced magnifying glasses to larger, more steampunky apparatuses. I tapped my foot in impatience and would have lit a cigarette, but Ruby had made me quit last year. I'd just been on the verge of forgiving her, too.

"Well?" Ruby asked eagerly when Jason leaned back.

"It really is," he said, sounding awed.

"Is *what?*" I said, wishing again for a cigarette.

"The antler of Golden Hind."

"You've heard of those," Ruby told me, as if I were an idiot.

"Remind me," I said.

"Mythical beings," she said. "Golden deer with magical properties."

"Long ago, when the Fae first started coming here—short trips, not like their recent migration—they brought some of the Hinds with them," Jason said. "Or maybe the Hinds came on their own, I don't know. Some legends say they're intelligent. The Hinds are all gone now, or I thought they were. This antler must come from the Fae Lands. Or..."

"Or what?" Ruby questioned, looking up at him. The profound respect and care she had for him was reflected on her face.

"Well, it could be one of the lost Hinds. The ones that came over all those years ago. Only why would this antler be surfacing now? Jade, you say you found this in a penthouse...of a human?"

"That's right. He's not even a mage or anything, although he employs them."

Jason rubbed his face. "That antler is a powerful thing, guys. It's not the sort of object people have lying around or even stored in a safe. If this Hawthorne guy had it at his *home*, that means he was planning to use it."

"What for?" Ruby asked.

"I don't know. Maybe..."

"Yes?"

He shook his head. "I'll have to study it more. If Hawthorne had hired a mage to begin some magical working with it, the imprint of that might still be embedded in the antler. Give me some time and I'll examine it closer. Then maybe I can figure this out."

"I don't know why it matters," I said. "Just name a price and I'll see if I like it."

Jason's jaw fell open. "You would *sell* it to me?"

"What else would I do with it? Use it as a paperweight? A back scratcher?"

That seemed to stump him. "Good question."

Ruby shook her finger at me. "Jade, we can't just sell it, or get rid of it. We nearly died getting this thing, and a very bad man—well, at least *a* bad man—was up to something with it that may or may not involve the Fae Lords. Something is *up* with this thing, Jade. Maybe..."

"Yeah?"

"Maybe something...*bad*."

Her words held a gravity and a level of doom I normally didn't hear from her. Now that she knew the antler belonged to a Golden Hind, something seemed to have changed in her. It was as if she saw things differently now, as if she were seeing a bigger picture than I was.

"Ruby," I said, trying not to sound irritated. "The last thing we need is to get mixed up in some intrigue involving the fucking Fae Lords."

She placed her hands on her hips. "Jade, this is bigger than you and your revenge."

"We weren't even talking about that, Rubes. And please, let's not start."

"We *were* talking about it. *You* said you weren't interested in what was going on with the antler, but *I* know the reason for that. It's because you can't see beyond your own—"

"Enough."

Jason's head swiveled back and forth from Ruby and me as if watching a tennis match, but it wasn't entertainment on his face. It was alarm.

"Whoa there, ladies," he said. "Calm down now." Then, to me: "Revenge? What's she talking about, Jade?"

I'd never told him the truth about my heritage or what I was doing in New York in the first place.

"Never mind," I said.

"Well?" Ruby demanded.

I forced myself to count to ten. "Fine." I sighed. "Let Jason examine it. You and he can even do it together."

She smiled, but Jason frowned.

"I'm sorry," he told her, and I could tell he meant it. "I need to work on the antler alone. It will require all my concentration. Give me a day and come back. Hopefully, I'll have some answers for you by then."

Ruby pouted, but she must have seen he was telling the truth, because she nodded. "Okay, then. See you tomorrow, Jason." Brightening, she turned to me. "Sis, I'm sorry about what I said."

"What?" I said. The last thing I wanted was to talk about our feelings. Ugh. "No, it's—"

She grabbed my hand and tugged me toward the stairs. "We need to go out," she said firmly. "We need to party."

"You mean, like to a club?"

She looked at me over her shoulder, and a smile had split her freckled face. "Hell yeah! We just stole some prize loot, saved a nice young woman from her nightmare, and may have landed ourselves in the middle of something interesting. I'd say a drink is in order."

"A drink! But you're underage."

She yanked a wallet out of her purse and flashed it at me. "Not after I cast just a little bitsy spell on my driver's license."

"You wouldn't!"

"I'm a stone-cold badass thief witch, babes. You'd better believe I would fudge my driver's license by one month."

I laughed. What the hell?

If only I had known.

"You are stone cold," I said in admiration. "Okay, where should we go?"

"I know just the place."

CHAPTER 3

Lights blazed, and I paused to admire the display. Pandora's Box was the hot new magical club in town, and it occupied the first few floors of a major building downtown. A magical mural had been painted across the façade, and not only was it very...lurid, depicting a lot of very healthy people with not much in the way of clothing cavorting across green rolling hills dotted with Roman columns entwined with ivy, but the figures in it moved, gyrating, thrusting, and posing provocatively. Also, the mural glowed, the magical paint not just lambent in the dark, but burning through it like a lighthouse beam through fog. It looked like one could just walk right into the mural, just step from the New York sidewalk into Orgy Hills.

Two actual centaurs—buff, shirtless guys with the lower halves of horses—stood to either side of the main club entrance, serving as bouncers. A lengthy line of hopeful partiers trailed down the street, eager to get in.

Ruby and I climbed out of the cab, which reeked of clove cigarettes, and joined the others in line. It was October and plenty cold, but the owners of the club had magically heated the sidewalk area outside the 'Box.' In fact, a few beads of sweat trickled down my back as I took my place.

We'd swung by our apartment to change before coming here, and we were all decked out, Ruby was in a short, glittery red skirt with a matching top featuring much cleavage—Mom would have thrown a fit. I was in a black mini-dress and thigh-high shiny leather boots with high heels. I looked good in black.

"This is going to be awesome," Ruby said. "I've been dying to come here."

I glanced up and down the line. Many here sported magical totems or symbols, or at least wore things that looked magical. Magic was the new cool, and everybody wanted in on it, whether they were part of the actual supernatural community or not. It was all alien to me in a way. I'd been born supernatural, but I had had to keep it secret or suffer the consequences, at least until the Fae Lords arrived and changed everything.

Of course, the consequences had caught up to me even though I kept the secret, and my gifts—well, most of them—had been stolen. Our father had died that day, and our grandmother not long after. When Ruby said I wanted revenge, she wasn't kidding, and I had good reason, too.

"Think any of these guys can do any real magic?" I asked, just to make conversation.

"Not like I can," Ruby said.

She lifted a hand, said a word under her breath, and a tiny ball of green fire jumped from her palm. Gasps of astonishment rippled up and down the line. That answered that question. If such a small display could awe them, they couldn't be magic users.

"Stop showing off," I said.

Ruby sniffed and closed her palm. The fire died. She brightened again. "Did you see what Jason was wearing?"

Here we go. "Not really."

"He had on a new top, and it was tight. Like, really tight."

"I didn't notice." Although I had.

"I think he's been working out." Her cheeks colored. In a lower voice, she asked, "You told him in advance we were coming, right?"

"Well, duh. I had to make an appointment."

She beamed. Her enthusiasm was both infectious and annoying. "I knew it," she said, hugging herself.

I tried not to roll my eyes. "Knew what?"

"Duh," she said, mocking me. "He worked out for me!"

She continued chatting happily about Jason as we advanced in the line and were at last admitted into Pandora's Box. I couldn't help but admire the meaty chests of the centaurs as we passed between them. They had smeared scented oil all over their torsos and thick arms, and their heavy slabs of muscle glistened tantalizingly. It was all I could do not to reach out and poke their abs.

We spilled into the club, which buzzed with noise, lights, and warmth. People packed the place, but there was enough room to dance, and couples thronged the dance floor, thrusting and gyrating not much more modestly than the people on the mural outside. The owners of the club had stuck with the whole Roman theme. I would have thought it was passé, but they made it work with Roman columns supporting jets of magical pink and blue fire, vines climbing stone walls on one side of the room—flowers burst from the vines, emitting magically intoxicating smells—and a grand Roman fountain that seemed to spout not water but…blood?

"Blood?" I said, surprised.

Ruby nodded sagely, as if she had known this all along. Maybe she had. She'd been reading about this place for weeks, dying to go there as soon as she turned twenty-one or had a good enough excuse to get me to take her earlier. Sucker me.

As we made our way toward the long, gleaming black marble bar along one corner, she pointed at the people decked out in black leather and wearing too much foundation.

"Vampires," she said.

I recoiled, but she tugged me along, bound and determined to reach the bar and her first quasi-legal drink.

"Vampires?" I repeated.

"That's right. Or their groupies, more like. They're allowed here, too—the vampires. Not the groupies. Although, them, too, obviously. I mean, vampires have to have their groupies, right?"

"I…guess."

"Why don't witches have groupies? I would *love* some groupies. Maybe those centaurs…" She bit her lower lip. "Anyway, it's not like there's a law against vampires or anything."

"There should be."

I had known about the existence of vampires even before the Fae-rival, but I'd been shocked when they "came out" along with the other shifters and paranormals after that event. Some things belonged in the darkness.

"Why?" Ruby said as we reached the bar and had to stand in another line to get one of the bartenders' attention.

"Because they kill people?" I suggested.

"Pfft. If they kill people, they go to jail just like any other murderer. But if they don't, why not let them be?"

I sighed. I wasn't going to win this argument. But that didn't mean I had to sit next to one of the creepy goths who were either real vampires or fang bangers. I couldn't tell one from the other, so I kept my distance. We finally signaled the bartender, a cute tattooed girl who had absolutely nothing Roman, magical, or goth about her, and ordered our drinks. I nearly leapt out of my skin when she handed me my daiquiri, because when she did she flashed me a smile, revealing a set of gleaming white fangs.

"Ack!" I said.

Even Ruby paled. "Are those real?" she asked, leaning forward. The vampire nodded. Ruby's face brightened. "Can I touch?"

The bartender laughed and indicated the tip jar. "Depends on how generous you are."

Evidently Ruby wasn't generous enough, because shortly after the bartender moved off to help someone else.

I downed a long swallow of my drink to calm my nerves. "Serves me right, I guess," I said. "Should've known that someone who looked so normal couldn't really be normal, not in this place."

Ruby nodded at the goths. "I bet that means they're just groupies. The real vampires probably look just like everyone else."

I flinched, suddenly looking around with paranoia.

Ruby laughed again. Her attention switched to her drink, and a grin crept across her face. At last, she would get to enjoy her first quasi-legal alcoholic beverage in public. I knew all too well that it wasn't her *first* first drink, as I'd caught her at my beer more than once and had warned her off it just as many times. Well, almost as many. I mean, I wasn't our mom.

"This is going to be glorious," Ruby said, and then placed her lips to her straw. She'd ordered a strawberry margarita. I watched as the red liquid traveled up her straw and past her lips. Her eyes widened, and her cheeks sucked in. Pulling back, she said, "Cold! Too cold!"

I laughed. "Serves you right."

She stuck her—very red—tongue out at me. "It's delicious."

We found a small table and sat down. "So," I said. "How long have you been hot for Jason?"

"Since I realized you weren't going to make a move on him. I mean, I always thought he was hot, but I never let myself get too far in my thinking, if you know what I mean. I kept expecting you to do something."

"I don't know why I never did. He *is* awfully cute."

"He's more than cute, sis, he's delish. But I guess he's not bad enough for you."

I shifted in my seat. "I don't know what you're talking about."

"Ha. I've never seen you go out with a guy that didn't have at least three tattoos."

"That's not true at all. Besides, when do I ever go out?"

She slurped her margarita noisily. "True," she said, making a face to show she was getting a brain freeze. "Why *don't* you go out more?"

I sipped my own drink, desperate to end this line of conversation. "I don't know. I just don't."

She regarded me with alarming soberness. She could go from bright and fuzzy to shockingly grim with ridiculous speed, and it seemed like she'd just switched gears. Uh-oh.

"It's not because of your…mission, is it?" she said.

Groan. "No. Can we talk about something else?"

But she had me speared in her gaze. She wasn't letting me off the hook that easy. "Sis, Dad and Gran wouldn't want you to carry on this way. Let it go."

A swell of anger rose in me. I tried to shove it down, because Ruby was the absolute wrong person to unload on, but somehow I couldn't stop it. She had pricked an old wound, and a deep one.

"Could *you* let it go?" I said.

"Yes." Her eyes glanced down. "If I had to."

"I don't believe you."

"Well, I could."

"If someone had stolen something from you that you prized above everything else? That defined who you are?"

Her eyes flicked back to me, hurt pooled in them. "More precious than *anything* else?"

Shit. I'd stuck my foot in my mouth again. "Ruby, I didn't mean it like—"

She set her margarita down and stood up. "I've got to go."

I reached out. "Ruby, come on, you know I didn't mean it like that. Sit down, let's talk about this."

Anger flared in her eyes, and pain settled on her face. I would have given anything to take my words back, but it was too late.

"I'll…" She swallowed one last sip of her margarita and seemed to be trying to shake it off. Her eyes strayed to the dance floor. "I'll catch up to you later," she told me, which was as much closure as I was going to get for the moment.

"Ruby," I pleaded, but she was gone.

The dance floor was sunken in the great main room of the club, so I could peer down on it from the bar area and watch Ruby melt into the throng of gyrating, sweaty bodies and vanish. *Real smooth*, I thought.

Ruby shouldn't have pushed me, I told myself. Why did she always have to push?

But she was right, and I knew that, too. Mom and Dad would want me to move on, to not obsess over getting justice for Dad and Gran. And myself. I'd been a victim, too. Hell, I'd been the target of it all. I still dreamt of flying, which was something I could never do again, not under my own power. A man named Vincent Walsh had taken that from me, and he'd also killed Dad and Gran, as well as turned Mom into a drunk. How could Ruby suggest I forget all that?

I downed my drink, my mind churning. The noise and the fury of the Box suddenly seemed repellent to me. I wanted to be alone to drink and sulk in private. Rudy said I did too much of that, but the truth was I just wasn't fit company to be around sometimes. I knew my limits. She needed to learn them, too.

But I shouldn't have lashed out at her.

Shit, I thought after I'd killed my second daiquiri. Ruby hadn't come back. I would have to go find her. As much as I hated to do it, I'd have to apologize. I really hated apologizing for stuff, even when it was my fault. Hell, *especially* when it was my fault.

Setting the empty glass down, I pushed through the crowd toward the dance floor. Almost immediately, I smashed into someone—well, not just *someone*. The most gorgeous man I'd ever seen. Steel-blue eyes stared coolly out of a strong-jawed yet beautiful face, and the lights of the club bounced off his short blond hair, making it burn like gold. He wore a fashionable brown leather jacket over a tight blue T-shirt that showed off stunning abs and pecs, which was what I'd bounced right off. He was tall, with broad shoulders tapering down to a slim waist and long legs clad in tight blue jeans.

I tottered off balance and nearly fell. He reached around me and grabbed my lower back, stabilizing me. Our eyes connected, and heat flooded through me. His eyes shone like molten silver, and yet they were cold at the same time. When he moved, he did so gracefully and smoothly, but I could feel the amazing strength in his arms when he steadied me.

"I…uh, thanks," I said as he set me back on my feet.

"No problem," he replied, but there was something slightly stilted about the way he said it. I couldn't figure it out. But it was almost like he was from another country and trying to use the local slang.

I frowned. There was something *familiar* about him somehow.

"Have we met?" I asked, hoping I didn't sound too drunk. I *felt* too drunk, and staring up into his ridiculously handsome face wasn't helping.

He fixed me with his steely eyes. "No. I would have remembered."

"Maybe we didn't meet, but I know I've seen you somewhere before."

His eyes tracked down my body, then back up to my face. I couldn't read his expression.

"I'm sorry. I can't help you," he said. "Now I really most go."

"No, wait—"

Too late. With a small, gentlemanly bow to me, he turned and slipped away, vanishing into the crowd. *Real good,* I thought. I'd scared both Ruby and Mister Steel-Eyes away in record time.

Sniffing, I called to his back, "Oh, you *better* run!"

I resumed my trek toward the dance floor. Who had that guy been? Somehow, he hadn't fit this place…or it hadn't fit him. I recognized him from somewhere, but I just couldn't remember where.

I stumbled onto the dance floor, suddenly regretting my choice of heels, and scanned the crowd for Ruby.

"Ruby," I called, edging around a trio of mostly naked dancers, two women and one man. They seemed to be clothed mainly in gold dust, and their eyes glowed purple—obviously they had taken some magical drug. Such things were mainly illegal, but that didn't stop people from selling them. "Ruby!"

I started to say her name again, but I almost collided—I blinked—with a fucking *bear*. Shock ran through me, and I reeled backward. A laughing boy shoved me back the other way, toward the bear. It danced with a woman, or at least shambled in a dance-like way, while she twerked her heart out, rubbing her butt against its shoulder.

A bear shifter. There weren't many of them in the city, but a few did live here. And this one had decided to take his girlfriend—mate?—out for a night on the town. The owners of Pandora's Box seemed to encourage shifters to shift. I just hadn't expected a bear. Then again, who does?

Laughing, I pushed on, calling out for Ruby, but I couldn't find her. I finally started asking people.

"Have you seen a cute young redhead wearing a short red skirt?" I asked, again and again.

It was the bear shifter's date/mate who came to my rescue. "She went that way, dear," the woman said, pointing to what looked like a rear exit. "She went with some guy with tattoos."

Great. I'd made Ruby so mad she took a page from my book, and that wasn't a book anyone should be taking a page from, let alone my little sister.

"Thanks," I told the woman before moving toward the back of the club.

After fighting my way through the crowd, I burst out the back door to an alleyway. The owners of the club hadn't magically heated this area, and I shivered in the sudden blast of frigid wind. Fortunately, alcohol and worry kept me warm enough. I had to get to Ruby before she made a mistake she would end up regretting.

Darkness cloaked much of the alley, but there were a few dim lights. My shifter senses proved more than adequate to spot Ruby moving away from me, arm in arm with a tall, black-haired man with a black leather jacket. Sure enough, he had a tattoo on the back of his neck.

"Ruby," I called.

She turned toward me, but the man jerked her roughly forward.

"Hey," she said, pushing away from him.

Alarm ran through me. I moved toward her more swiftly.

"Ruby," I said again, injecting a note of toughness into my voice. I wasn't sure how successful I was, half-drunk as I was and, honestly, a bit frightened.

"Sis—" Ruby started, but the man hauled her even more roughly forward, almost dragging her off her feet.

"Do it," the man said to the shadows around him.

Four dark shapes emerged from the gloom and stalked toward me. Danger glimmered in their all-black eyes, and their pale skin swam in ghostly fashion against the darkness.

Vampires—and not the humanized kind like the bartender, but the real-deal, no-frills monster kind. The kind who killed.

And they were coming right for me.

CHAPTER 4

"You're not going anywhere," the lead vampire said. He was dressed all in black, with ratty black hair and a mustache. His long arms ended in wicked talons, and he could barely speak for the enormous fangs bristling from his mouth.

"Ruby!" I shouted. "I'm coming, just hold on."

These vamps might think they could keep me from my sister, but they were wrong—dead wrong. Just the same, I had gone even colder with fear. Countering it, I felt that familiar blaze of anger well up in me as I kicked off my heels, tossed my purse aside (hoping it wouldn't get ruined by alley filth) and raised my hands to fight.

The vampires paused, perhaps surprised that a lone woman would put up such a defense. Then they fanned out as much as they could in the narrow alleyway and rushed me. I leapt at the leader, my foot crashing down on his thigh. Bones snapped. He howled and went down.

The second bloodsucker grabbed me by the neck and lifted me off the ground. I kicked her in the face, hard. She let go and was hurled backward, striking the brick wall with terrific force.

I hit the ground with my butt and rolled as the third vamp

kicked and stomped at me. The fourth grabbed me by the ankle and swung me around. I sailed through the air and smashed into the opposite wall. The blow would have crippled a human, but my shifter abilities made me stronger and more resilient. Just the same, pain flared through me, and I hit the ground groaning in pain.

The two vampires still in the fight advanced, their fangs gleaming in the scant light.

"I don't think so," said a voice to my right.

The two vampires and I glanced toward the exit from the club. Framed in the lights of the doorway was the tall man I'd slammed into earlier and then promptly alienated.

I grabbed my ribs, which felt like they were broken. "Who…are you?"

"My name is Davril," he said. Suddenly, even though he hadn't been holding or wearing anything that I'd seen, he was holding up a long sword that shone with an inner radiance. Its light pushed back the shadows and illuminated the pale, unwashed vampires in an almost holy glow.

They shrank from the light, hissing and screeching.

"You don't scare us," one said.

"Then you're fools," Davril said.

The other two, the ones I'd temporarily put out of the fight, picked themselves up and joined their fellows. The four advanced on the sword-wielding maniac, or whatever he was.

He'll get himself killed, I thought. Only a supernatural could fight those vamps. I had to do something.

Lurching to my feet, I grabbed a nearby trash can and hurled it at the back of the vampire on the far right, a man with a shaved head. The can caught him on the dome and sent him to his knees.

Davril launched himself forward, bringing his sword around in a blur, and the vampire leader's head fell in a different direction than his body. Instantly, both burst into flames and dissipated into ash.

A third vampire jumped at Davril's back, meaning to take him from behind, but Davril spun, and his sword decapitated this one, too. The fourth leapt straight for Davril's jugular, knocking him backward. His sword flew through the air.

I moved to help. The vampire I'd hit with the trash can sprang up, growling, and put itself between Davril and me.

"Out of my way, asshole," I said.

Davril and the vamp rolled around on the ground, and I knew Davril's human strength was no match for the bloodsucker. He might be ridiculously brave, but he only had moments to live. Part of me wanted to rush off after Ruby, but I couldn't let this man die.

I stalked straight toward him, right at the vampire. Baldy scowled at me, then sprang. I expected it and turned sideways as he moved through the air. Grabbing him by the jacket as he sailed past, I dashed him against the wall, caving in his head. That was all it took to kill a vampire—decapitate it or destroy its head. The vamp burst into flames.

I didn't pause but rushed toward Davril and the other vamp… just in time to see Davril clamp his palm on the vampire's forehead—*and for Davril's hand to blaze with light*. The same sort that had emitted from his sword. The light suffused the vampire, who screamed. Smoke wafted up from his head, and he suddenly burst into flames. Davril kicked his charred corpse away, stood, retrieved his sword, and thrust it through a scabbard hanging from his belt. As soon as it went in, the sword and belt both disappeared, becoming invisible.

I stared. No human could have done what he had. He hadn't even spoken a spell or used any magical device. He had incinerated that vamp with his own power. That meant…that meant…

"You're a *Fae*," I gasped, studying Davril with new eyes.

He wiped a bit of ash from his cheek. "I'm Davril Stormguard, Knight of the Queen's Court."

I swayed on my feet. "A Fae Knight…"

I couldn't believe it. I knew very little about the Fae or their queen, but their knights were the stuff of myth and legend—grand, heroic figures battling demons and sorcery that threatened the Fae crown or its interests.

In a way, they were the cops of the Fae world. Well, maybe FBI.

And I was a criminal.

So it should have been no surprise when he whipped out a pair of handcuffs and marched toward me, stepping around the blackened body of the vampire he'd just dusted.

"You're coming with me," he said.

Realization hit me. "It was you...*you're* the one who was on the penthouse roof!"

"That's right. And I saw you in the act of committing theft. Theft committed against a vassal of the Throne."

I thrust out my chin. "I don't have time for this."

Turning, I ran. He called out, but I ignored him as I splashed through muddy puddles and around broken beer bottles. Freezing wind whipped at me, but I barely felt it. Where was Ruby?

"Ruby!" I shouted. "Ruby!"

Hearing a sound, I paused as I reached a cross-alley. The tattooed vampire who had abducted Ruby pulled her toward a shimmering green magical portal. Fear filled me. If they passed through that portal, it would close behind them and Ruby would be gone.

"Ruby!" I screamed, hoping to encourage her to fight the bloodsucker. Why was she just going along, damn it?

Abruptly stopping, the vampire yanked her around to look deeply into her eyes. "Do not react," he commanded in a booming voice, and she continued stumbling along with him.

Shit, I thought. *He's got her hypnotized.* A vampire's thrall could be a powerful thing. Most vamps wouldn't have been able to enthrall a witch like Ruby, though. That told me these assholes had come prepared. They must have some magical charm or other mojo that boosted their thrall, at least for a little while.

The vampire dragged the unresisting Ruby toward the portal. They were just inches away now. I didn't waste time screaming her name anymore but lunged for her instead. Behind me, I could hear Davril enter the cross-alley, then came the patter of his feet.

The vampire grabbed something at his waist, and I saw the glimmer of steel. He half-turned, hurling a knife at me. I ducked and heard it clatter off the wall behind me—it hadn't hit Davril, darn it—but the move had slowed me just enough.

The vampire dragged Ruby through the glowing portal.

It immediately closed, sealing me off from my sister and plunging the alley into darkness.

"*Ruby!*" I screamed, feeling my throat go raw and tears burn in my eyes.

I sank to my knees where the portal had been and nearly dissolved. She was gone. Ruby was really gone. The vampires had taken her. *Bastards. I'll get you, you motherfuckers.*

Behind me, I could hear Davril draw close.

"I'm sorry," he said.

I wanted to snap at him but held myself back. My real anger was for the vampires. And, honestly, some for myself, too. My last words to Ruby had been in anger. *I can't let those be the last words I ever say to her.*

"Who could be behind this?" I said, having to force the words out. Even so, they came out ragged. "Why would they take Ruby?"

"I'll look for her," Davril promised, but then he added, "Once I take you in."

I impatiently wiped my eyes and stood, then turned to glare at him. "You really mean to *arrest* me?"

"Yes."

"Bastard."

"It will go easier on you if you don't resist."

He started to take a step toward me. I turned and ran. I reached the street, crossed it, and plunged into another network of alleys. I hit a turn, then another, then another. A few drunks and criminals edged out of my way, not wanting me to call attention to them, and once a man with a knife even tried to mug me. I punched him in the face, and he collapsed onto the crate he'd been sitting on. Sometimes, shifter strength could be a very good thing.

At last, breathless and crying, I drew to a stop. I could hear Davril's footsteps on the asphalt around a corner. I jumped onto a dumpster and shimmied up a fire escape, moving with all the speed and silence given to me by my shifter abilities.

"Come back here!" Davril shouted from the street, although he couldn't have seen where I'd gone.

As if.

"I'll find you," he said. "Come now and it will go easier on you!"

To hell with that. Wishing I still had my shoes, I took off across the rooftops, my entire world in tatters about me.

I ran and ran, my eyes streaming tears and my chest heaving. An awful pain curdled inside me, and my mind spun like a whirlwind. Ruby was gone, taken by who the hell knew, and I was being hunted by a Fae Knight.

I made my way home, eventually creeping down the fire escape and entering the apartment Ruby and I shared via the window. This was in a poor area of town, one rife with much underground and illegal magic. Many people called the area Gypsy Land. Ruby and I were no gypsies, but we'd always liked the name and the atmosphere of the place, even if there was crime.

Ruby had warded the doors and windows, so we didn't fear burglary. I knew the words to unlock all the spells, and I had no trouble getting in. Once inside, I flipped on all the lights and went to the kitchen, where I poured a stiff bourbon.

I tried to calm my overactive mind. Terrible images stormed through my brain, of Ruby in terror and pain, and it took me a long time to get hold of myself.

Then, suddenly, I heard a voice.

It came from the bathroom.

"Jade, come here."

A chill ran down my spine. I had been sitting at the breakfast table, sipping my drink, but I shot to my feet.

"Who's there?" I asked, grabbing up a scimitar from the wall. Its enchanted blade could cut through almost anything, and I knew how to use it, too.

"Come...*here*."

The voice really did sound like it came from the bathroom. Just as puzzled as alarmed, I crept to the bathroom and kicked the door open. It banged against the wall, then swung back, but not enough to obscure the mirror, where a huge, otherworldly face stared back at me.

A face. In the mirror.

I stepped back, trying to hide my fear, but I must have done a poor job of it to judge by the expression of the thing in the mirror. It was white and skeletal, and its eyes burned with an unnatural green light. Only its face showed, or what passed for its face. Its skin was withered and drawn tight.

"We have your sister," the face said, speaking with a curious accent. The voice battered against my ears, enfolding me in waves of malice. I could taste the bitterness on my tongue.

I raised my sword, then, realizing it was useless, lowered it. The owner of that face, if there was one, was far away, only using the mirror to relay his signal. He could even be on another plane for all I knew.

"Who are you?" I demanded.

"Never mind that now. Concentrate on what we require of you and only that."

"What you...require?" I shook my head, dizzy with it all.

"You must perform a task for us, a simple one, in order for us to return your sister Ruby."

My mouth had gone dry. "Let me talk to her."

"No."

"You've got to provide proof of life," I said.

"*We* don't have to do anything. *You* must do what we tell you, or we'll kill Ruby."

"No!" I raised the sword again, although I wasn't sure why. What was I going to do, break my own mirror?

"Bring us the golden antler."

I scowled at the floating white face. "I don't know what you're talking about."

"We know you stole it. Bring it to us or suffer the consequences."

"Leave my sister alone!"

"Bring it to us. We will make contact soon. Do not disappoint us."

"Hey! Wait!"

The head rippled and vanished, and the mirror was once more just a mirror. I gazed at myself, seeing a shocked woman with tears in her eyes who held a shaking sword. Damn, I looked bad. I glanced away and staggered back, my spine striking the opposite wall.

Who could that have been? I tried to figure it out. This didn't feel like Walter Hawthorne or one of his agents; nor did it feel like the Fae Lords. This felt like another party entirely. But who? I couldn't make any sense of it.

Maybe—

The front door exploded inward. Shocked, I whirled to face the threat, raising my sword again. Framed in the doorway was Davril Stormguard.

Seeing my sword, Davril raised his, too. Coming inside, he kicked the remains of the door behind him. We were alone.

"What are you doing here?" I demanded, my voice shaking as badly as my blade.

His eyes narrowed, and an electric spark passed through me.

"You left your purse behind."

The unexpected comment brought me up short. A disbelieving laugh came out when I saw it hanging from his belt.

He hadn't brought my shoes, though, or at least I didn't see them.

"What about my shoes?" I countered.

He moved toward me, and I danced back.

"You can get your own shoes."

I moved, being careful not to trip over anything.

"I guess you got my address from my purse," I said.

"Yes. And your name. Jade McClaren."

"That's my name. Don't wear it out." I nodded my chin at the remains of the door. "How did you get through the wards?"

"I'm a Fae Knight."

I rounded a corner and kept going. I almost darted into a room so I could lock it behind me—the room was warded and could probably protect me for a couple of hours, anyway, even against the likes of him—but that would only be making myself a prisoner. I needed to get out.

"I'm not going away to fucking Azkaban," I said. "Fuck that."

"You already speak like a convict. And this isn't *Harry Potter*."

"Fuck you."

His lips twisted, just slightly. "Come with me, Jade. You will not be harmed, and you will stand a fair trial."

"I'm not going any—"

His sword came in, sharp and fast. Breathlessly, I batted it way, then jumped back, almost tripping on the carpet.

"Come quietly," Davril insisted.

"Damn you," I said. "*They have my sister.*"

"I know. I'm sorry. I will do my best to deliver her to safety."

"They told me I have to—"

He thrust at me again, aiming for my shoulder. I batted his sword away and leapt back again.

"What did they tell you?" he asked, wrinkling his brow. "The people in the mirror?"

"That Fae Knights are assholes!"

He slashed again. I didn't bother parrying the blow but jumped back. There was no way I could defeat him or even hold my ground against him any longer. He was *bad ass*.

My own ass slammed against the window. In a moment, I had it opened and was scrambling onto the fire escape. The wind howled icily about me, misting my eyes.

"Where do you think you're going?" he said.

I slammed the window down and said a spell under my breath. He reached it before he could counter Ruby's warding spell. When he stretched a hand toward the glass, sparks flashed out. The blow flung him down the hall.

I scowled, unhitched Ruby's spell-cloaked broom from the fire escape, and fled into the night. The wind shrieked even louder around me.

CHAPTER 5

"Shit," I said, banking hard to the right as I swerved around a building. I tore through the city, my chest hitching. "How can Ruby fly this thing?"

I used to be able to fly without a broom when I could sprout wings, but I couldn't do that anymore. This sort of flying made me break out into a fierce sweat. I had only attempted to fly Ruby's broomstick a couple of times and never for so long. I nearly dashed myself against one building after another.

Ruby's spell cloaked the broom from anyone who wasn't one of us...or that wasn't a powerful magic-user. I had to watch out for the griffon-mounted police, too. I *thought* Ruby's magic was a step ahead of theirs, but I couldn't be sure, and both sides, police and criminal, were always leveling up.

"Shit shit shit," I said again, but not because of the flying. I couldn't believe everything that had just happened—Ruby gone, me being hunted by a Fae Knight, a strange skull-like face in the mirror giving me an ultimatum that would get Ruby killed if I didn't comply.

It'll be all right. I'll just go get the antler from Jason, and they'll give

Ruby back. The knight would see I no longer had the antler or whatever and he'd leave us alone.

I repeated that to myself all the way to Queens, but when I finally reached Jason's pawnshop, I saw flashing police lights and squad cars camped outside. What now? A sick feeling rose in me, and I tried to push it down.

I landed the broomstick on the roof and took the access stairway down to Jason's murky workshop, where I heard activity and noises. That sick feeling welled in me again, even stronger than before. I said a spell to make myself invisible for a few minutes, which was as long as the incantation would last, and that was using expensive ingredients I wasn't sure I could replace. Stepping into the main room, I found police officers interviewing the pawnshop employees and technicians snapping photos.

A great hole gaped in the side of the building, wind fluttering through it and bringing leaves and dust. I stared. Had something *smashed* its way in here?

Fear shot bile into the back of my mouth. *No,* I thought. *Please no. Anything but this.* Then I saw it—a form on the floor draped with a white sheet blotched with crimson. Grief twisted through me. *This is too much. This is all too much. I can't take anymore.*

I staggered off into a corner and puked as silently as I could. No one seemed to notice.

Poor Jason. He had been a kind and good man. The world would be a worse place without him. And Ruby, when I could get her free, which I was determined to do, would be devastated.

But how had this horrible thing happened? I saw overturned tables and busted magical items that Jason had been repairing or inspecting prior to selling them. The beautiful cuckoo clock he'd been showing us earlier lay in splintered pieces on the floor, and the sight brought me to tears. He'd been so excited about it.

I waited until a police officer finished interviewing one of the employees, a woman named Mindy, and approached her.

"Mindy," I whispered.

She jumped. "Who's there?"

"It's me, Jade McClaren. Don't look around or they'll know I'm here."

"Where…?"

"I'm invisible. It's a spell. Come on."

I gently tugged her toward a hallway, and she came willingly. Giving her directions, I succeeded in getting her into the women's restroom and locked the door behind us. Decloaking to save my limited magical mojo—derived from items in my belt pouches—I said, "What happened?"

She swallowed, then hugged me tight. Her body trembled.

"He's gone, Jade, just gone!"

"I'm so sorry."

I pulled back and studied her. Tears glittered in her eyes, and her face had gone pale. In a quavering voice, she said, "It just barged right in…right through the wall…and went after him."

"*What* did?

"No one knows. Some sort of creature, we think. The police have found claw marks and what might be drool stains."

"Damn. Where did it go?"

"I don't know, dear, but there was ice on the floor."

I wrinkled my brow. "Ice? I don't get it."

"Jason's ice wand, remember? He was so proud when he acquired it last year. Well, he still has it. *Had* it."

I snapped my fingers. "The wand that only does ice spells. Yeah, I remember. You think he used that to freeze the creature?"

"I don't know, but I think so. It didn't help Jason, but the police are trying to track the ice particles to see if they'll lead them to it. I doubt they'll have any luck."

I nodded. "They need more witches on the payroll. I guess they'll get the point eventually. What about the antler, the golden one?"

"I looked for it earlier—I knew how excited he was about it and was kind of wondering if it was the cause of the attack—a big magical thing like that's got to be dangerous—but I couldn't find it."

"So the creature killed Jason and stole it." I stuck out my chin. "Maybe I can track the ice particles and get it back."

"Don't! The creature..."

"You let me worry about that."

"Promise me you'll stay safe," she said.

I couldn't make any such promise. Jason would never have been in danger if not for me. I was the one who stole the antler. I was the one who caused all this.

"Thank you," was all I said.

I said a magic word and cloaked myself again. Stepping lightly, I returned to the workroom and tiptoed through the activity. The medical examiner had just arrived and was taking photographs of Jason's body. I tried not to look but edged around them, through the gaping hole the creature had torn in the wall, and stepped outside. Wind shoved against me, and I inhaled deeply, letting it stream through my hair and clothes as if it could cleanse me.

My stomach bunched in knots. I hoped I didn't throw up again. Just what the hell was going on in the city? Things seemed to be spinning out of control, and it all had to do with the antler of the Golden Hind.

Several police officers inspected the thin trail of water that led across the parking lot away from the hole in the wall. Presumably, the melted ice. By the way they were frowning and shaking their heads, I could tell they weren't making much progress, and how could they? The drops of water would only be trackable to a human for so long, but perhaps with my shifter senses, I could make more progress. I could find the creature, steal the antler from it, and save Ruby.

Guilt at what had happened to Jason ripped through me as I slipped past the cops, my nostrils quivering as I caught the scent of magic-laced water and...something else. The creature reeked of unwashed hair, sweat, and decay. It was revolting. Now that I was concentrating on it, I couldn't smell anything else. I followed it down a street, then an alley, then ducked up a cross-alley. The pawnshop and the police were far away now. Where had the thing gone? Where had it come from?

A sudden tingle on the back of my neck made me spin around.

The icy eyes of Davril Stormguard stared back at me. His sword shone a pale yellow in the murk of the alley.

"You," I said, and braced myself.

"Me," he affirmed. "And you *are* coming with me."

"I don't think so. That monster killed a friend of mine, and I mean to do something about it."

"You think *you* can defeat it?"

His pompous tone made my hackles rise. "I may not be able to beat it, but I can damn well make sure it didn't get what it came for."

Davril gave me a measured look. "Do you even know what you're fighting for? What the antler is for?"

"Well…no. What *does* it do?"

"Never mind that now." He fished out a pair of handcuffs, which glittered faintly by the light of his sword. "Put these on and come with me."

"Didn't you hear me? I'm going after the creature!"

His eyes held no pity. "It will kill you, Jade. And no, you're not fast enough to steal the antler back from it. It will only reduce you to the same state as your friend Jason. Did you see his body?"

I swallowed. "I…tried not to look." Images of wet redness flashed before my eyes anyway.

Davril nodded slowly. "I think you understand, at least on some level. What you're on is a suicide mission. And if you commit suicide, you can't answer for your crimes."

"And my crimes are so important, aren't they?"

"They've already gotten one man killed. How many more will follow?"

I tore my eyes away, guilt rising once more.

Davril used my distraction to his advantage, stalking toward me, his gaze unwavering and determined. His palely burning sword lit the way before him. I stumbled back and turned to flee, but before I got two steps, he kicked my feet out from under me and dropped me onto my back. I felt his weight crushing me into the asphalt.

"Get—off—you—stupid—cop," I said, but it was hard to talk with a Fae Knight on my back.

His breath teased at my ear. "I told you, Jade. You're coming with me."

Cold cuffs snapped around my wrists.

CHAPTER 6

I cursed as he hauled me to my feet and removed the belt containing my spellgredients.

"You won't be needing this anymore, thief," he said.

"I'm not just a thief," I said, struggling to break free of his grip on my arms. He had twisted them behind my back. His hold was too strong, though. "I help people."

"Tell it to the Queen."

Ice flooded my veins. "The...Queen?"

I couldn't figure out why the Queen of the Fae would personally sentence me. Then again, the Fae were sort of medieval, and ancient kings used to settle legal matters among their subjects, didn't they?

I kicked and struggled, but Davril didn't even slow down as he dragged me from the alley and into the street. At some point along the way, he'd disabled my cloaking spell and I hadn't even noticed. People stopped and stared as he paused on the sidewalk and thrust his sword through his sheath. Instantly, both vanished.

"Fae business," he told gawking passersby, then placed his fingers in his mouth and whistled.

"Who do you...?" I started, but stopped in midsentence as a

flying car—it had *wings*—swept gracefully down from the skies and landed on the road, then coasted to a stop before us. I sucked in my breath. It was gorgeous, like some 1960's muscle car mixed with a modern Lamborghini, and all of silver chrome like the armor of a knight. Did Davril have armor? I wouldn't put it past him. White wings like a swan's arced out to either side of the car, but they folded up when it landed, and the doors opened by themselves.

"Meet Lady Kay," Davril said, a small smile tugging at one corner of his lips. I could see that he really loved that car, and no wonder. It was a miracle.

Still, I sniffed and tried to act unimpressed. "It would look better if it only had two doors," I said. The car had four.

His smile widened slightly. "Yes, but then I couldn't do *this*." He placed his hand on my head and shoved it down, propelling me into the rear seat of Lady Kay. Polished leather enfolded me, and I breathed in the scent of it. Mm, new leather. Just like a cop car, the rear doors didn't have knobs on the inside, and though there was no physical barrier between the front and the back, I could sense a magical shield dividing the space. No way I could smash my way forward and escape.

Damn. I'm really caught this time.

Davril slid smoothly behind the wheel and gunned the engine. It purred like a cat, almost sounding eager. *It likes his touch,* I thought, mortified to realize I was a little jealous. Of a car. *Get it together, Jade. Jason just died!*

The car bucked under me. It took off, flying through the airspace above New York. Below, people were stopping to point. They had seen enchanted flying cars before, but few of them would have seen the car-steed of a Fae Knight as it took a dangerous criminal off the city streets. Yeah, I was a real terror, all right.

Angrily, I kicked the back of his seat, but a magical shock

blasted me and I winced in pain. The blow didn't seem to have affected Davril at all. In fact, his laughter taunted me.

"What are you laughing at, you bastard?" I said. "I have to track down that creature before it kills again! I have to get the antler back!"

His laughter died. Suddenly sober, he said, "That's Fae business, Jade. And *you* won't be going anywhere anytime soon."

I smacked my lips. "Will I really be…imprisoned?" The thought of being confined terrified me.

"That will be up to Queen Calista."

"How did you find me, anyway?"

"I'll tell you later."

We reached the upper levels of the city, and I couldn't help but stare in amazement out over the metropolis. I rarely got to see it during daylight, not from this height. I could see the city all laid out before me, from the harbor to the sea, from demon-haunted Central Park to Mandesti Witches' University to the north. The sun heaved upward to the east, casting a golden glow across the spires and shining on the envelopes of dirigibles in the distance and on the gorgeous white wings of Lady Kay, which pumped slowly up and down to either side of us, stroking the air like the fingers of a lover. The wealthy piloted their airships or flew their enchanted animals along the traffic corridors of the sky, but Davril didn't pay attention to the prescribed traffic lanes. He flew where he wanted, as only Fae Knights and other Fae could do.

I jerked my eyes away from the sights when I noticed Davril watching my reaction in the rearview mirror. Making my face hard, I straightened my spine. Cops had been my enemies for years, but a Fae cop, or whatever he was, being so high and mighty, well, that just made it worse. It meant he and I really were on the opposite side of the world, intrinsically opposed to each other.

As we flew into the center of the city, we began passing Fae castles perched on the tops of skyscrapers, bristling with towers, domes, and crenellations. My eyes drank them in despite myself. I saw one glittering like crystal in the rays of the morning sun, another sparkling like ruby. Another was black and spiked, while still another had ramparts that seemed covered in brilliant peacock feathers. I had always longed to visit one of those castles. Like a dream, they loomed majestically over the rest of the city. All knew that inside those walls, the real power of the world resided.

Ahead of us, the Palace drew nearer. Constructed of stone, it was covered in ivy that flowered all year long, and its lofty white towers soared high and seemingly weightless, as if defying all known laws of gravity. Its windows winked like icicles. Flying horses and car-steeds came and went from its balconied garages and stables, and Davril flew to the highest of these.

I couldn't believe it. I was actually going into the Palace! For as long as the Fae had been around, I had dreamed of this moment, along with everybody else on the planet. Now here it was and I was in handcuffs. Shit.

Davril drove through the great hangar doors and set down in a huge chamber filled with activity and morning light. Fae of all kinds went about their business, their clothes flowing and colorful, their skin flush with health and power. Think the elves in *Lord of the Rings*. Only Davril was more Aragorn than Legolas. But with Legolas's smooth skin and nimbleness.

Lady Kay pulled her wings in. Davril shut the engine down, climbed out, then opened the rear door.

"Come out," he said, then stepped aside as a gentleman would when escorting a lady on a date, only I wasn't a lady and he certainly wasn't my date.

I sniffed, half tempted to stay in the car. It was certainly comfortable enough. I had a tough time believing the dank cell that awaited me would enfold me with soft, aromatic leather. But if I stayed, he would just have to drag me out, and I couldn't handle more embarrassment today. Although part of me wouldn't have minded the feel of his body pushing against me.

Grinding my teeth, I climbed out of the car and planted my feet for the first time in a Fae castle. Nearby, some Fae were feeding a row of lovely winged white horses, giving them each an apple. I admired the play of sunlight on the muscles and flowing manes of the steeds.

Davril surprised me. "The pegasi are beautiful, aren't they?" he said.

I turned to find him watching me, not the horses. He didn't look away when I caught him, but his face didn't tell me anything, either.

I sniffed again. "They're okay, I guess. Are we going to do this thing or what?"

The merest hint of amusement glimmered in his eyes. He grabbed my arm and propelled me through the hangar, and I narrowly avoided stepping right in a big steaming pile of pegasus shit. The animals were amazing, but man, their poo was stinky.

"Hey," I told Davril. "Watch where you're steering me, hotshot."

"You're the one who's in a hurry."

He guided me through a doorway and into the hallways of the palace proper. At first, I saw Fae coming and going in substantial numbers—the hangars were a hive of activity, apparently—but then the traffic dwindled and I focused on the intricate bas-reliefs and molding of the Palace. The walls were high and the stone fitted with such skill it almost looked all of a piece. At times, long, narrow windows poured sunlight into the halls or ivy could be seen curling along ornamental columns and fountains in the frequent courtyards. We passed through large open areas tangled with splendid vegetation, most of which I didn't recognize. The plants must have been imported from the Fae Lands. Some boasted strange colors or gave off exotic scents.

Magic pulsed all around me, invisible wave after wave of it, and my head swam with the power of it all. I was almost floating. I wanted to ask Davril how he could stand it—it was just too much—but I refused to speak with him any more than necessary. He probably didn't notice it, anyway. Being a Fae, he probably detected the absence of magic more than its presence. It was his natural element, after all.

Besides, I had other thoughts to occupy my attention. Ruby. Jason. A deadly creature on the loose. And here I was, possibly going to prison! I seethed with the injustice of it all. Well, sort of unjust. I *had* stolen the mirror and the antler. But still.

The halls grew grayer and grimmer in the direction we were going. We soon passed an official checkpoint of guards in uniforms, then moved into a darker, more depressing area of the palace.

"Shit," I said. "The dungeon."

He found a cell, unlocked it, and then opened the door for me. Once more it struck me how gallant he was acting. Shrugging, I stalked past him and into the cell.

"What about my—?" I started, but he was already ahead of me. With a wave of his finger, my cuffs unsnapped from about my wrists, then flew into his hands, where he clicked them into place on his belt.

He slammed the door.

I stared at him through the barred window. Suddenly, I felt very alone.

"What now?" I said.

"Not in such a hurry anymore?"

I glanced away but didn't answer.

He sighed. "I'm sorry. That was callous. In any case, this is only a temporary holding cell. I will make my report to the Queen, and we will proceed from there."

"I…"

His blue gaze speared me. "Yes?"

I forced myself to look him in the eyes. "What I said was the truth. I do help people. Well, we do. My sister Ruby and me. We steal things, sure, but only objects that bad people use against the helpless."

"Who was the antler being used against?"

"I...well... That was an exception. A spur-of-the-moment thing. I thought, well, if that asshole needed it for something, then it couldn't be a good thing, whatever it was. I mean, what he was using it for. Not the antler. The antler itself might be fine—good, bad, or neutral, I don't know." I cleared my throat. "Anyway. I just wanted you to know, for when you make your report to the Queen. I wasn't in it for greed. I wasn't hurting anyone. I was..."

"Helping?"

I felt my eyes start to sting. "Yes." My voice came out thinner and more fragile than I'd expected, and I tried not to wince.

Out of the corner of my eyes, I could see Davril regarding me strangely. I had the feeling he wanted to say something, maybe something kind, but if so, the mood passed. He bobbed his head and merely said, "I will put it in the report."

With that, he spun on his heels and marched away. When the sound of his footsteps was gone, I examined the cell. It wasn't quite as dark or dank as I had feared, but it was still dim. And small. I had never really appreciated how tiny a prison cell was before, but I could already feel claustrophobia setting in. I eyed the hard, narrow cot and shot the finger at the ceiling, as if the Fae Queen herself might be watching, magically peering through the stone, perhaps with the aid of a scrying mirror like the one I'd stolen last night.

"Screw you, Fae hag," I said. "I know you could make these cells nicer if you wanted."

But obviously, they didn't want to. Because in their righteous minds, criminals deserved this fate.

The dam holding back my emotions broke, and I collapsed onto the cot in tears.

CHAPTER 7

I jerked up at the sound of banging on the bars.

A face peered down at me, stony and unreadable. It wasn't Davril but another Fae, female, with auburn hair pulled back in an elaborate braid twined with tiny flowers, but her eyes were even flintier than Davril's.

"So you're the thief," she said.

I'd been trying to rest on the cot, unsuccessfully, but now I stood up. "I prefer heroic rogue," I said, straightening my back. "But yeah, that's me. Care to teach me how you do that braid?"

She sniffed but didn't reply. I heard locks popping and the door swung open. The Fae woman wore a suit of glinting armor, delicate-looking but surely harder than steel, and amazingly form-fitting and flexible, giving her full range of movement. This was another Fae Knight—Davril's more aloof, lamer twin sister.

My tears had dried hours ago, and my rebellious nature had reasserted itself. "So I'm to be released and given the keys to the castle, is it?" I asked jauntily.

The she-knight held up a gleaming pair of handcuffs. "Do I need to put these on or will you come quietly?"

"I don't know about quiet..."

She shook the cuffs meaningfully.

"Oh, very well," I said. "But this better be good. I was just about to catch some Zs."

"It will be good," she said, but the way she said it didn't make whatever "it" was sound very appealing. In fact, it made it sound rather sinister. "You're to go before the Queen of the Fae herself, Lady Calista."

I tried to suppress the flurry of panic that rose in me.

"A proper greeting, then," I said. "About damned time. I don't have all day, you know."

I emerged from the cell, and she allowed me to walk beside her as we passed back through the halls I'd just come through hours ago. It must have taken that long for Davril to submit his report to the Queen and for it to be processed. Or maybe they'd just wanted my time in the cell to soften me up a bit. That was probably more likely. Well, screw that. I wasn't going to be softened up for anything or anyone. If they wanted to chuck me in some dark hole, I sure as hell wouldn't go quietly. I'd go kicking and screaming, and I'd escape the first chance I got. Or die trying.

That was the thought that had dried my tears, and it stoked a fire inside me now. It was the only fire that could be stoked inside me these days, after the arch-fiend Vincent Walsh had done what he had. I forced myself not to think about it.

The she-knight, whose name turned out to be Jessela, led me through enchanted halls and courtyards, and I attempted not to look impressed. There were some amazing sights to behold, for sure, but I could only focus on the meeting to come. The Fae Queen? Damn it all, just what had I gotten myself into?

Jessela ushered me down a huge hall lined with Fae soldiers in niches along either side. Each held wickedly sharp swords at their sides. At the head of the hall stood a grand, beautifully worked metal door, and at a wave of Jessela's hand it swung open, revealing the awe-inspiring sight of the Throne Room. I gasped and took a step backward, and I only moved forward again when Jessela propelled me. She didn't look sympathetic at all to the wonder I felt.

And it *was* wonder. Sunshine shone down from the glass dome above, glinting on the marble floors and on all the golden detailing on the walls and windows. Grand statues stood here and there, wonderfully worked figures of what were probably Fae legends—beautiful women (and men, too) in flowing garments and flowers in their hair ... but often with weapons in their hands, too. Magic was baked into the great chamber. It simmered on the air and coursed along my arms as I stepped inside. Some of the statues moved, but that was only the beginning to the fantastic vision. Scented green water jetted high from numerous fountains or trickled down from the waterfalls that cascaded along the walls at intervals, the water coming from who knows where. Birds of brilliant and often shifting plumage flew over trees—yes, trees—that grew out of the marble floor, and from the thick limbs of these trees hung fruit of dizzying colors and scents. I had never seen their like before.

There was a whole forest, really, and grass, too. Beings that might be nymphs darted among the tree trunks, quick, lithe, and hard to see, and there were other shapes there, not all of them friendly-looking. An animal that looked like a huge, severely scowling owl perched on a hillock not far off, and a creature that resembled a horned tiger glided along at the base of the hill.

On the far side of the great chamber, a series of crystalline steps led up to a crystal dais upon which loomed a huge crystal throne that seemed like a snowflake exploding. The sun shone down from the dome overhead and made the whole thing sparkle like a dream, especially making the crown, armbands and other jewelry of its occupant gleam like stardust. The occupant of the throne had to be the Queen, of course, and she was the most beautiful woman I'd ever seen, tall and long-limbed, with flowing golden hair, and she sat on the throne as if born to it, which I guess she was. She wasn't cold like Jessela, but she wore an air of gravity and care about her that precluded much warmth and fun. She looked like a woman who had troubles—that was my take, anyway.

Jessela led me down the broad avenue that wound through the enchanted forest and finally to the base of the stairs leading up to the crystal throne. My heart slammed against my ribs, and I was breathing too fast. This was all too much for me, and I was reeling from sensory overload.

Then I received yet another shock. Standing right beside the throne was Davril Stormguard. He stood in his own gleaming, beautiful armor, with his sword visible at his hip, and he peered down at me with an expression I couldn't read. Was he the Queen's protector or something more? Maybe he was simply present to serve as a witness in my case.

"Welcome to my Court, Jade McClaren of the Highland McClarens," said Queen Calista.

I blinked. "You know my family, ma'am? Er, Your Highness?"

"Your Grace," Jessela hissed at me.

"Uh, Your Grace?" I said.

The Queen's smile was small but real. "I do. There was a famous Highlander witch named Rose, if I recall."

"That's right, ma'am. The legend was passed down through my father's family. My sister Ruby inherited that propensity. I received...another gift."

The Queen's nostrils flared, just slightly. "I smell it. You're a shifter, aren't you?"

"Yes...Your Grace."

"Please, approach."

When I stood stock-still, not knowing what to do, Jessela elbowed me toward the stairs. I almost stumbled on the first step but caught myself. I turned a nasty look on Jessela to see her smirking. Fuming, I faced forward again and ascended the crystal stairs, conscious of not just the Queen's gaze but also Davril's. In addition to the two of them, several other courtiers stood upon the dais, all dressed in shimmering, elegant, and very form-fitting finery. Some of it was obviously magical and changed color moment by moment.

As I drew closer to the throne, I was struck by the force of personality in Queen Calista's gaze. Her eyes were the blue of plunging mountain rivers. She was not just beautiful but formidable, as well. As I ascended, she seemed to regard me with greater interest, and her nostrils quivered slightly as she breathed in my scent.

At last, I reached the dais and stood before the throne awkwardly, trying not to shuffle or, hell, pass out. My head still swam. Davril watched me, so I returned my gaze to him. He didn't look away, but I could get no sense of his thoughts. He was as hard as the stone the castle was composed of. I had the impish urge to stick my tongue out at him, but I didn't think the Queen would approve of that, and I (just barely) resisted.

I turned back to Calista to see her staring at me, surprise on her face.

Alarmed, I said, "Yes, Your Grace?"

She rose from her throne. As soon as she did, Davril and the others on the dais knelt. I realized I was supposed to kneel, too, and awkwardly managed it without falling on my ass. *Why am I kneeling to her?* I asked myself. *She's not MY queen!* The Fae had great power, true, but they hadn't taken the country over, at least not officially. It might not be long, though. The people *wanted* them in charge.

"Dear gods," Calista said, approaching me, her face still full of amazement. I had a distressing notion why, too.

She knows, I thought. *She's smelled me and she knows.*

Shit.

As if to confirm my suspicions, Calista said, "I haven't encountered a dragon shifter in many years. Well...except for one."

A muttering stirred among the gathered dignitaries, and I glanced around to see shock in their faces, even fear. Davril's face turned even grimmer, the lines around his mouth hardening.

"My kind is rare," I admitted. "At least here. I kind of thought they were more common in your world. The Fae Lands."

She paced back and forth before me, stalking like a lioness. "How much do you know of the Fae Lands, Jade?"

"Very little, ma'am. I mean, Your Grace." My mind spun. *Just what the Sam Hell is this all about?* Surely it wasn't every criminal who was granted an audience with the Queen! There had to be something more at work here.

She stopped pacing and spun to face me. "Did you know that we didn't leave the Fae Lands willingly?"

I opened and closed my mouth. "Then...why did you?"

She regarded me in silence for a long moment. "We were forced out."

That sounded ominous. Suddenly, I realized I'd been right; there *was* something bigger at work here. Something *huge*.

"What could force the Fae out of the Fae Lands?"

"I will keep that under wraps for now. Tell me, when was the last time you shifted? I imagine it must be infrequent. It's difficult to transform into a dragon in the middle of New York—at least without causing mass panic." She sort of smiled, and I was relieved to feel some of the tension drain from the room. When I looked to Davril again, he had relaxed somewhat, though the other Fae still looked as if something had just walked across their graves. Maybe not walked—slithered. With slimy appendages flailing.

I lowered my eyes, grief and shame welling up in me at the Queen's question. It was the same wound Ruby had picked at earlier, and it didn't hurt any less now.

"I can no longer shift," I said. "I was only a half-shifter. But that ability was stolen from me years ago."

A puzzled divot appeared between Calista's arresting blue eyes. "Stolen from you? Explain."

"I don't want to bore you with the details..."

She returned to her throne and reclined on it elegantly, her hair falling perfectly into place. The sun shone down on her sparkly leotard-like outfit and made it gleam like a silver waterfall. It threw glints of heaven off the sharp points of her diamond crown.

"I would hear the story," she said.

I sighed. The last thing I wanted was to relive the tragic events of the past. "I'd really rather not," I said.

Her eyes speared me like a fish. "I'm sorry, Jade McClaren, did you think I was asking?"

I swallowed. "No, ma'am. I mean, Your Grace."

She waited. "Yes?"

Speaking in a clipped, strained voice, I said, "A mage did it. Vincent Walsh. He...stole my fire."

"I am very sorry, Jade. Is there more to tell?"

"I..." *More than I can say.* At least more than I could say without balling like a baby. "No, Your Grace."

"Very well. In any case, I am most sorry for what befell you." She let a beat go by, and clouds passed across the sun overhead, then moved on. "Now, to business." She waved a hand around the dais, drawing my attention once more to my situation, as if I might have forgotten. "Do you imagine it is every day that I entertain thieves in my court? That I clear the room for them?"

That hadn't occurred to me. But she was right. If this was the heart of her hive, and she was the queen bee, then why weren't there any drones buzzing about?

"I...guess not," I said lamely.

"Good. Because I don't. But there is something sinister threatening my court, and I have reason to believe it derives from the great evil that drove us from our lands and into your world ten years ago. This is a threat to us all, even your kind—humans, that is, not half-dragon shifters—and you would do well to take this as seriously as I do." She turned to Davril. "Isn't that so, Lord Stormguard?"

Lord Stormguard. A new flutter worked in my belly.

Davril had stood when she had retaken her seat, and so had the other courtiers. *I* was the only one still kneeling. *Idiot.* Hastily, I stood and dusted myself off, not that there was any dust in this place.

Looking vaguely amused at my discomfiture, Davril said, "I was assigned to watch the man you stole from last night, Jade. You don't need to know why, only that it has something to do with all this."

"Do tell," said a voice, and I turned to see Jessela. At some point, she had ascended the stairs and now stood behind me and to one side. One of her hands rested on the pommel of her gilded sword, and I didn't like the thought of her at my back.

Davril didn't respond to her provocation, though, if that was what it was. Just what was their relationship, anyway?

"You stole the item I was there to monitor," Davril told me. "I knew how to track it and followed you to the man, Jason Mattox, who I believe served as your fence. I eavesdropped on your conversation and knew where you were bound, so I inserted myself into the crowd at Pandora's Box. I had meant to see if you met any other underworld contacts in an attempt to trace your network. Make a map of this underworld of yours." He let out a breath. "I should have simply retaken the golden antler and let you be."

Jessela sniffed. "Something about her interested you, Davril. Just what was it?"

Davril ground his jaw—I could see it bunch—but he refused to take her bait. There was something there, something to their relationship. But also something to what she said. Davril had jeopardized his mission because of me. *That* was a shock.

"Lord Stormguard could not have known what would happen to Mr. Mattox," Queen Calista said, but the pain in her eyes was obvious. She mourned for the loss of Jason, for the loss of an innocent mixed up in all this. That endeared me to her, if only a little. I was still her captive, after all.

I decided to speak up. With more boldness than I felt, I asked Davril, "If you can track the antler, why not just go find it?"

A flicker passed across his face that might have been a wince. "Whoever stole it is masking its signature, Jade. Our antagonist is no novice, unfortunately. This was well planned and, so far, well executed. There's no way to find the antler now, at least not in that fashion. But we have reason to believe that whoever did do this is using the human criminal underground in some way—though *how* exactly we don't know."

Queen Calista once more swung her gaze to me, and I could see the terrible weight in it. Something in me went cold.

With deceptive mildness, she said, "We *could* use someone associated with the human underground. To help us track down the antler."

I rocked back on my heels as the meaning of it came crashing home. *This* was why the court had been cleared, why I had been given a special audience with Her Majesty.

"You..." Once more, I opened and closed my mouth, but only a squeak came out. When I could talk, I said, "You want *me* to help you find Jason's killer?"

"And retrieve the antler, yes." Queen Calista flicked her eyes to Davril. "Lord Stormguard can use all the help he can get."

I almost laughed. "You want me...*to team up with Davril*...I mean, Lord Stormguard...to do this?'

Davril scowled at me, and the urge to laugh only grew. I half-turned to see Jessela looking amused, too, if only at Davril's discomfiture.

"That is the situation," Davril said, sounding as if he wished he could say anything else. "If you agree, and if the mission is successful, you will be pardoned and free to go. As long as you promise not to steal anything else from a subject of the Fae."

I crossed my fingers behind my back. "I promise," I said. "Now let's go get Jason's killer."

And get my sister back, I thought but didn't say.

CHAPTER 8

"I can't believe this is happening," I said as Davril led me through the halls of the palace. He looked thoroughly put out by it all. "We're going to be working together!"

"I wouldn't get too excited," he said dryly.

"I'm not *excited*; it's just interesting."

"Anyway, it will be brief. We're not becoming partners or anything."

I flashed a smile. "Aren't we?"

He frowned at me. Staring up at him, I was suddenly aware of how huge he was, how wide his shoulders were, and how deep his chest. The shining armor made him even bigger, of course, but he didn't need its help; he was a giant. I felt tiny standing in front of him.

"I mean, we *are* working together," I said. "Doesn't that make us partners?"

His cold eyes stared at me out of that ridiculously chiseled face. "No," he said curtly. "It doesn't."

He continued striding up the hall, and I scurried after him. We were passing through a lovely high passage filled with magical displays. Currently what looked like an aurora borealis shimmered overhead, fantastic waves of color rippling like the waves of the ocean, red and green and blue and yellow. Warmth tingled along my skin, and the scent of baking apples filled my nose. Fae magic was awesome.

"You will be quartering here until the task is accomplished," Davril said, his eyes forward, not looking at me.

"I'm going to *live* at the palace?"

He hedged. "You will *stay* at the palace."

We marched up a delicate-looking spiral stairway and down another hall lined with handsome wooden doors. He stopped before one and swung it open, revealing a small but very pretty apartment complete with a plush bed and a window admitting a shining shaft of light.

"This is where you will stay," he said. "I'll leave you now."

He started to turn, but I touched his arm. "Why didn't the Queen ask about Ruby, my sister?"

Davril stared at me for a moment, then glanced away. Sounding somehow subdued, he said, "Because that would have raised questions in her mind. It certainly does in mine. *Why* was she taken? It makes no sense."

I could have told him she had been taken to use as leverage against me, but that would only alert him to the fact that my loyalties were divided. If push came to shove, I would do whatever I had to in order to save Ruby, even if it meant going against the mission of retrieving the antler of the Golden Hind.

"I wish I knew," I lied.

He shook his head, as if shrugging the questions away. "In any case, it would have made the Queen doubt you. She might have thought you had more to do with this than the rest of the facts would indicate."

Shock ran through me, and I took a step backward, then stared at Davril in wonder. He avoided my eyes.

"You lied to the Queen," I said, then realized I had spoken too loud. Whispering, I said, "You lied to the Queen to protect me!"

He looked like he regretted starting this conversation. "To get you released, yes. I didn't imagine she would *team you up with me*. I work best alone." He didn't have to add that he would work even better not saddled with a criminal, a half-human and an utter amateur in all things Fae Knight.

Acting impulsively, I reached out and squeezed one of his hands. He wore gauntlets, but the palms were leather, and I knew he could feel the pressure.

"Thank you," I said, and meant it.

"Well. If that is all, I'll leave you now. Someone, not me, thank the gods, will fetch you to dinner later. Tomorrow morning, we will begin investigating the case. I want you to be thinking about what steps to take next."

"*Me?*"

The seriousness in his look sobered me. "Remember, Jade, the reason you're assigned to me is that we need your insight. Your connections."

"You mean...you'll go wherever I say?"

His mouth quirked in annoyance. "Within reason."

I tapped his chest, indicating his armor. "You'll need to lose this."

"Done." He paused. "You weren't entirely forthcoming about having your fire stolen."

"That's my own business."

"Actually, no."

"No?"

He laid a hand on my shoulder, and I jumped at the contact. His hand was strong, and I could feel the great power in it. He didn't squeeze, though, at least not hard.

"No," he said again. "You are, however temporarily, my partner. Sort of. And I need to know who I'm partnering with. What makes you tick. That makes it my business. I can sense there's a lot you're not telling us. And whatever that is, it's what drives you, Jade. What motivates you."

"I don't know..."

He held up a finger, silencing me. "I *know*." He withdrew his hand and stood back. Almost ruefully, he added, "I don't know *what* I don't know, but I know I don't know everything I need to."

He lied to his queen about me, and now he wants to know me better. "I'll...think about it," I said.

"See that you do. I want the truth tomorrow. Along with our destination."

He marched away, the faint clanking of his armor receding down the hall, and I watched him until he rounded a corner, for some reason thinking he might look back, but he didn't. Sighing, I passed into the apartment and shut the door behind me. The suite was simple enough, but homey for all that. It was certainly a far cry from the dungeon. And I owed it all to Davril for lying on my behalf. What did that mean? What did I *want* it to mean?

Nothing, I told myself. *Anyway, the last thing I need is to get hooked up with a magical cop who hates my kind, or more likely, to start obsessing about a magical cop and then never attain the object of my affection. Besides, I have other fish to fry.*

Not knowing what to think, I flung myself on the bed and stared up at the stone ceiling. Ivy twined across it, bursting with red flowers.

I pictured Ruby. Where was she now? How was she doing? I prayed she was safe and well. But there was something that made no sense to me. If Ruby had been taken because the nefarious party who had spoken to me in the mirror needed the golden antler, then who the fuck had killed Jason and taken the antler? Were there *two* nefarious parties at work here, both wanting the antler? I couldn't make heads nor tails of it. But that did seem to be the situation. The skull-like face in the mirror had contacted me after Jason had been murdered, which mean that it, or the powers behind it, did not have the antler.

There *were* two villains, I thought, or maybe even more. Maybe two whole *sets* of villains. Skull-Face was Villain One, and Creature Summoner was Villain Two. Villain Two had the antler, but for what purpose? No one had ever really explained to me what use the antler served. Obviously it fulfilled some magical function, but what that was, I couldn't imagine. I wasn't a real witch, after all, and certainly not a Fae.

No, I thought. *I'm a dragon.*

A long, sad sigh escaped my lips. For a moment, I remembered being a young girl before my fire had been stolen. Back then, I could shift, at least as much as I could. Wings would burst from my back and I could fly into the air as high as I wanted. I was free and weightless and happy. I could defend myself, too. I could breathe fire.

I laughed to remember Mom beating out the flames on the Christmas tree one year after I had belched (due to too many pancakes) and accidentally set the tree on fire. Ruby had been the one to finally put it out. She had been tiny then, but she had gravitated toward magic early on and knew just enough to turn the tree to ice. That had killed the fire, true enough, but it had also caused the tree to shatter into a million pieces.

My laughter turned to tears as I thought of little Ruby with her bright red hair covered in ice particles, trying to stamp out a little spark of fire that still jumped from the carpet. She'd still had a little blueberry on her cheek from the jam she'd smeared on the pancakes, and she'd been about to cry. She kept saying, "I broke the tree, Mommy! I broke the tree!"

I'll find you soon, Ruby, I promised.

Somehow, despite my fear for my sister and the general turmoil in my mind, I must have fallen asleep, because before I knew it, knocking jerked me out of slumber. Rubbing my eyes, I said, "Come in."

It was Jessela, accompanied by two other women who were obviously not knights judging by their livery. Of course, Jessela didn't look much like a knight at the moment, either. She wore a flowing, elegant blue dress that might have been chiffon, all lace and ruffles, and her hair had been put up with a dozen glinting pins.

"What's this?" I asked as the two women began measuring me. One had brought along a bright purple dress and laid it on the bed while I stood and submitted to being fussed over.

"They're some of our dressmakers," Jessela said. "Geniuses, all of them, if they can make me look like this." She indicated her dress and hair with a rueful smile. For a moment, I began to like her. Then I remembered how frosty she'd been to me earlier and held myself back.

"But what's the occasion?" I asked as one of the women brushed my hair.

"Dinner, of course," Jessela said. "Queen Calista likes us to look our best. 'Respect yourselves and others will respect you, too,' she likes to say. But really, I think she just likes us to look nice. *She* certainly likes to look nice."

"Strip this off," one of the women told me, tugging at my cat-burglar outfit. "We'll incinerate it."

"Don't you dare," I said, but I allowed them to peel it off me. It had become grimy in the dungeon, sweaty and a bit torn from my misadventures. "Just clean it and mend it if you can, then return it to me. I'll want to wear it tomorrow." I laughed. "My friends in the underworld wouldn't know what to do if I showed up looking like...that." I smiled and pointed at Jessela's outfit, and she rewarded me with an amused look.

"That I would like to see," she said wryly.

I hadn't been dressed by others before, at least not since my mother used to dress me for church, and that had been a hell of a long time ago. I bore it all with only the occasional curse and elbow jab, and finally emerged like a butterfly from a cocoon. Gasping in delight, I stared in the mirror that hung from one wall and ran my hands along the purple dress, which was becoming more form-fitting by the second thanks to the spells the dress-makers were laying on it even as I watched. Its hue accentuated the purple highlights in my black hair, and even as I admired the dress, one of the women was dabbing purple glints onto my eyelashes. I was getting all purpled up.

"You look splendid," Jessela said. "I never would've known it was you."

I shot her a look. *There* was the cattiness I'd been expecting. "Excuse me?"

To her credit, she seemed to realize what she'd said. "I only meant…you look nice," she said, trying to recover, and I had to give her props for trying.

"That's okay," I said. "I'm not used to looking this good, either." The fact was that I'd never looked this good. "And you do this every night?"

"No, but often. Just as often, I stand guard while others eat. We knights rotate shifts."

"Is that what you do, mainly—protection?"

"Different knights have different duties, and some of us rotate through those, too. The higher-level knights serve the Queen's interests outside of the Fae sphere."

"Like Davril."

"Right. Sometimes, I'll take up duty outside the palace, too, but I'm mostly stationed here, or at least in the realm of the Fae. I don't go much into the human world." She bit her lip, and I was surprised to see her act a bit…well, not intimidated, but at least humbled, or hesitant, or something. I couldn't quite place it. "The truth is, you're one of the first humans I've ever interacted with."

That explained some of her frostiness. To her, we were an alien species. I guess we really were, too, in a way. Although we looked so much alike that obviously there was some common ancestor at one point.

"And I'm guessing that most of the humans you have interacted with have been criminals, am I right?" I said.

"True," she admitted, then cast a look at the dressmakers; they were pretending not to listen as they made last-minute adjustments to my dress and makeup. Apparently, they weren't just dressmakers but make-over artists—gods knew, I needed the help.

"You're the first human I've met who was given free rein in the castle."

"Is that what I've been given, free rein? You mean I can go…anywhere?"

She actually laughed. "Well, not *any*where, but you can wander about without supervision."

"I think that's about it, miss," one of the make-over artists told me. "You're ready to go."

I flashed another look quick in the mirror, shocked at just how good I looked, then thanked each of the women profusely. They took it all with wide smiles, then left.

"Are you ready for the feast?" Jessela asked.

My heart fluttered. "I'm ready."

We left my little room and marched through the corridors of the palace toward the dining hall. As we went, others joined us, all Fae decked out in their finery. Each Fae was beautiful, whether male or a female, and their clothes would have dropped jaws on Fifth Avenue.

"So how well do you know Davril?" I asked Jessela, careful to keep my voice casual.

One of her eyebrows shot up. "I've known him for centuries, my dear."

Centuries. Jesus. I had forgotten the Fae were practically immortal.

"How well have you known him during that time?" I asked.

"You noticed my dodge, eh?"

"Yes." *Just answer the question!*

"Why do you ask?" She cast me a sidelong glance, then returned her attention forward. More and more people were joining us in the halls, or we had entered a well-populated area, and there was noise and conversation all around. Just the same, she had lowered her voice, which I appreciated.

"No reason," I said, hoping my voice didn't creak.

Still looking annoyingly amused, she said, "Then I have no reason to answer."

I resisted the urge to strangle her. "I just wondered, that's all. I mean, he is going to be my, uh, partner soon."

She frowned. "I hadn't forgotten."

I sighed. She was still holding back, and holding answers, too. For some reason, I found myself wanting to be friends with her. She was a beautiful (of course) badass Fae Knight, and she knew all the ins and outs of this place. What's more, she knew my future partner much better than I did, and I wanted all the information I could get on him. Which was the *only* reason I was asking, I told myself. I was just collecting information. Intelligence gathering. Right.

A grand archway appeared around a bend, and we all poured into a great open room that seemed half ballroom, half immense dining room, with several large tables on various levels and a great open dance floor to one side. Magical balls of white-gold light hovered over the tables, and others shone from the fruits of the enchanted trees that sprang up throughout, giving the space an almost arboreal feel. The sap of the trees emitted a pleasing, cinnamon aroma, and it brought a pleasant lift to my mind. Better than smoking cigarettes.

Jessela and I ascended to the highest level and gathered around a huge polished-wood table with radiant red bark, along with many other handsome people—all Fae, no humans. Queen Calista took a seat at the head of the table first, with some fanfare—but not much—and then the rest of us sat.

Lord Davril Stormguard, looking most handsome indeed in his velvet and silk finery, with the light of the hovering orbs glowing on his golden hair, sat close to the Queen. He wore no sword. Or at least not a visible one. He wore tight leggings, which showed off every bulge of his muscular legs, buttocks, and, erm, other parts to great effect. At least the effect was great on me. I couldn't speak for Jessela or the others.

As we sat down, he swung his gaze toward me, and I hastily looked away. My cheeks smoldered.

"Well met, friends," Queen Calista said. Even though she hadn't raised her voice, it echoed throughout the chamber. People at the other tables had found their seats by this time, and they were listening respectfully. "As many of you know, there are dark forces at work here lately, but have no fear. We have just taken steps to counter our enemies and drive them back." Her blue eyes fell on me, and I shifted in discomfort. Could she possibly be talking about *me?* "So relax and enjoy yourselves," Calista went on. "We will eat and dance and celebrate being alive."

While she talked, her guests had been pouring wine into their glasses (I had been so bewildered I'd barely noticed) and now they lifted their glasses and said, "Hear, hear!"

Dully, I reached for my still-empty glass and raised it, echoing their words.

Dinner came, one course after another, but I didn't comprehend much of it. My head was swimming with the heady magic radiating all around me, throbbing in my bones and filtering throughout my body. I felt like I was being irradiated, but in a good way, if that made any sense—completely fried by magic.

"Just breathe, my dear," said the Fae Lord next to me. He was a handsome fellow with brown hair and a thick mustache—one of the few Fae I'd seen sporting facial hair.

"I'm trying," I told him.

"Allow me to introduce myself. I'm Lord Gerwyn Seafoam."

"Er, nice to meet you. Jade McClaren."

We shook hands, though his was a little hesitant, and I realized Fae must not shake hands like humans did. Or maybe it was a Western thing, I wasn't sure. Did Chinese people shake hands? If not, it made sense that Fae wouldn't, either.

"Is it true that you're going to work with Lord Stormguard?" asked a female Fae from across the table.

I started to answer, but Jessela leaned in and said, "Beash, she probably doesn't want to be peppered with questions."

The other female Fae bowed her head, accepting this. "But of course."

"Forgive her," Gerwyn Seafoam said. "She's just curious. I'm afraid we all are."

"I didn't know the Fae gossiped so much," I dared to say.

"I'm afraid we do, dear," said another Fae Lord, a handsome fellow with hair as long as Jessela's and as blond as Davril's.

"That's Lord Greenleaf," Jessela whispered. "The Queen's Grand Vizier."

"We gossip a *lot*," Greenleaf added. He said this glancing at the Fae all around, as if warning them not to pester me with questions. They nodded respectfully, and the conversation moved on to other matters. I nodded to Greenleaf, showing my appreciation, but he just smiled.

The courses were light and delicious, with lots of fish, elegant sauces, and crunchy bread. I tried not to drink too much, partly because I didn't want to get even more out of sorts and partly because, for me, this wasn't a day to celebrate. A friend of mine had just been killed and my sister had been abducted by God knew who. These Fae might be in a festive mood, but to me their cheer felt remote and strange.

Jessela seemed to sense my mood. At one point, she indicated the great windows that covered half the chamber.

"Isn't it lovely?" she said.

From here, we could see the stars shimmering in inky blackness above, and lights that were almost like stars winking from the many towers of the vast city below.

"It really is," I admitted. I pictured the comparative rat hole where Ruby and I lived and could only shake my head in amazement of the change one day could bring. Thinking of Ruby only depressed me, though, and Jessela looked disappointed when I didn't brighten.

I remained quiet as the Fae finished their meals and migrated to the dance floor. Music had sprung up from somewhere, and it was like nothing I'd ever heard, faster and more challenging than I'd expected, but very classical, too. Somehow, the Fae musicians had found common ground between Beethoven and Bon Jovi. To my surprise, the music made me tap my toes, but I was shocked when I found Davril looming over me, his hand outstretched.

"Would you care to dance?" he asked.

"Uh…"

I shot a look to Jessela, but she waved a hand as if to say *This is between you two.*

I turned back to Davril. His gunmetal eyes drilled into me. *Think of Ruby,* I thought. *Think of Jason.* But his eyes continued assessing me, and all other thoughts slipped from my mind.

"Um, okay," I said. But only to continue my research. I needed to get to know my future partner better.

I took his hand, and he led me down the various daises to the dance floor. I was only a little surprised to see the Fae Lords around me begin to lift off from the floor and float through the air as if gravity were only an illusion, or maybe as if they were fish swimming through the sea. Gorgeous, stately fish shimmering with fantastic scales. Okay, maybe not like fish at all. But I did feel like I was underwater. Being bombarded with magical energy was bad enough, but having a bunch of well-dressed dancers waltzing over my head? I was simultaneously about to barf and weep with joy at the beauty of it all.

Davril's hand went around my back before I could prepare myself, and he pressed me against him. My other hand was still firmly in his.

"Shall we?" he asked, wearing an infuriating smile, and like that—snap—we were lifting off the ground.

"Ack!" I said, flailing my feet.

As I did, I lost my balance. His arm tightened around me, holding me close.

"Don't do that," he said. "Your feet still control how you move. Pretend there's a floor under you."

"So you're not flying?"

He laughed, and I kind of loved how his face crinkled up when he did, and how his muscular throat flexed.

"Fae can't fly," he said. "At least not on their own. There are beings that can, of course," he added, but he didn't elaborate—at least not in the way I'd hoped. "Witches, too, need a little help, but they seem to get around okay."

"I'm not a witch."

"That broomstick you were riding says differently."

"It's my sister's."

"The one who was abducted." He frowned.

I had to change the topic. We were dancing now, sailing through the air twenty feet above the ballroom floor. Other dancers spun and twirled around us. Davril was leading me, his hand on my back light and firm at the same time. Pressed against him, I was annoyingly aware of just how firm he was, and how large—tall. And his shoulders were very broad.

"You look nice," I said, which had to be the worst diversion ever.

His frown continued for a moment, then lightened. "As do you."

I felt my throat swell up. "Really?"

"Really."

He smiled again, then led me in twirl. I laughed, surprised at how smooth it was, and felt even hotter when he caught me and dipped me. Our faces were very close. I hoped my breath wasn't rank.

Straightening, we continued to dance, both quiet for a moment. Then he said, as if to kill the mood, "Have you decided where we're going to tomorrow?"

Damn it. *That* was why he'd asked me to dance. He hadn't wanted to dance at all—not that I had, either, sheesh, come on—but to grill me about tomorrow's activities. Or to push me into planning it out.

"Actually, I don't have any idea," I said. "I mean, I've got *some* ideas—haha, you don't need to put me back in jail or anything." *So funny, Jade.* "But, um, I haven't narrowed them down."

"You're trying to pick the best lead."

"Exactly. I—"

Before I could go lamely fumbling for an excuse, a high-pitched scream cut the air.

CHAPTER 9

My head snapped in the direction of the scream. It had come from the daises leading up to the one the Queen's table perched on. Some huge ogre-like thing, complete with tufts of hair sticking out all over its muscular body, was striding up to the top dais, sword clutched in its hand.

"A troll!" Davril said.

Ice flooded my veins. "Get us down," I said. The last thing I needed was to be stranded in the air during combat.

Davril lowered us to the dance floor. Other dancers were alighting on the floor, as well. Meanwhile, the troll marched up the daises.

A Fae Lord sprang at the creature, yanking out his dress sword, but the blade shattered on the tough hide of the monster. The troll grabbed the Fae Lord up in the hand not holding the sword and flung him against an ornate column. I winced as I heard his body crack.

Another Fae Lord jumped at the monster, then a Fae lady. He swatted the first down, then stabbed the second.

Davril ripped out his own sword, which appeared from nowhere like before, and launched himself at the troll. I screamed for him to stop, hardly believing what I was doing, then rushed to help him.

The troll had reached the highest dais. It raised his bloody sword high over Queen Calista, who glowered at it in defiance. I was amazed by her calm demeanor and bravery. She didn't even lift a finger to defend herself. *She's crazy*, I thought.

But no.

The troll swung the sword down at her head, hard, with all the strength the brute possessed. There came a flash of light right before the blade struck her shining crown, and a blast of energy flung the troll back. It landed on its back, groaned, and sat up, still clutching its sword.

Two more Fae Lords jumped at it—well, one was a Fae lady. It grabbed the lord and bit his head off, then smashed the Fae lady in the head, snapping her spine.

Davril ran toward the monster. I was right behind him. I didn't see how either of us could stop the beast.

Davril cocked his arm back—the one holding his weapon—and then launched the sword like a missile, right into the troll's eye. The sword sank all the way to the hilt. The monster gave a last groan and toppled backward. It struck the floor with a mighty *bam!* and didn't move again.

"You did it!" I cheered.

He didn't acknowledge my praise, and we turned back to the dead monster.

Queen Calista stormed down the stairs, a deep scowl on her face. By her side was Lord Gerwyn Seafoam, the Fae with the brown mustache, holding his sword in hand. Queen Calista started to say something else, but someone shouted, and several of the Fae pointed toward the windows. Davril, Calista and I turned to see two witches on broomsticks hovering beyond the windows. They must have been watching the action. I couldn't imagine how they'd gotten so close to the palace without being seen; even the best cloaking spells couldn't overcome the magic of the Fae Lords. Unless...

But no, I thought. *Surely not!*

In any case, the cloaking spell had dissolved and the witches were plain to see.

"Get them," Calista shouted.

Several Fae Lords ran to the balconies and jumped on their steeds. Davril clearly wanted to join them, but he knew his place was to guard the Queen. He stood by her even as the other Fae Knights gave chase to the witches. The two figures on their broomsticks vanished into the night, pursued by Fae Knights on winged horses and riding in winged cars.

At last our attention returned to the fallen troll...which was no longer a troll.

"Huh?" I said.

Because even as we watched, it was slipping forms, transforming from a huge, hideous brute to a young man in the clothes of a Fae Lord. He was handsome enough to pass for one of them, but I sensed he was only pretending.

"A mortal," Davril said, as if to confirm my suspicions.

"He must have slipped in somehow," Calista said.

"But how?"

That was Jessela, approaching the scene with her sword still unsheathed and a lock of hair out of place. She looked sweaty and tense, and I didn't blame her.

"That's the question of the day," said another voice, and I turned to see Lord Greenleaf, the Grand Vizier.

"If he was an assassin," I said, daring to speak up, "then he had help. Those witches may have been able to give him spells to turn him into that thing, but no way could they help him sneak in here. At least, I don't think so," I added shakily as all eyes turned to regard me.

"I agree," Calista said, and I let out a breath in relief. She had come to my aid.

"But who could have let him in?" Davril said.

No one had an answer.

"How did you resist that blow?" I asked Queen Calista. "When the troll struck at you, he just rebounded."

She touched a jewel in her crown. "I am protected."

"Did *he* know that?" I pointed my chin at the body.

No one had an answer to that, either.

"Maybe that's what the witches were observing," Davril said. "They sent the troll in to attack you, Your Grace, to find out what would happen. This poor creature was their sacrifice to discover what protective wards you have."

"If so, then now they know," Gerwyn Seafoam said.

More Fae Lords and Ladies had gathered to the scene of the carnage, gingerly stepping over and around the dead bodies. Several of the Fae were kneeling over the corpses, checking for signs of life or trying to heal them, but I didn't think they'd have any luck. Fae were said to be immortal, but even they couldn't live with a snapped neck, although I was sure it would take a lot of force to snap. But the troll had that power and then some.

Suddenly, I spied something.

Crouching down beside the body of the assassin, I peeled back his sleeve, exposing a network of tattoos. One was an unusual snake tattoo, or possibly a dragon. I unbuttoned his shirt, revealing a muscular chest also covered in ink.

"What are you looking for?" Jessela said, squatting next to me.

Davril peered down at us critically, as did various other Fae. I itched to be out from under their scrutiny.

"Gang signs," I said. "Or some underworld symbol. Or maybe —ha!" I laughed as a tattoo caught my attention.

"What is it?" Davril inquired.

Despite the horror all around us, I grinned and pointed to the tattoo of a beautiful young woman with flowing black hair and liquid dark eyes.

"That's Moody Maria," I said. "Can someone bring me my phone? It's in my belt. I need to take a picture."

"Moody who?" Jessela sounded confused, and the Queen frowned. The Fae Lords were muttering to themselves.

To Davril, I said, "I know where we're going tomorrow."

~

"This is crazy," Davril said as we flew through the lanes between buildings. He hunched behind the wheel of Lady Kay, his face stoic but just slightly brooding and judgmental. I was getting to know him well enough to read his expressions.

"Crazy or not," I said. "That's where we're going."

"A brothel! Really?"

I rolled my shoulders. I was once more in my (dead sexy) cat-burglar outfit, complete with my utility belt full of spellgredients. They were all cleaned and pressed.

"That's where Moody Maria works," I explained, "and our would-be assassin obviously sees her regularly. Enough to have a huge tattoo of her face etched over his liver. It's not his heart, I'll grant you, but I bet he used his liver more than he ever did his heart."

Davril let out an annoyed breath. "I can't believe I let you talk me into this. No Fae Knight should be caught dead in such a place."

I threw my legs on the dashboard and laced my fingers behind my head. "That's why you hired me, though, isn't it? Because I'm *not* a Fae Knight and I *wouldn't* do the sorts of things Fae Knights do."

"We didn't hire you. You're a felon, or close enough. And get your legs off my dash."

"*Our* dash," I said, but obeyed. It wasn't worth causing a fight over, even if I did enjoy watching his face turn, just subtly, red. "We're partners, remember?"

"We're not exactly partners," he grumbled.

"No?"

"Partnership implies equality, and we are not equal."

I put my hand over my mouth, pretending to yawn. "I know, I know. You cop, me robber. Here, turn right."

He muttered something under his breath but complied...with a little more alacrity than necessary. I resisted a curse as the car banked too swiftly, then righted itself. Davril and Ruby had a similar sense of humor, evidently.

Thinking of my sister again, I stared out the window. Morning sunlight stroked the wings of two griffons to the right, and the policemen on their mounts nodded once to Davril—he nodded back—then flew off. Two sets of law enforcement officers acknowledging each other. All I could think of was Ruby.

Be safe, Sis, I thought. *Be well and be safe.* I had to believe she was alive and okay. It was the only way I could get through this.

When would Skull-Face contact me again? He'd said it would be soon and that I'd better have the antler by then. I started to ask Davril what he thought about the situation, then remembered I couldn't tell him. He shouldn't know our enemies were using Ruby against me. Then he'd know he and I might not be on the same side, after all.

"You never did tell me your secret," he said suddenly, and I jumped.

Trying not to look guilty, I muttered, "What?"

"About how your fire got stolen—your dragonfire. How you lost the ability to shift. You told me you would tell me the whole story. Well, what is it?"

"Are you ready to tell me *your* secrets?"

He said nothing, which disturbed me. His silence seemed to imply that he did have secrets. What could they be? Thinking about it made me frown. I'd just said that to nettle him, but I seemed to have touched on something real.

"I meant your kind," I elaborated. "Why you fled the Fae Lands. Just what dark power drove you out of them?"

He seemed to relax. It was subtle, but I noticed it. All his expressions were subtle. But he did have them. Knowing he had emotions was empowering somehow. He wasn't some alien, remote god. He was human, too, in his own way.

"I'm afraid some of that is a state secret," he said.

"Turn right," I said.

He banked the wheel.

"Now left," I told him two blocks later, and he obeyed. Slowly, I said, "But not all of it is secret? What part isn't?" When he remained silent, I pressed, "You *said* you'd tell me."

His jaws bunched. "I will. In time. First, you tell me yours."

I laughed. "I show you mine and you show me yours?"

"I don't understand."

He probably didn't. I resisted a sigh.

"Go down," I said, and pointed to a line of brownstones. "That's where we're going. Last one on the right."

He set Lady Kay down along the curb, and we emerged into the bright morning. Warm sunlight stroked my skin, and I inhaled deeply, loving the smell of the tall trees that lined the road. Augmented by sorcerers, their flowers gave off a scent like vanilla.

"That smells awesome, doesn't it?" I said.

Davril scanned the street, then the brownstones. "Is that the one?"

No small talk, then.

"That's the one," I said.

Going up the stairs, we passed a man heading the other way. He looked drained but happy, and he was buttoning his shirt as he went. Davril suppressed his own discomfort, and I tried not to look too smug. Pushing through the doors, we came into a foyer in which three men sat on a couch. The room was ornate and old-fashioned, with a hanging chandelier and Persian rug, all rather fancy for a foyer, really. But I knew that this was the only room in the house...other than the small guardroom that stood off to the left, where guards would watch TV and thumb through magazines. When they weren't surfing porn.

Currently, two bare-chested and very hot male guards stood beside the grand, lacquered door that stood opposite the entranceway.

"Maria has good taste in guards, doesn't she?" I asked Davril, but he only gave me an annoyed look.

Striding up to the guards, he said, "Allow us entry. We wish to speak to Maria."

"I don't think so," said one of the guards, a tall man with deep brown eyes. "You're not on the list for today."

"We're on the business of Queen Calista."

"Even so."

Davril's hand strayed to the handle of his sword, which was currently invisible but which was about to become all too clear as soon as he touched it.

Acting quickly, I sidled past him and put on my biggest smile. Tracing a finger up the guard's firm bicep, I said, "James, you remember me, don't you?"

He looked me up and down. "Yeah. You're one of those McClaren sisters, aren't you? Ruby and Jade?"

"She's Jade," said the other guard, giving me an approving leer, which was both creepy and complimentary. "Can't you tell the difference?"

"I'm a friend of Maria's," I told James. "Mind letting us in, just for a moment? We have a quick question to ask her."

James and Bobby, the other guard, exchanged glances, then James said, "I'll ask Madam, but I know what she's going to say. *You* will be able to go in," he said to me, then flicked his eyes to Davril. "*You'll* have to stay out here. She doesn't want cops in her private place."

"This is my investigation," Davril said, "and I will go where I will."

James flexed his big hands. When he did, the golden bracelets he wore on his wrists shimmered. They were magical and would give him superhuman speed and strength. Bobby wore them, too. Maria outfitted all her guards with them—just in case. It meant they could give Davril a run for his money if they wanted. The bands also made the guards look super hot.

"Easy, boys," I said. "Easy. We're all friends here."

"I highly doubt that," Davril said. His fingers had curled around the hilt of his sword, which was now visible.

The three johns on the couches were glancing from the ensuing scuffle to the exit, perhaps wondering if they should make a break for it. Such were the charms of Maria, though, that none of them did. At least, not yet.

To James, I said, "Why don't you contact Maria and let her know I'm here…with Davril?" Thinking quick, I said, "Tell her he's smokin'."

"I will not," James said, puffing out his chest, and even Davril looked unsure at this new stratagem. He wanted to pass the threshold under his own authority, not his good looks. But he would have to learn that one used what one had.

Tracing my finger down James's seriously hard abs, I batted my eyelashes. "Please?"

At last, he relaxed. "Oh, alright."

We had to wait until Maria signaled James that she was ready for the next client, which wasn't long—after all, we'd just seen the last one leave. James opened the door, revealing strong sunlight, but Bobby was the one who ushered Davril and me through it. Davril mashed his eyes against the sun.

"I don't understand," he said as we stepped through. "Is it a magical sun? It's almost like we're…"

"Outside?" I said, and swept my arms before us. As my eyes adjusted, I could see that we stood in the desert sands before a sprawling green oasis filled with waving palm trees, luscious grass, and a lovely pool the same shade as the crystal blue sky.

The door slammed behind us.

Spinning, we could see that it had vanished. We were now trapped in the desert, somewhere other than New York. *Far* from New York.

"Ah," Davril said, nodding. "The door was a magical portal. Clever."

I surveyed the oasis, noting the seashell path leading into the heart of the palms.

"I think that's where we're supposed to go." I started down the path. After a moment, Davril followed. Just for something to say, I told him, "We can only return when Maria lets us. *If* she lets us. So be nice. It's a long walk back to Manhattan."

"How long has she located her services here?"

"Not long," I said. "She changes it all the time. Last time, it was on a mountaintop in the Alps." I mock shivered. "Very cold. This is much better." But even as I spoke, sweat welled up from my pores and beaded my skin. I turned to Davril to see him looking just the slightest bit flushed, too. It was *hot*.

We began to hear noises ahead—at first, I wasn't sure what to make of them, but as we pushed forward through the dense palms, the noises resolved into the unmistakable sounds of combat: the ringing of metal, the thump of flesh, and someone crying out.

"Shit," I said.

I sprinted forward. I may have lost my crossbow back at Hawthorne's penthouse, but I still had my spellgredients, and even as I ran, I was mentally preparing to use a spell. I wasn't sure which one would be called for, so I cycled through the options in my head.

"Jade, wait," Davril called, and I heard him running after me. I might be a lowly criminal in his eyes, but that didn't mean he would let me go to my death. That might have warmed me, but I knew he just saw me as a tool to help his queen. *She* was the one who had his loyalty, not me.

The path opened up ahead. Breathless, I ran out into a

clearing near the lagoon. At first, I wasn't sure what I was looking at. In the middle of the space was a patio mounted with a cute table laden with wine bottles and what looked like wine bottles in a basket, while to the side hunched a huge four-poster bed. Or at least that was what I thought I *should* be seeing; instead, the table was broken, the wine bottles smashed, and the bed in ruins.

Two bodies sprawled on the cobbles of the patio: two handsome, swarthy men with bare chests and pantaloons. Definitely Maria's servants.

They had apparently been struck down by the creature advancing on Maria.

The lady herself, no mere damsel in distress, had grabbed one of the fallen guards' guns and was even then taking aim at the creature that loomed above her. It looked like another troll of the same sort that had attacked the Queen last night, huge and brutish, with knotted muscles and a drooling mouth crammed full of uneven brown teeth. As I entered the clearing, Maria fired the pistol. A spurt of red appeared on the troll's chest, but it didn't pause in its attack.

"Livecta," I shouted, hurling a pinch of dust from one of my pouches at the monster's feet. Instantly, the feet turned to ice. The troll tried to take another step forward, clearly meaning to kill Maria, but its legs snapped off and it plummeted to the ground.

Maria screamed and jumped out of the way, having to dive to the ground to avoid being squashed. The troll landed hard, fortunately avoiding the two downed guards.

Groaning, drooling, it dragged itself toward Maria with one hand, the other hand reaching toward her...

Davril sprang out from the palm trees, sword flashing, and drove his blade through the monster's temple into its brain. The beast groaned again, shuddered, then, just like last night, shifted shapes, shrinking to become a normal-sized man. Davril's sword clattered to the ground. He picked it up, wiped it off, and replaced it in his scabbard, never taking his eyes off what had been the creature.

"Are you okay?" I asked Maria as I helped her up.

"I-I'm fine," she said, and dusted herself off. She cleared her throat, obviously gathering herself, then crouched beside the nearest fallen servant. He had a bit of blood on his head but looked otherwise unharmed. She slapped him lightly on the face. "Taru, wake up! Taru!"

He murmured something.

"Taru," she repeated.

His eyelids flickered, then parted to reveal beautiful dark eyes fringed with long lashes.

"Mistress, are you all right?" he said.

She let out a deep breath. "Thank the goddess," she said, then helped him up. Together, they checked on the other man. After a few moments, they were able to wake him, too. Only then did Maria approach Davril and me. We'd gathered over the body of the dead assassin and were searching him for clues, just like last night. So far, nada.

"Thank you so much, Jade," Maria said, and hugged me. She was an attractive woman with dark hair, dressed like a harem girl, complete with silks, veil, and tiara. She might charge her clients a small fortune, but she sure put on a show for them. I mean, an oasis, really?

"It was nothing," I said, but my heart was still jackhammering.

"You saved my life!" Maria glared down at the body. "Who was he?"

"We were hoping you could tell us," Davril said.

I tried not to roll my eyes. Davril was all business, all the time.

"*Me?*" Maria said.

"Never mind him," I said. "He's Davril Stormguard, Fae Knight and asshole. He can't help it; it's genetic, I think."

Maria giggled, her eyes darting from me to Davril, then back. Her smile seemed a little too knowing for my taste.

"Anyway," I said, eager to change the subject. "A guy like that attacked Qu—"

"Attacked someone important," Davril said. Clearly, he didn't want to admit his queen had been endangered. It would make the Fae Court look weak, and he couldn't allow that.

"Um, yeah, someone important," I said, then showed her the picture I'd taken of the assassin from last night with my phone. "He had a tattoo of you—see?"

"Goddess," Maria said, putting a hand to her chest. "That's Marko!"

"Marko?"

"Do you have a last name?" Davril said.

Maria shook her head, looking disturbed. "No, but he was into some bad stuff. He's been coming to me for a while, but lately… well, I always knew he ran with a rough lot, but in the last few months, he's seemed especially stressed and…excited." She shook her head again. "I can't explain it. When he came to visit me yesterday, I just knew something was wrong."

"He came yesterday?" I said. "But that would be right before…"

Maria's eyes strayed sadly to the body, as if imagining Marko lying there.

"He must have wanted a last night in heaven, just in case," Maria said.

Davril arched an eyebrow, something I couldn't do. "Heaven?"

Maria didn't answer, but I said, "*Trust* me. From what I've heard, she ain't joking."

"Did he tell you who was employing him?" Davril asked. Back to business again. Couldn't he give her five minutes to get herself together? For Pete's sake, she was still holding the pistol, her hand trembling. I was half afraid it would go off again at any moment. Too bad those bottles of wine were broken.

Maria tapped her chin. She didn't say anything for a long moment, and I enjoyed the sound of the wind sighing through the palms. I *didn't* enjoy the smell of sand and blood mixing in my nostrils to create a cloying perfume.

"He didn't say who he worked for, no," Maria said.

Davril shot me a look as if to say *This was all for nothing.*

Then she added, "But he did say that if he saw tomorrow—I guess that would be today—that he might regret it."

"He knew the mission to kill the…person…might get him killed," I mused. "But he thought there might be a chance of survival. I mean, he was changed, after all—a monster. Maybe he thought he could do the deed and escape. But you're saying that even if he did that, he'd still be in danger?"

Maria nodded. Tears glimmered in her eyes. Somewhat to my surprise, I realized the tears were for Marko. The man Davril had killed yesterday. The man who had tried to murder the Queen. But he'd still been human, at least most of the time, and evidently his time with Maria had meant something to her, even if he'd had to pay for it.

"He said the Voris Cemetery was his worst nightmare," Maria said, then turned away from the new corpse with a last sniff.

"Voris Cemetery?" I said. "That's where he thought he was going? I've never heard of it."

"I have," Davril said, and there was a dark tone to his voice. His gaze raked the forest of palms all around us. "Let me scout the area. If this man traveled here the long way, he might have a vehicle. Those same witches from yesterday might have helped him. They could still be around."

"I'm coming with you," I said.

While Maria and her guards saw to the body and began straightening things up, Davril and I prowled the oasis for witches and winged steeds, but we turned up nothing. Maria didn't know anything else, so we thanked her and returned to the magical portal leading out.

"Why would they send someone to attack Maria?" I said.

Davril didn't hesitate. "Obviously to silence her."

"But that would mean they knew what we found last night. They knew about the tattoo..."

Davril and I stopped in our tracks and stared at each other.

"They have a mole in the palace," Davril said, and his voice thrummed with anger.

CHAPTER 10

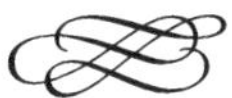

"So what's Voris Cemetery?" I said, once we were back in Lady Kay and flying through the steel canyons of the city.

Davril stared straight ahead. "A cemetery for witches and wizards."

Something cold traced fingers up my spine. "Why would Marko expect to go there?" I thought about it a moment, then answered my own question. "Because his employers were going to send him there."

"Exactly. Whoever's behind this is sending people to a secret, supposedly haunted graveyard of magic-users."

"Tonight."

His jaw bunched again. He let a long beat go by. "We know there's a mole at the palace. We can't afford to return there to give a report. We have to go straight to the cemetery and stake it out."

"You and me…on a stakeout?"

"In a haunted cemetery with mysterious and magical villains en route, yes."

I hid a grin. "Sounds like a party."

"You have a strange definition of party, Jade McClaren."

"Maybe I do." I glanced sideways at him. I couldn't help but remember him in action, taking down two trolls in two days—the way he'd leapt at the monsters, sword swinging, eyes like lasers, every muscle bunched...

"What is it?" he said.

"Nothing." I cleared my throat. "So why is there a cemetery for wizards and witches, and why the hell are the bad guys going there?"

"To the second question, I have no idea. But, as to the first, magic users know their body parts and various belongings, like magic rings, totems, and so forth, will be highly sought after by the...criminal element interested in magical artifacts and ingredients for spells." He jerked his gaze to me, then snapped it forward again.

"Don't know what you're talking about," I said.

"You probably don't." He swerved (too sharply) to the right, then gunned the gas, shooting us forward, slamming me against the seat.

"Hey!" I said.

He eased off. "Sorry. I forget you're still half human."

"Then remember that the *other* half of me is a dragon."

A dark look passed across his face so briefly I almost thought I'd imagined it. "I will," he said, and his hands gripped the wheel a bit too tightly. What the hell? Was he some sort of dragon-hater? I'd have to feel him out on this issue when he was calmer.

"Anyway, you were saying?" I said.

"Well, the wizards and witches don't want criminals tampering with their graves, so they put their graveyards in secret destinations and place a great number of wards, haunts, and magical guardians on them. I'm surprised your sister Ruby didn't tell you about it."

"I don't think she knew. *Knows*," I made myself add. "She pretty much had to pick up the whole witch thing on her own." I hesitated. "Haunted, you say?"

"That's right. It will be dangerous, Jade. Are you sure you wish to come? I'll give you this last chance to back out."

What were my options, though? To go back to the jail cell and face punishment? "Screw that. Besides, I can't let you go in alone, especially not if we can't trust the other knights in the palace."

"I doubt it was another knight who informed our enemies that we wished to interview Maria, but..." He sighed. "I admit, I can't discount the possibility, either."

"That sucks."

He made several more twists and turns, and my gut tumbled with each one. Gradually, we moved into a darker and more decrepit area. Greasy smoke belched out of grime-encrusted chimneys, and strange things with rust-colored wings flapped down the alleys. We were far from the graceful skyscrapers of downtown now, and the denizens of the area went about their business furtively and, I was sure, fully armed. In other words, I felt right at home.

Well, almost. This place looked even scarier than Gypsy Land.

"We're in the Shadows, aren't we?" I crossed my arms over my chest as if that would protect me.

"That's right."

"Great." The Shadows were where the most outlaw magic-users and buyers went to operate. There were said to be homunculi factories and dark-side witch schools, among other sordid things. *Not* the place for a first date. Which this was emphatically not.

Davril brought Lady Kay low and parked her along the street.

"You're not afraid of her getting tagged or ripped off?" I said.

One side of Davril's mouth curled up. "I'd like to see them try."

His humor—so rare!—was infectious, and I laughed. "Me, too."

We climbed out, and I nearly gagged at the sour smell wafting up from a nearby sewer grate.

"What died in there?" I said. "Never mind. I probably don't want to know."

"Probably not."

The sun shone brightly overhead, seeming as if it came from another plane of existence altogether. There was certainly nothing bright or shiny down in the Shadows. It seemed cloaked in a perpetual gloom. It also seemed colder than it was outside of the Shadows, and I couldn't resist a shudder.

My belly growled suddenly, and a flash of embarrassment made me cringe as Davril looked over.

"It's about lunchtime," I said. "And we do have the rest of the day. The bad guys aren't supposed to show up for hours. Hell, we have time for lunch, then a movie, then dinner, too."

Davril's face was hard. "I'm in charge here, Jade. I set the schedule." Then he relented. "That said, I understand it is mealtime for you mortals."

"What, Fae don't have to eat? Bullshit. I saw you scarfing it down last night."

"I was not…scarfing it down. I was eating properly. You were scarfing it down. You acted like a wild goblin."

"Well, sorry, I didn't know I was being scrutinized." Suddenly, a picture floated into my brain, of me seated at the dinner table in the Queen's dining hall, my face lathered with bits of food as I chomped down on succulent quail I had gripped in my bare, greasy hands. More grease and chunks of quail dripped down my dress front. *I wasn't that bad,* I told myself. But I couldn't escape the nagging feeling that I had been from Davril's point of view.

Something caught my eye, and I pointed.

"A pizza place?" Davril asked doubtfully.

I grinned. "You'll love it. Pizza's my favorite."

I tugged him inside, where it was much warmer, and the smell of grease and pizza sauce instantly made my mouth water. I ordered a slice of the Meatlover's Special, while Davril ordered a salad. He paid. I hadn't even known the place sold salads, but I wasn't surprised when it came served beneath a gallon of creamy ranch sauce. Davril poked at it skeptically as we sat down at the window counter right before the neon sign which read *Pizza by the S ice*. The *L* was missing.

"If you don't like your ranch, I'll help," I said, and dunked my slice into his salad. It came away with a dollop of ranch on the tip. I shoved it into my mouth and munched on it greedily. "Mmm."

He was watching me eat, and I shifted in my seat.

"What?" I mumbled around my next bite.

He blinked. "Nothing."

He returned his attention to his salad. Experimentally, he prodded it with his fork, then took a bite, careful to shake off the ranch. "I've had better," he said with obvious diplomacy after he'd swallowed. The very obviousness of his diplomacy made it somewhat less diplomatic.

"Well, sor-*ry*," I said. "If I'd known you wanted salad, I would have suggested a salad place."

"Would it have less of this…dressing there?"

"Probably. You could put as much or as little of it on your salad as you'd like, and they'd have various kinds of dressing, too. Not all of it would be ranch."

"Ranch?"

"Yeah. That white stuff. I love grabbing a salad and sandwich at salad restaurants. Maybe we can find one of those for dinner."

"We are not going out to dinner, too."

"I wouldn't call this *going out*," I said. "I mean, it's just a pizza place, although it's pretty damned good. Going out is like with tablecloths and stuff."

"Well, we're not doing it."

"Why not?" I said around another mouthful. God, the pizza was good. I was coming back here for lunch tomorrow. I might have to move in.

"Because we need to arrive at the cemetery early and survey it," he said, careful to keep his voice low, not that the guy behind the counter, currently taking another order, was going to listen in on us. "We need to grow familiar with it before our enemies arrive, so we know the lay of the land. And any potential traps, magical or otherwise."

"Do we have to?" I whined, then flashed a smile I was sure was wall-to-wall cheese and half-eaten pepperoni. "Just kidding. I just wanted to see your reaction."

"Why do you insist on needling me?"

"You're so dour; one of us has to try to keep our spirits up. It's funny, because Ruby is always telling me how dour and broody *I* am. But then I get around you, and you make me look like a bunny on crack." That image made me giggle, and I put a hand over my mouth in case I started spraying pizza chunks.

Instead of being amused, Davril looked away. The expression on his face was sad, somehow, but I sensed it wasn't a sadness that had anything to do with me. It was always there. It always *had* been there, ever since I'd first met him. I just hadn't noticed it, or I'd attributed the expression to other causes. But it was true, I instinctively knew. Some tragedy had impacted Davril heavily in his past, and he wore its echoes with him always.

There was much more to him than I knew. Suddenly, I wanted to know all about him. Just who was he? A badass Fae Knight, check. A handsome, troll-slaying hero, check. A broody, self-righteous prick, check. But there was more. Much more.

I crammed the last bite of pizza into my mouth. "Well, if we're not going out for dinner, I'm getting seconds," I garbled around the bite.

Davril sighed.

Ten minutes later, we were back on the streets. We meandered down a couple of blocks, and I tried to hide my belches. That pizza had been good, but it was kicking back on me. The sunlight on my skin, however muted by the general weirdness of the Shadows, felt warm, unseasonably so, and I was basking in it. I had begun to think Davril didn't know where we were going, which would have actually been refreshing—it would have shown him to have some faults—but then he turned down an alley and seemed to expect me to follow. Warily, I did.

As the alley's shadow engulfed me, the temperature plunged twenty degrees, and I shivered, no longer warm at all.

"What the hell?" I said.

"We're nearing a magical barrier of a very specific kind," he said. "You may experience some discomfort."

"Good to know. You should consider being an airline hostess if that whole Fae Knight shtick goes south."

I had come abreast him, just in time to see his grimly amused expression.

"Good to know," he said, imitating my tone. Again, I was strangely glad to see his sense of humor.

We pressed deeper into the shadow, coming to a cross-alley. The gloom thickened around us. We were now surrounded by some sort of weird smoke that sparked and hummed with magical energy. Davril waved a hand, and the sparks glowed more fiercely.

Grabbing my hand, he guided me deeper into the cloud. I coughed and waved it out of my face, then slapped my hair as one of the sparks buzzed through it, thinking for a mad moment that it would catch my hair on fire. Thankfully, it didn't. At last the smoke thinned, then dissipated altogether, and Davril and I found ourselves standing before the immense Gothic gate of what appeared to be a vast cemetery stretching away into the gloom. The smoke had vanished, but an acrid fog rolled over the low hills the cemetery had been built on.

At seeing the hills and the size of it all, I said, "Where are we? Is this another portal, like with Maria's oasis?"

"Not exactly. This is more like a bubble dimension."

"Those old witches and wizards went through a lot of trouble not to be disturbed."

"That they did. They didn't want random people stumbling across their places of rest and spreading word of its location. They knew that if it happened, their bodies and tombs would receive no rest. Grave robbers have no respect." Again, he shot me an inscrutable look.

I held up my hands, palms out. "Hey, I never robbed any graves." *Because I never knew about places like this!* The tombs in here were probably worth a goldmine. Hell, two or three goldmines. It was all I could do not to rub my hands together greedily. But as soon as this business with Davril and the Fae Queen was done and Ruby was safe, well...

He seemed to read my expression. "Don't even think about it."

I rolled my eyes. "Let's get on with this, shall we? I sacrificed dinner for this."

"I would not be so flip if I were you. We're after the ones who killed your friend and, presumably, abducted your sister for reasons unknown."

I could have corrected him—I was quite sure Skull-Face had nothing to do with Troll-Maker—but I bit my tongue. Besides, the mention of Jason sobered me. Davril was right. If I wanted to avenge Jason and steal back the antler, I needed to put my game face on. This wasn't a date. This was possibly the post important assignment I'd ever taken on, and Ruby's life hung in the balance.

I straightened my spine and gave him a salute. "Shall we go in, then?" I gestured at the grand, rather spooky gateway. Think Halloween on steroids. This world might exist in a bubble dimension, but it had stars and a sky. Currently a yellow moon glared down at us. With a start, I realized it was a different time here than it was outside. Hell, for all I knew, this bubble of reality didn't have a sun. It might be night here permanently.

Davril shook his head. "The gateway will be warded very strongly." He pointed to the wall of high, sharpened iron stakes that went all the way around the graveyard, disappearing into the mist to either side. "We go over the hard way."

I wanted to roll my eyes again, but my game face wouldn't allow it. "Then let's do it," I said, starting toward the wall. He laid a hand on my shoulder.

"Wait."

I looked back at him. "What?"

He stepped forward and held out his palm, closing his eyes as he did, and I realized he was sensing, or at least trying to sense, any magical traps ahead. At last he flicked his fingers in a curt gesture, and the air sort of shimmered around the wall directly ahead.

"There," he said. "I've created a window, but we must be quick."

As if to illustrate his point, he leapt onto the wall, grabbing two of the iron poles, and began pulling himself upward. I admired the play of his muscles under his shirt and pants for a moment (just a moment) then followed him up. He made it look easy, but my own muscles had been honed by years of catburlgaring, and I had shifter strength to draw on, too. He didn't get too far ahead of me. We eased over the sharp tips of the posts, then descended quickly down the other side and dropped to the ground.

Not speaking, he moved off, threading his way between two mausoleums, and I followed. An eerie stillness lay over everything. I understood why he didn't talk. In total silence, we navigated our way between tombs and mausoleums, moving deeper into the cemetery—no, he was circling its perimeter. I was about to ask why when he did move deeper in...and began a circuit of this layer, too.

He's scoping out the joint. Moving in ever-narrowing circles. It was clever, I had to give him that. I wanted to tell him he would have made a good burglar, but we were still being quiet. Also, I didn't think he would be pleased at the idea.

As we went, the mist enfolded us. At times, I lost sight of Davril even though he was just a few feet ahead. Seeing this, he started to move slower, and I tried to move in tandem with him. Since we were bunched in tight in the narrow lanes between mausoleums, occasionally our shoulders or sides would brush against each other. He was very warm.

He stopped suddenly and crouched low, and I did the same.

"What is it?" I whispered.

He pointed. I narrowed my eyes to see some wispy objects, only half solid—if that—gliding through a break in the fog ahead. The apparitions sailed right through the stone wall of a vine-encrusted tomb as if it had been made of air and vanished from sight.

"Ghosts," Davril said, keeping his voice low.

The fine hairs rose along the nape of my neck. "Ghosts? You mean, of the dead wizards and witches?"

"Maybe. Or slaves or vassals of theirs."

"Slaves?"

"Some wizards had slaves, yes, and some of those slaves were sacrificed when their masters died so their spirits could serve as guardians for their tombs. This could be some of them. Let's go back another way."

I nodded.

We retreated, then cut down a narrow channel. Overhead, the moon passed behind thick black clouds. Gargoyles leered down at us from the corners of mausoleums, and obscene statues loomed from grim, lichen-infested courtyards. This place was seriously creepy. It occurred to me that, since it was eternal night here (at least as far as I could tell) it would be difficult to determine when nightfall in the real world was. I pulled out my phone, but of course there was no signal. The Twilight Zone was for landlines only.

I started to open my mouth to mention this, but just then a great shadow eclipsed the moon. A strange and foul smell wafted to us.

I glanced up just in time to see a many-legged horror drop right down on us.

CHAPTER 11

"Watch out!" I cried, trying to shove Davril out of the way. Instead of going, though, he ripped out his sword. It glowed white in the dimness of the nightmarish alley.

The horror fell on him.

Giant and many-legged, it resembled something like an enormous spider, but with too many legs and too many red, multifaceted eyes.

Davril slashed at it, gashing its abdomen, and then the weight of it drove him to the ground. I had leapt to the side, but I picked myself up and looked for a way to help him. God, but I wished I had a weapon! Well, I did have a knife, but it was a puny thing to use against this bastard.

I still had my utility belt, though. *Batman, eat your heart out.* I unzipped a pouch, pulled out some dust, and then mixed it with the crushed basilisk eye I retrieved from another.

"*Garona,*" I shouted, and hurled the dust at the spider. Instantly, it turned to stone.

I heard what sounded like Fae swearing, and then the spider broke into a hundred pieces. Davril jumped from the ruins, spitting out spider dust. Dusting himself off, he nodded his thanks to me.

"Well done," he said. "You'll have to teach me that sometime."

"I wish I could. That was my only basilisk eye."

"Your—"

Another shadow fell on him. Glancing up, I saw three more enormous spiders scuttling over the top of the mausoleum to our right. Were they pouring out of its top? I pictured them nesting in the sarcophagus of some long-dead sorcerer, growing fat and powerful off his or her magic, then boiling out of some crack in the mausoleum's roof.

"Shit," I said.

By the light of Davril's shining sword, I could see their fangs glinting. They wanted to trap us, spin us in their webs, and suck us dry.

"I don't think so," I said, and pulled out my knife. It was better than nothing.

Davril glared up at them. Slowly, he took a step back. Above, they moved with him. Another many-legged shape joined them, then another.

"A whole swarm," he said, disgust in his voice.

"Can you take them all?"

"Maybe," he said, "but maybe not. And even if I could, I couldn't do it without a great deal of destruction, which would be obvious to our enemies when they arrive. It would give our presence away."

"Then let's try to do this my way," I said.

"I thought you were out of basilisk eye."

"That was only for emergencies. My usual way is sneakiness, and I have several spells for that."

"Very well."

We continued backing slowly away down the alley while the spiders jockeyed for position above. As we moved, I mixed another spell, then spoke a magic word. When I did, the shadows around us thickened, and we became less visible to anyone outside the shadows. Taking Davril's hand, I led him down one alley, then up a cross-alley, and down another. The spiders spread out overhead, looking for us, but they didn't seem to be able to see us. Gradually, we saw them less and less, and then not at all.

Breathing heavily, I drew to a stop in a courtyard beneath a huge withered tree bowed with white fruit that looked suspiciously like skulls. Man, I couldn't wait to get out of this place.

"That was too close," I said. "I mean—"

Davril lunged past me, sword flashing. I spun, breathless, to see that the roots of the tree had lifted out of the ground and were questing toward me like tentacles. Davril struck one root with his sword, severing it, then lopped off another.

The whole tree listed toward us. Its fruits *were* skulls, and each one was snapping, trying to eat Davril up!

His sword flashed, again and again, and skull-bearing branches fell to the ground along with root tentacles, some still writhing. At last the tree quit its assault and listed back, its surviving roots plunging underground once more and its skulls becoming quiet fruits again.

"Jesus," I said, wiping sweat out of my eyes. "Now *I* owe *you*."

He grinned and made his sword disappear. "That's the way I like it."

My heart fluttered in my chest. Staring at him with his face flushed and eyes agleam, with that wicked smile on his face, I realized that he was a man of action, that he only really came alive when there was danger about, or at least that's when he was *most* alive. And something in me drew toward him, inexorably.

Because I was the same way.

We stared at each other for a long moment, but then our heads snapped to the side as new sounds sprang from the darkness. The sounds of footsteps and conversation.

Davril and I pressed our backs against the nearest tomb wall and held our breaths. This was it. Our enemies had arrived. He looked sideways at me as if to say, *Are you ready?*

I nodded.

Carefully, we moved toward the sounds. My stealth-shadow spell still held, but I knew it would dissipate soon. When I whispered this to Davril, his eyes grew flinty and he nodded once, curtly. We crept down a narrow alley between death houses, making for the noise. As we approached, the sounds grew louder. Shouts and curses, then strange, eerie wailing.

"What the hell?" I whispered. I knew I wouldn't be overheard what with all the other noises.

Davril didn't answer, and we approached the mouth of the alley slowly. There, before us, in a small, creepy courtyard watched over by four monstrous gargoyles on the top of four tall stone columns was a truly strange and macabre scene, straight out of my nightmares. Or at least somebody's nightmare's. Stephen King's, maybe.

A group of maybe a dozen people had formed a defensive circle in the courtyard. The group was mainly composed of rough-looking sorts with scars, tattoos and leather, men and women but mainly men, all of the type Marko had been, as well as the other one, the one who had attacked Maria. The criminal element, as I thought of them, were all brandishing guns and knives, and some were stabbing or shooting at the enemy that assailed them.

Ghosts ringed them. Howling, phantasmal, see-through ghosts —probably the same ones Davril and I had avoided earlier. This group had stumbled across them, or maybe stepping within the ring of gargoyles had summoned them, much like a similar set of gargoyles had served as an alarm back at Hawthorne's penthouse. Whichever, the ghosts were tearing at the criminals with phantasmagorical claws and gnashing at them with half-substantial teeth. Wherever they struck, the criminals screamed and writhed, and I saw smoke trail up from some of the contacts. The ghosts, however ghostly, were able to inflict damage on the material world.

Well, duh, I thought. *They wouldn't be much use as guardians otherwise, right?*

The group of criminals had some defense, though. Two women I instantly pegged as witches by their affected, Gothic-style dresses and haughty demeanors were speaking spells and hurling invisible missiles at the ghosts, driving them back and setting up magical force fields to defend themselves and the thugs.

One of the women was taller, with flowing chestnut hair and a beautiful, oval face. I put her in her early thirties. She seemed to be the leader, and her face was set in a determined scowl. In one hand, she held—I stared—*the golden antler.* She seemed to be using it as a magic wand. I glanced to Davril to see that his eyes had fixed on the antler of the Golden Hind, too. What could it mean?

The other witch was much younger, barely into her twenties, and she was sort of chubby, with a cute round face that she had painted white and had on black lipstick, too. *A total goth poser.* The spells she cast didn't seem nearly as effective against the ghosts. Ultimately, that didn't matter, though.

"Evecta cothrum," shouted the tall witch as she stomped her foot on the ground hard. At the impact, the ground seemed to shake, and I could sense a magical ripple radiate out from the blow. That magic must have come from the antler.

The ghosts screamed and withdrew, stopping their assault but still circling in a nightmarish tornado, with the witches and their lackeys (at least, that's how I saw it) being the eye of the storm.

Biting my lip, I glanced to Davril, but his attention was firmly rooted on the spectacle ahead. Part of me wanted to rush to the women's defense. The other part of me realized they were my enemies. It had been their goons, transformed by magic, that had killed Jason and assaulted both Maria and Queen Calista. If the ghosts killed them, they'd only be doing me and the Fae a favor. Just the same, it didn't feel right just watching it happen.

The ghosts started to close in again, but the tall, auburn-haired witch stomped her foot once more, even harder this time, and thundered, *"Evecta THRUM!"*

A wave of power radiated out from the golden antler in her hand. The ghosts shrieked and scattered into the cemetery, vanishing from sight. I hadn't realized I'd been holding my breath, but as soon as they left, I sucked in a deep lung-full. A bit of sweat had popped out on Davril's brow.

"That was close," said one of the thugs in the courtyard, and his mates nodded and muttered agreements. Some shoved their weapons away, while others scouted out the nearby buildings, making sure the ghosts were really gone. Two of the thugs had fallen, stricken by the phantasms, and a small group of the others gathered over them. I tried to get a look at the two men on the ground, but it was too dark and the mist was starting to rise again. All the activity had dispersed it for a few moments, but it was rolling back in.

"Look, they're still alive," said the young goth witch as the two magic-users drew closer to the spot where the downed men were.

"Heal them, Mistress Angela," one of the female thugs said to the tall witch, and others took up the cry.

"Heal them!"

"Heal them, please."

The tall witch—Angela—paused over the bodies, then swept the antler over them. I knew she must be scanning them with her powers, augmented by the power of the antler. At last she sniffed and said, "I could heal them, but it would deplete my stores of magic, and I cannot be without them in the middle of Voris Cemetery. Stand back."

"But Mistress—"

"Stand back!"

The thugs drew back warily, shooting each other dark looks.

Moving the antler back and forth, Angela began speaking a

spell under her breath. Below her, the two wounded men began to scream.

The chubby goth girl opened her mouth to protest, then seemed to think better of it. She closed it and looked away.

"Please, Ms. Blackfeather, tell her to spare them," one of the thugs pleaded with her. "She'll listen to you."

Blackfeather, if that was her name (but of course it was—look at that makeup), frowned at the man. With more venom than strictly necessary, she said, "Don't tell me what to do, loser. Mistress Angela will make their ends quick."

There came a sudden scream, and the downed men burst into green flames. The flames blazed brightly for a moment, then went out in a flurry of green sparks and ash. There was nothing left of them.

A few last cinders swirled around Angela, who stood tall and serene amid it all, her eyes slitted cat-like and a small, repugnant smile on her face. "They knew the risks," she said, then shoved the antler away. "Now to the mission at hand. We are very close to our goal."

She turned and strode off briskly down a broad aisle of the cemetery. Blackfeather scurried immediately behind her. The thugs glanced at each other, then at the dark, dangerous cemetery in all directions and, as one, ran after the two witches. I didn't blame them.

"Well, shall we?" whispered Davril with an ironic smile, waving his hand as if to say, *Ladies first.*

This really does get his blood going, I thought. But I was numbed. Well, chilled really. I had just seen two men die, and they might not be the last before the night was over. Grimly, I moved to Davril's side while the witches' party continued through the cemetery.

Darkness pressed around us, thick and cloying, hiding unseen dangers, and I could barely see through the fog. Luckily, I could see just enough to prevent barking my shins on some obstacle, and our quarry made enough noise that we could still track them. I couldn't believe I was really here, in Voris Cemetery, in pursuit of witches and who-knew-what-else.

This is madness. We must be mental.

I couldn't deny that the only thing that made it bearable was Davril's presence. If he hadn't been there I wasn't sure what I'd have done—probably run screaming back over that wall. Hell, I wouldn't have gone over the wall in the first place. Then again, I wouldn't have *had* to, either. I wouldn't have even been able to find the damned cemetery. *Thanks, Davril.*

Careful to keep my voice low, I asked him, "How are they even here, anyway? It's not nightfall yet in the outside world...is it?"

"Time does strange things in places like this," he said. "Many hours could have passed in the outside world."

"You tell me this now." When he didn't reply, I said, "What are they after, anyway?"

"I haven't a clue. But they're using the antler of the Golden Hind to help them navigate the dangers of this place. We must stay close enough to them to derive its benefits or all is lost."

"*That's* what they wanted the antler for?"

"Apparently. It was just a tool to help them achieve their real ends."

"So what did your people want it for?"

"We knew it was a powerful thing and could easily be misused. We simply wanted to keep it out of the wrong hands."

Then what the hell does Skull-Face want with it? This mystery just got deeper and deeper.

"Okay," I said, "So last night, at Hawthorne's penthouse..."

"We'd sent one of our number to collect the antler from Hawthorne after having discovered he possessed it. We'd already made payment and the Fae was simply on his way to pick it up."

That was why a Fae Lord had been coming to the party, I realized, remembering Lydia's excitement.

"So why were you there?" I asked. "On the rooftop?"

"As I've told you, I was simply monitoring the transaction…in case of mischief. We knew there were other interested parties inquiring about the antler and suspected…"

"Yeah?"

"Quiet. I think they're slowing down ahead."

Indeed, the witches' group was reaching a stop before what looked like a grand mausoleum complete with ornate stone walls, gargoyles perched on the corners, and a heavy metal door inset with a bas-relief of flames. That was it, just huge, roaring flames. The Inferno, I thought. The dead sorcerer beyond had put a picture of the place he was going on the door of his tomb. Funny fella.

Mistress Angela issued orders, and several of her thugs made a circuit of the mausoleum, then reported back to her. Others fanned out, setting up a perimeter, while more began sentry patrols. Meanwhile, Angela waved the golden antler before the metal door while she and Blackfeather muttered strange words. I knew a little magic, just enough to get by, but their words were completely foreign to me. Angela's magic was on a whole different level than anything I was familiar with, and I suspected that anything Ruby was familiar with, either.

"What now?" I whispered as Davril and I crouched in an alley between two huge, vine-overgrown tombs. The vines moved like bloated, sluggish snakes, and I was eager to be away from them.

Davril frowned. "They're trying to get access to that mausoleum."

"Thanks for the heads up, genius."

"Which means that whatever they want, it's in there."

"Again, thanks for the newsflash."

His eyes roved up and down the mausoleum in question. Even then, Angela and Blackfeather were increasing the volume and pace of their chanting. It wouldn't be long before they were able to break through whatever magical wards guarded the dead dude's resting place. He may have been formidable, but they had come prepared to deal with exactly this. That was what they'd needed the antler for, after all.

Davril's eyes stopped moving when they reached the roof. "Is that a skylight?"

I squinted. My shifter senses helped see into shadows, and I could just make out what Davril was indicating. Due to the slope of the mausoleum's roof, I saw a sheet of what might be stained glass set into the roof.

"I guess the dead guy wanted a view of the stars during his eternal rest," I said. "So what?"

"So that's how we can spy on them. We can see what Angela and Blackfeather want with the late mage. Then we can plan a defense accordingly."

It wasn't a bad plan, and I nodded. "Let's rock."

"You're the thief," he said. "How are we going to get on that roof?"

There were too many thugs on patrol for us to cut through them, no matter how dark and foggy it was. I studied the scene, then indicated a rope of vine trailing from one gargoyle-festooned corner of the roof to the edge of another mausoleum's roof.

"If we can get up to that structure, we can shimmy along that vine to the mausoleum," I whispered. I had to speak especially softly because one of the patrols was nearing our hiding spot. My cloaking spell had dissipated, and we were at risk for being seen if we were careless. I wasn't worried, though. The shadows were deep, and Davril and I were both good at blending in with them. This wasn't his first rodeo.

"Then let's do it," he said.

We waited for the patrol to pass, then doubled back down the alley, up a cross-alley, and approached the structure I had indicated from a roundabout route. It was a tall mausoleum, half-buried in mist, covered in gargoyles and bas-reliefs and overgrown with weird ivy that moved, just slightly, and emitted a sort of buzzing noise. Perfect for climbing, in other words.

Davril and I waited for another patrol to pass by, then dashed to the building and scaled up its side. One of the vines moved as I went to grab it and I nearly lost my hold, but I quickly grabbed another, then stuck my tongue out at the offending plant. In moments, Davril and I had reached the roof. I led the way over to the rope of vines—and some roots, too, since a couple of spindly trees sprouted from the top of both mausoleums—then tested the rope to make sure it would hold.

"It's solid," I whispered.

I shimmied out onto the leafy bridge, feeling it creak under me, then stiffened as four of Angela's thugs passed below. I held my breath until they were gone, then continued. Reaching the far side, I scrambled onto the roof of the mausoleum that held whatever Angela's party had come for, then turned to gesture Davril forward. He was already moving. He crawled out onto the rope-and-root bridge with more dexterity and poise than I would have thought for a man of his size, but then again, he was a Fae, and they were graceful and nimble, every last one, or at least it always seemed so on television whenever they were featured, which was often.

As Davril neared, I heard a noise behind me.

I spun just in time to see one of Angela's thugs rounding the corner of the pyramidal glass roof. The glass was overgrown with dirt and grime, so I hadn't seen him through it, and he obviously hadn't seen me. His eyes widened and one of his hands flew to the gun in his shoulder holster. Evidently Angela had dispatched him to serve as a sentry up here, just in case. I would have to remember that she was no dummy.

Before the man could draw his gun, I whispered, *"Vectalis molun!"*

He still moved, but his movements suddenly slowed way down. The spell would only last three seconds, though. Meanwhile, the goon seemed to move in molasses. I rushed forward to knock his legs out from under him. Before I could, the second goon rounded the bend. He'd been just behind the first one, both making a circuit of the roof. As I swept the legs out from under the first goon (he seemed to fall in extra-fast-motion as the spell collapsed) the second goon crouched into a fighting stance. A ring on his finger glowed orange and a magical axe popped into existence in his hands.

Shit.

The first goon hit the roof. Reached for his gun. I kicked him in the head. The gun-reaching hand fell away.

The second goon stepped over the inert body of the first one and raised his axe high, meaning to slice me in two like a bagel.

"Vectalis molun," I said.

The ring on his finger glowed brighter—that was the only change. He wore a charm that would protect him against certain spells. *Damn it all.* I moved backward, tripped on a vine, and hit the roof with my back. *Crap.*

The axe drove straight at my face.

Davril arrived.

Straddling me with his powerful legs, he grabbed the axe shaft in both hands, gripping it tight, and shoved it back against my attacker. The goon growled, low in his throat, and shoved down harder on the axe shaft. The blade of the axe was now perilously close to Davril's handsome face.

I rolled to the side and tried to stand, but the first goon, stirring feebly, reached out and grabbed my ankle. I stumbled.

The second goon, using strength surely drawn from his ring, shoved even harder on his axe, and I could see the strain in Davril's face as he resisted. The blade of the axe neared his cheek...closer...

Acting with sudden violence, he kicked the kneecap of his opponent. The man groaned in agony, then wilted to the roof. The axe spun out of his hands. He reached for it, but Davril had ripped out his own sword, luminous in the gloom, and was bringing it down. I glanced away as it connected with the goon's chest, but I heard the *thunk* and saw a spray of blood.

The first goon had drawn his knife and was attempting to slash my Achilles' tendon. Little bastard. I kicked him in the face, hard, and he went limp. The blade clattered to the roof.

"Are you all right?" Davril asked, coming to me.

I nodded raggedly. Glancing to the dead man, I said, "Did you have to kill him?"

As if it was an easy answer, Davril said simply, "He was an enemy engaged in mortal combat. You would have given him quarter?"

"I…maybe." I waved it away. We could worry about such things later, if we survived.

Getting on my stomach, I crawled to the edge of the roof and looked down. The roof was of the same stone as the rest of the building save for the pyramid of glass at its center. Below the patrols still cut through the cemetery, and Angela and Blackfeather still stood before the main door. Good. No one had noticed our fight with the sentries.

BOOM!

The main doors crashed open.

Angela threw back her head and laughed. "You thought you could keep me out?" she shouted into the night. "You'd better think again!"

She stepped boldly into the interior of the mausoleum, and I couldn't help but be a little admiring of her courage. Tough or not, she couldn't know for sure what awaited in there, but she was determined to lead the charge inside. Blackfeather looked more timid, but I saw her swallow, square her shoulders, and follow her mistress in. Half of the goons had been waiting behind the two witches, obviously ready to storm the building with their mistresses, and they glanced at each other tensely, then moved inside.

I turned to Davril, who was already sweeping some of the dirt and grime away from one of the panes of the glass pyramid. Crawling over to him, I raised myself up on my hands and knees. Shoulder to shoulder, we stared down into the interior of the tomb. Instantly, I felt my face go numb.

Below us, a bizarre scene played out. Angela had entered a strange, circular chamber made of what looked like marble, with niches lining the walls. Each of the niches contained the upright corpse of a man or woman in flowing, brilliant ceremonial garments. Each was skeletal but containing some withered remains of flesh. In the center of this grisly circle, the only other thing in the room, was a stone bed upon which stretched the long, gnarly body of a demon.

CHAPTER 12

I clapped a hand over my mouth to prevent my gasp of shock from sounding too loud. Heart hammering, sweat stinging my eyes, I turned to Davril. His face had gone hard and flinty, and he stared down at the scene below with great intensity.

I turned back to study the body on the slab. Seven or eight feet tall (or long, lying down) it was clad in bronze-looking armor. Hooves jutted out where its feet should have been, and the skeletal remains of its wings stretched out behind it. Angela had to move around one as she neared the body. But the most telling features of all were the two grand horns curling up from its temples.

The flames, I thought. The flames on the mausoleum door. *That was what they meant.*

When I could, I said, making sure to keep my voice low, "Holy shit. That's a demon. I…I didn't even think they were real!"

"They're real," Davril said. "But what in the world is she doing with it?"

Angela had moved around to the demon's head and was inspecting the horns. She turned and said something to Blackfeather—I couldn't hear what she said from here—and Blackfeather handed her (I gasped again) a handsaw.

"Oh. My. God," I said as Angela began sawing at the base of one of the dead demon's horns.

I was aware Davril and I were shoulder to shoulder, our faces very close together as we gazed down upon the surreal scene below. When I turned to see how he was taking this, my lips almost grazed his cheek. Almost. I was so surprised I momentarily forgot what I'd been about to say, so when he turned to see what I had been turning toward him for, my halfway parted mouth was very close to his own...as he opened his to speak.

"Yes?"

"I..." My heart pounded. *Focus, Jade! The witch is sawing off a demon horn.* Getting myself together, I said, "Whatever she wants that thing for, it can't be good."

"No," Davril agreed. "She had her minion attack the Queen, failed, then went to retrieve this horn." He frowned. "No, that's not right. Marko said she intended to come here whether the attack was successful or not. Something's not adding up. But in any case, she needed one horn to find another."

We turned back to watch the scene unfold below. Our cheeks were almost pressed together, and I could feel heat radiating off him. I could smell him, too, a sort of sandalwood aroma mixed with clean sweat.

Below, Angela finished sawing off the demon's horn, then held it aloft. Her goons muttered and made expressions of awe. Blackfeather produced a carefully embroidered and surely warded cloth bag, then held it open while Angela very slowly lowered the horn into it, then removed her hands from the bag. Once she was clear, Blackfeather jerked the strings around the bag's opening, sealing it shut.

"I don't think so," Davril said.

Abruptly, he stood and ripped out his sword, which glowed whitely in the night.

I stared up at him with wide eyes. "What do you think you're doing?"

“Preventing that witch making off with the horn. She obviously means the Queen harm. Now stand aside.”

“What…?”

He didn’t wait for me but kicked at the glass pyramid, raining glass down on the witches and their thralls below. I heard cries and swears rise through the hole in the glass.

“Davril,” I said, “please don’t do anything stup—”

He jumped down through the opening he’d created in the roof of the tomb and sailed through the air. Heart stuttering, I pressed my face through the gap to see him alight nimbly on the marble floor, shattered glass shining in the light of the flashlights under him, bright sword making his steel blue eyes seem to spark.

“You will give that horn to me,” he demanded.

Angela had drawn back from the rain of shattered glass, and now she eyed Davril up and down. “Who are you?” she said.

“Lord Davril Stormguard, Knight of the Fae Court, and you will have your apprentice drop that bag and order your people to surrender. Do that and I can assure you that things will go easier for you.”

Mistress Angela half-smirked. To Blackfeather, she said, “Take that and go.”

Blackfeather nodded. Gripping the bag tightly, she spun about and left the chamber. Half the goons detached and went with her, obviously knowing that safeguarding the horn was key. I knew they would be joining even more guards outside. Shit.

Sweat stung my eyes even more fiercely as I watched Davril face off against Mistress Angela. Should I leap down there and join him? I was strong and nimble for a human, but I didn’t think I could survive the drop, at least not without breaking my legs. The fall had to be at least twenty feet onto solid marble strewn with broken glass. I had rope in my utility belt, though.

As I flipped the pouch containing the rope open, Angela was turning from watching Blackfeather depart to Davril advancing on her.

"I don't want to hurt a woman," he said.

"Then you're a fool." Waving her golden antler at the upright bodies of the demon's priests that lined the circular wall in their niches, she said, "*Gurum pilgaza!*"

To my shock, the bodies stirred in their niches…then stepped out of them.

The goons swore and jumped away from the walls, gathering around Angela as if to protect her, though I knew they really wanted protection *from* her.

Smiling hideously, the witch pointed at Davril. "Get him!"

Without hesitation, the dusty, decrepit but still horrifying corpses swiveled to face the handsome, daring Fae Knight, and I could see something that looked like hungry malice flicker across their withered, skeletal faces. Davril's eyes narrowed, and his jaw set grimly.

"Eat well, darlings," Angela told the zombies. With that, she shot Davril the finger, spun about, and swept from the chamber, taking her wide-eyed goons with her.

"You will face justice!" Davril called at her back. "You—"

The stone door slammed shut, magically sealing him in with the dead ones.

The undead things closed in on him, their hands gnarled like talons. Their ancient, half-broken teeth, jutting like filthy knives from their jawbones, flashed as they snapped their jaws with surprising strength. They might be dead, but they weren't weak. They possessed unnatural strength.

Davril swung his sword, slicing through the neck of the first one. The creature wobbled for a moment, then listed sideways and fell. The other four closed in, hands clutching and mouths snapping.

I ripped out the rope, attached the grappling hook to the lip of the hole in the roof, then dropped the line down, meaning to swing down and join Davril in repelling the zombie priests.

Before I could, something grabbed my ankle. Startled, I turned to see the sentry I'd rendered unconscious gripping me tightly.

"Damn you," I said. Maybe Davril had been right to kill the other sentry.

I kicked him in the face—again—and the man collapsed backward, but he still gripped my ankle. When he went backward, he yanked my leg out from under me. I toppled, almost going through the hole in the glass, but at the last moment I adjusted my weight and fell to the stone ceiling.

The sentry and I scrambled to our feet at the same time. He had lost his gun in our first encounter, but now his eyes scanned the roof for it. With my shifter senses, I could see better in the dark than he could and I picked it out right away.

It was behind him. *Shit*. No help to me.

"It's behind you," I said.

"What?"

He glared at me, then, unable to help himself, turned his head around to peer backward. I sprang forward and kicked him in the chest, hurling him back...over his gun...and past the edge of the roof. He screamed as he fell through the air, and I couldn't help but wince as I heard him smack the ground below.

"Serves you right, asshole," I said.

I hurried to the hole in the glass. Below, Davril was swinging his sword and kicking out. He rolled and punched and slashed as the undead priests tried to rip and bite him. He had no armor and he was surrounded, and they were possessed of unholy strength. He cut off one's head, then another one's outstretched arms.

Only two left. I cheered.

Then, as I was preparing to swing down to join him, the dead demon on the slab stirred. The empty eye sockets blazed with fire, and one of the hooves kicked. Davril had been backing away from the last two zombie priests...right toward the slab. I think he'd meant to climb onto it and make his last stand there.

"Behind you," I called, only belatedly realizing that that was what I'd just told the sentry.

Davril quickly glanced over his shoulder, saw the demon lurching up into a sitting position, and adjusted his path around the stone bed. Good call.

He was in real trouble. He might have been able to take on five zombie priests, but I had serious doubts whether anyone could take on that demon. I sure as hell—pun fully intended—didn't want to find out.

I grabbed the rope and jiggled it, drawing his attention to the cord.

"Climb up!" I said. "Climb!"

Davril hesitated a moment, his face shiny with sweat. He was reluctant to retreat even in the face of overwhelming odds. He was too macho for his own good.

"Don't be stupid," I said. "Climb!"

He hacked one last time, chopping through the wrist bone of a zombie, then thrust his sword back into its sheath and grabbed the rope with both hands. He began climbing hand over hand even as the zombies closed in around him and the demon struggled to his feet. It shook its now-one-horned head as if to clear away the cobwebs of death, then seemed to see Davril climbing to safety.

"Hurry!" I shouted.

The two zombies clutched at Davril's ankles, trying to drag him off the rope to his death.

"I don't think so," I muttered, digging through my pouches.

Selecting a tili seed, I threw it down toward the marble floor of the death chamber and said the words, *"Avructa si lumpath!"*

As soon as the seed hit the marble, tentacles burst from it, grabbing up anything in their way. One went round the waist of the demon and lifted him while others snatched at the zombies. I knew the tentacles couldn't hurt them—it wasn't that kind of spell, unfortunately—but it could slow them down. I nearly panicked when one of the tentacles reached toward Davril.

"Fuck," I said, unable to stop myself.

Davril kicked the tentacle away and kept climbing. I grabbed the rope and heaved, straining my muscles, trying to pull him. I could feel an intense pressure in my back, and my arms quivered. Davril was heavy. Fortunately, he was agile and quick, and he reached the top much faster than I'd anticipated. Even while I was still straining, his hands fastened onto the lip of the roof and he surged up and over, knocking me down.

Gasping, I stared up into his face. His body was pinning me down. Red-faced and sweaty, clearly on fire from the fight, he stared down into my face, and I could see that he was sort of smiling. He had nearly been eaten by zombies and God-knows-what by an undead hellspawn, and he was grinning!

My legs had gone around his waist. For a breathless, eternal moment, we stayed that way, and I couldn't help but relish his touch just a little. I thought he was enjoying it, too. Judging by the lusty glints in his eyes, he was.

He cleared his throat, rolled off me, then stood, holding a hand out for me. I accepted, let him pull me up, then tried to cover my unease by dusting myself off.

He peered down into the chamber. "How long will that hold them?"

"Not long," I admitted. "We'd better get going."

He nodded. I retrieved my rope, then we moved to the edge of the roof and began climbing down, using the vines and gargoyles for handholds. The two witches and their goons had vanished, having gotten what they came for. They apparently hadn't bothered sending out a search party to look for the two sentries Davril and I had taken care of. Mistress Angela was all heart.

Just as Davril and I touched the ground, I heard a deep, unearthly roar, and a chill ran down my spine.

"The demon," I said, knowing it must be true. "That was the demon!"

Davril opened his mouth to reply, but just then glass shattered loudly. My head snapped up as a dark figure flew upward, and a swell of dismay ran through me when I saw those skeletal bat-like wings spread out from it. They may be skeletal, but apparently they worked well enough. Then again, their ability to fly came more from magic, I sensed, than physics. The undead demon paused, silhouetted against the strange stars, and I could see its eyes burning in its skull.

Those eyes fell on Davril and me.

"Run," I said, and tugged Davril in the direction of an alley. He hesitated, still clearly hating to flee an enemy, but he obviously knew his duty was to his queen, not his pride, and that he had better live through this if he was going to help her. He obeyed.

We plunged into an alley between mausoleums. I turned my head, just once, to see the demon tuck its wings and dive after us. Its two surviving undead priests, meanwhile, were just scrambling onto the roof of the mausoleum, possibly having used the tentacles as ropes, or hell, who knew, maybe they could fly, too. Then I faced forward again and nearly stumbled. Davril righted me and we ran on.

My heart thumped so hard and fast I thought it would rip free of my chest and fly around the cemetery to join the demon.

"What now?" I said, laboring for breath. "I don't—think—we can make it out—before they—catch us."

"We will," Davril said beside me. "We must."

Suddenly, an idea occurred to me.

"The spiders," I said.

"What?" Even he was beginning to pant a little.

Grinning tightly, I said, "This way!"

Adjusting my course, I ran in the direction in which the spiders had ambushed Davril and me earlier, and Davril followed.

He ripped out his sword as he ran, and its light lit the path before us.

It would also let our enemies know where we were. Pumping my legs, I ran faster.

"You will die!" roared the demon behind us. "You have awakened Lord Mortock, and you will rue your mistake bitterly. And briefly."

I saw reflected firelight on the wall ahead of me and turned to see the demon—Lord Mortock—barreling down on us, a fireball growing in the palm of one clawed hand. His eyes glimmered with the reflected light, too, making them dance with flame.

"Shit," I said. "Fireball!"

I said this just as Mortock hurled the flame at us. I tripped on a root as I turned my head back around. The wall of the tomb we were passing was almost at its end. Davril and I ducked around the corner of it breathlessly, and the fireball exploded on the granite mausoleum we'd been facing. Granite exploded everywhere, and the statue of a man on a horse (well, half man, half horse) that was on the tomb's roof tilted to the side and fell to the ground, where it shattered.

Mortock hit the turn and swung around, more agile than I would have thought; I saw this in the reflection off an aged brass façade of a tomb ahead. I thought I recognized it from the area of the spiders. We were close.

"This way," I said, taking a turn.

Davril followed.

I heard the whip of air as Mortock banked around the corner after us, then the roar as he launched another fireball. This time, it was Davril who grabbed me and knocked me aside. He slammed me up against the wall just as the fireball whizzed past, exploding brightly. We panted into each other's faces for a moment, then hastily separated. Mortock approached.

We pelted down the avenue and made a turn. This was the lane we'd met the spiders on. Davril recognized it, too, I could tell by the way he slowed and lifted his sword. I slowed, too, but not out of fear—although maybe that, too, I'll be honest—but because I wanted to give Mortock time to catch us. Sure enough, I could see the stirring of multi-legged shadows on the edges of the roofs above.

Davril and I ran on, taking one turn, then another, but always letting Mortock catch us. At last, he had to leap and duck to evade the great webs that spanned the spaces between buildings, and Davril had to slice down one giant spider that came for us after another. They leapt on us like horrors out of a nightmare, but Davril swung his sword, ichor spurted, and they fell twitching to the ground.

After one attacked us and was similarly dispatched, the demon laughed behind us. Davril and I spun from standing over the body of the just-defeated arachnid. Mortock hovered right over us, a fireball gathering on his palm.

"Now you die," he said.

Before he could hurl the fireball, a great spider leapt over the rim of the roof and dropped right on him. The fireball died on his palm, just flickering out like a match. He let out a wail as the spider's weight drove him to the ground. His claws lashed out, tearing off one spindly limb, then another. Before he could rip apart the spider, however, another arachnid dropped down, then a third. In seconds, he was swarmed by the horrors. I saw one go up in flames, multi-legged limbs burning, then another. But there were many of them and I didn't know if he could prevail.

I didn't wait to find out.

"Let's go," I said, peeling away a section of webbing and clearing the path for us.

"I'll go first," Davril said. I had to admit I liked his gallantry.

Sword leading the way, he stepped forward down the dark, misty, spiderweb-filled lane as demonic screams sounded behind us, as well as the eerie wailing and hissing of the terrible arachnids.

Davril and I rounded a bend to come face to face with a true terror, a spider twice as large as any of the others we'd encountered. Its carapace was stained with age, and madness glimmered in its many red eyes. One had a scar through it.

"The queen," Davril said.

His sword darted out just as it pounced. Its fangs sank into his forearm even as his blade stabbed through its head and punched out the other side, showering gore. He grunted as it bit into him, and I could see blood gushing down his arm.

"Davril!" I said, rushing forward.

The spider quivered, ichor running down from the wound and hissing on the ground. With a sound of disgust, I heaved it off Davril's sword. He helped, shoving against it with one foot as he drew his sword back. He panted raggedly, sounding more tired then he should. When the great spider had collapsed dead to the ground, I wheeled to Davril.

His face suddenly clammy, he sank to his knees.

"Jade..."

My heart wrenched. "God, Davril, what..." I stared at the wound on his arm. Yellow fluid bubbled there, mixing with his blood. "Damn," I said. "Venom."

CHAPTER 13

I dropped to my knees beside him.

In the background, the demon Mortock unleashed another bellow. Somewhere, a spider shrieked, but I had eyes only for Davril. He stared at me stoically, but I could see the pain tightening his face. Also, I could tell he was growing weaker.

"Jade," he said. "Leave. Go now."

"But…"

"There's nothing more you can do."

"Bullshit."

"You'll die, Jade. Go now while you can. Soon the spiders will be back, and Mortock, too."

"They can't go beyond the cemetery, though. Right?" When he nodded weakly, I said, "Then that settles it."

I shoved myself under one of his armpits and heaved upward. With a groan, he stood, leaning against me for support.

"Now just one step in front of the other," I said.

I marched forward, letting him lean on me as we went. I tried not to let him see how scared or worried I was. God, he couldn't die now. Well, not ever, hopefully, but not now, just when I was beginning…well, never mind.

We reached the fence, and I paused. I stared skeptically at the top of it, then at Davril, his face hanging right by mine. His eyes were half closed, and his cheeks were turning yellow. I had to be swift.

"Screw going over the top," I murmured.

Mortock's fireballs gave me an idea. Saying a quick spell, I withdrew a certain feather from a pouch, set it along the wall, and then snapped my fingers. The feather exploded in purple flames, and bits of rock and metal hurled everywhere. I raised an invisible shield to protect us. It only lasted a few seconds, but that was enough. Coughing on the dust cloud, we stumped out into the real world—or at least, *my* world—alley, then kept going.

When I looked back, the cemetery was gone, replaced by the streets and alleys of the city.

Wheezing, I managed to bring Davril to Lady Kay on the street. Perhaps seeing how badly her master was wounded, she opened her doors even before I could reach her, and I carefully lowered Davril into the backseat. His chest was very warm, and clammy sweat beaded his cheeks and forehead.

"Jade…" he muttered, and I lingered, thinking he was trying to tell me something. But he just rolled his head and said it again, as if in a dream. "Jade…"

I pulled myself up, closed the door and slid behind the wheel.

"To, uh…" I tried to think of a destination. At last I settled for: "Lady Kay, take us to Davril's home."

Please, I thought. *Please be as alive as I think you are.*

The engine rumbled to life, the wings unfolded, and Lady Kay rose into the air. I tried to fight that same giddy feeling I'd felt the first time as the streets and buildings realigned around me. I put my hands on the wheel, but the truth was I had no idea where to go. I couldn't steer Lady Kay back to the palace. That place was infiltrated by the enemy, whoever they were. Was Mistress Angela working with anyone? The evidence seemed to suggest she was.

And I couldn't take him to a human hospital. They would be clueless in the face of magical venom.

The only other place I could think of was wherever Davril lived; I didn't think it was the palace. He didn't strike me as the type who would live in someone else's home. Hopefully Lady Kay knew where to go.

She did.

I gasped as, after navigating our way through the city, we approached a castle perched atop one of the highest skyscrapers in Manhattan. My belly flipflopped, watching the moonlight bathe its handsome towers, proud gray walls, and great metal gate. Ivy covered much of it, hugging its ancient, pitted walls. Coming close, I could see the great age of this place. Whoever lived here—and I was beginning to realize who that was—must have brought the structure over with them from the Fae Lands. The building looked scarred and blackened in spots, and I could just tell it had seen a great deal of battle. There were patches and assorted colors of stone in certain sections, hinting at hasty repairs. Some of it was lumpy and uneven, and I could sense a general sort of gloom or neglect hanging over it. It had a strange sense of…well, sadness. But it was handsome and commanding for all that.

Frowning, I turned back to Davril. "Davril," I said, tempted to poke him. "Is that…can this be your castle?"

He only moaned and muttered something beneath his breath, so I turned back to Lady Kay.

"Lady Kay, is this place…his?"

If she understood, she gave no sign. I gasped again as the great gate yawned overhead, revealing a dark interior lit with only a few braziers. As I flew in, I realized it was the courtyard, but shadows from tall, twisted trees drenched most of it. The lord of the castle had even brought soil and trees from the Fae Lands. They weren't like anything I'd ever seen before.

Knights rushed down from the walls and met us as Lady Kay

settled onto the ground. I climbed out, opened the back door, and tried to drag Davril out. He was heavy, and I strained my back to get him halfway out. A knight arrived and helped me. We laid him on the ground.

"Get back," said a voice, and I saw the knights who had gathered around part like the Red Sea, and four women in white cut through them. All were beautiful and blonde, and one said, "Out of the way."

Nurses, I thought. Magic-users. Maybe both.

They knelt over Davril, ushering me back. One took his pulse. Two others readied a stretcher. Then, all working together, they heaved Davril onto the stretcher, lifted him up and carried him toward one of the inner towers. Most were along the wall, but several stood inside it. A particularly tall and white-haired woman had come out to supervise them, and as they disappeared into the tower, she turned to me.

"You're not his partner," she said.

"He has a partner?"

"Well...once. Can you tell me what happened to him? Was that venom in his wound?"

"Yes, spider venom, from the spider queen in the Voris Cemetery." Fear gathered in my heart, and I had to force the next words out: "Is he going to die?"

"I'm not sure." When she saw my crestfallen look, she reached out and squeezed my shoulder. "I think he'll live," she added. "Thanks to your quick thinking."

I brightened, then impatiently brushed a tear away. "Can I go to him?"

"Let us heal him first."

I studied her. She seemed old—that was, aged. Most of the Fae seemed young—immortal, or practically so. That must mean she was truly ancient, perhaps tens of thousands of years old. The thought dizzied me.

"Who are you?" I said. "You and the other women?" Around us, the knights were returning to the walls and their other stations; many cast worried glances at the tower the women had taken Davril into.

"We're the Sisters of Elshe," the white-haired Fae said. "I'm Liara. Welcome to Castle Stormguard."

I swallowed. "So this *is* Davril's castle."

She smiled, maybe seeing more than I wanted her to. "That's right, dear. I don't think there's ever been a human here before, so you're quite unique. Although..." She leaned forward, just slightly, and I saw her nostrils quiver faintly. "You're not entirely human, are you, girl?"

"No, uh, ma'am."

She nodded, then glanced me over, obviously curious—but not quite enough to ask me. Besides, she had bigger problems.

"Stay here," she told me. "I must see to Davril, but I'll send a sister to you shortly." She squeezed my shoulder again, and I sensed genuine goodness in her, just a touch of surprise and caution. I immediately liked her, and I was more than curious about her, too. I watched her disappear into the tower. What was going on in there?

When a knight passed by, I said, "Wait! Who are the Sisters of Elshe?"

"An ancient Fae order," he said. "Part of our religion. Healers."

With that, he moved off, leaving me to wonder what sort of gods the Fae worshipped. I didn't have long to think on it, though, for within just a few minutes a "Sister" emerged. Beautiful, blond, and wearing white, she approached me, took my hand, then led me toward one of the other towers—the largest one. Not just a tower, really, but a large building with more than one tower: a tower with a square roof and four more towers.

"Why aren't we going into the hospital?" I said. "Or the Order building, or whatever you call it?"

"Davril needs time to recover," she said, opening the door for me. Hesitantly, I entered, finding myself inside the foyer of the keep, all stone fireplace and gleaming wooden floors covered in animal hide rugs. Some of the hides looked quite exotic. Suits of armor stood propped in the corners...along with cobwebs. This place could *really* use a woman's touch. Davril must not let the Sisters clean his home. Not minding my unease, the Fae woman tugged me up the long flight of stairs, then down a passageway lined with rich tapestries to a room at the end. "You'll stay here until he's ready to see you," she added.

"But he's okay?"

She paused, and a trace of worry flashed across her face. "I think so. The venom was deadly, but we extracted it and have given him powerful healing spells. He should make a full recovery." Just the same, I could hear doubt in her voice.

Her fear made me afraid, too. Davril could still be in trouble.

The woman squeezed my hand sympathetically. "He will be okay," she said with more confidence than before.

I smiled at her and tried to hold in my emotions; I could see her doing the same. Now wasn't the time to dissolve. Moments later, she left, leaving me with the room. It was simple and neat, and I flung myself on the too-comfortable bed and tried not to cry. I wasn't entirely successful.

After a few hours, someone knocked on the door. It was Liara, the white-haired Fae. I sat up straight, wiping at my eyes. Perhaps seeing my distress, she came in and wrapped me in a hug. I crushed her against me, sniffling and embarrassed.

At last, I pulled away. "How is he?"

"He's awake," she said. "And he wants to see you."

CHAPTER 14

My heart sped up as I approached his room. Liara was escorting me through the high bright halls of the Order of Elshe. Night had ended, and the red light of dawn cast glimmers of fire on the gilded mirrors and paintings. She flung open the door, and I stepped across the threshold.

Instantly, I gasped. Davril lay propped up in bed, bandages around his forearm and on the cuts and bruises on his torso. He was bare-chested...and he was *ripped*. His abs went on for days, each one harder than the other. He grimaced when he moved, and I could see his tight skin sliding over that eight-pack and knew he must hurt, but he was still the most masculine thing I'd ever seen. His arms were thick and his pecs hard and well-developed. He'd looked powerful in his clothes, but unclothed, he was a downright superman. I have to admit feeling a flutter stir in me at the sight of him.

Liara cleared her throat behind me. Flushing, I moved into the room, and she closed the door. I turned, but she was gone. It was just Davril and me in the room together. Heart hammering, I went to the window, and he watched me. I couldn't go to him directly. I just couldn't. I had to work up to it.

The room was all of stone and wood, but the bed looked comfortable and some scented candles flickered in a candelabra shaped like a deer head, each candle jutting from what would have been an antler. Instantly, I was reminded of the golden antler. Turning away, I looked through the window. The city was laid out before me, glimmering and beautiful. I couldn't believe I was in a fricking castle on top of a fricking skyscraper, locked in a room with a heroic knight, lord of the castle himself.

Slowly, I swiveled away from the window to find Davril still watching me. He seemed to have endless patience.

I went to him. Gently, I sat down on the bed beside him and touched his wounded arm. His skin was hot, and an electric thrill ran through me.

"How do you feel?" I asked, hoping he didn't hear the hiccup in my voice

Was there a grin tugging around his mouth? "I feel fine," he said, and sat up straighter. When he did, his pecs jumped. Feeling my face grow warm, I wondered if he'd adjusted his position just so they would.

If so, it worked.

Swallowing, I said, "I was…worried about you."

"I thought I was just a 'stupid cop'."

I rolled my eyes. "That was yesterday."

He grinned, and it was a real grin this time. "A lot has happened since then, hasn't it?"

I nodded. My hand was still very near his arm, and I could feel his heat. His large chest rose as he breathed, and his eyes bored into mine. Despite myself, my core turned molten.

I had to look away. *Don't get involved,* I told myself. *The last thing you need is that. Focus on Ruby. Focus on saving Ruby. Everything else is a distraction.*

To change the subject, I said, "Is this castle really from the Fae Lands? I mean, did you, like, relocate it here?"

He tilted his head, and a sort of sadness overcame him. I was sorry to have asked.

"I mean, don't tell me if you don't want to," I hastened to add.

"No, no, it's fine. This is my family castle. It's where those of my line have ruled from for thousands of years."

"Ruled?" I said. "But I thought Calista was the Queen."

"Once my kin were kings. We ruled a great kingdom in the Fae Lands, and only much later did we bend the knee and allow our kingdom to become part of Queen Calista's empire."

"This place…it looks like it's seen war."

A sigh escaped his lips. Again, I could see sadness in him. "It has. A great deal of it. The castle was located on the northern edge of the Realm of Nine Thrones—although now there's only one throne, really—right up against the Gilgorst Forest."

"Doesn't exactly sound like a vacation spot."

"It's not. The eternal foe of the Fae of the Nine Thrones is the Dark One, Vorkoth, who has tried to sweep our world in shadow for thousands of years. He and his foul hordes reside in the far north, locked away in his mountainous realm of Ongar. The only way south into the Nine Thrones is…"

I was starting to see it now. "Through Gilgorst Forest."

He smiled, relieved. "That's right." The smile faded. "It's a dark and cursed forest. Periodically, his goblin hordes will boil out of it and try to overrun the Nine Thrones. Well, my family and the kingdom it rules—or ruled—has been the bulwark against the dark tide. We've kept the Thrones safe for many, many years. This castle was the seat of our power, the great bastion of the city of Corwyn. My city. My home."

I could hear the love for the place in his voice. Unconsciously, I reached out and grabbed his hand, silently encouraging him to go on.

Fortified, he said, "My father fell fighting with the legions of Vorkoth, and the crown of Highgard—that's what my kingdom was called—came to me. My brother Nevos, whom I loved deeply, said the crown should have come to him because he was the oldest. He was right, too, at least according to our traditions. But Father had seen something in him that made him appoint me as the heir instead. At the time...well, I was sympathetic to Nevos, but I respected Father's wishes, and I accepted the crown."

"That must have been hard," I said. "Brother against brother."

A dark look crossed his face. "It's worse than you know, Jade."

His sudden seriousness chilled me. Breathless, I asked, "What happened?"

"He..." Davril cleared his throat and seemed to be summoning his strength. I could tell this was costing him, both spiritually and physically. He was still weak from the venom. "Nevos betrayed me. Behind my back, he colluded with agents of the enemy. With agents of Vorkoth."

"My God!"

Davril nodded gravely, and sort of grimaced. Pain was evident in him, not a physical discomfort but the agony of a bitter memory. A most bitter memory indeed. Suddenly I realized just how much he was sharing with me, answering all these questions I'd had about him, and something moved in me. He was opening himself up to me in a way I never would have been able to imagine.

Feeling my eyes sting, both at Nevos's betrayal and Davril's willingness to share, I said, "What happened?"

"I'll probably never know, not exactly, Jade. Nevos kept his dealings very secretive, and it was only much later that I could begin to put things together. I had ruled Highgard for fifty years—a long time to your kind but only a brief flash to mine—when I was roused in the middle of the night. The enemy was attacking. Corwyn is a walled city, and this castle, Wyngard, is perched along the northern arc of the wall, the part facing the forest. The great gate, the gate from which our troops would pour from in order to join battle, stood open."

"Nevos!"

Davril passed a hand across his face with the hand I wasn't gripping—and I was gripping it tighter than ever. "Somehow, he conspired with the enemy and had the gates opened just when the hordes of Vorkoth struck. They burst out of the haunted forest and streamed right through the gateway. I threw on my armor, grabbed my sword and fought them, meanwhile calling for my generals and troops to muster. They fought, and fought hard, but it was too late. The enemy was already inside the walls." Davril gazed off, and I knew he was seeing something far, far away, something that ate at him. I would have done anything in that moment to ease his pain, if only a little.

"I saw my brother, Jade," Davril said, his voice raw. "I saw Nevos. He was leading an army of Vorkoth's goblins...*against his own people.*"

Davril's eyes glimmered with unshed tears, and my heart wrenched. I knew then that I felt something for him, something powerful.

"What did you do?"

"I tried to reach him, to fight him. The goblins were too many, though, and I had to safeguard the city. I had to protect my people." Air hissed from between his teeth. "To my great shame, I had to evacuate the city. Even with the goblin hordes assailing us, I had to lead my people to Yasli, a more southerly town, but one with a strong wall protecting it. Once there, my people were protected. It...it was only the beginning, though."

"Don't tell me..."

"That's right. The reason the Fae came to your world...at least some of them. Many are still trapped in the Fae Lands, subject to the ravages of Vorkoth. At any rate, Nevos's treachery gave Vorkoth what he needed, the wedge with which to pry open the Nine Thrones. Once the breach was made, the Shadow poured in, blighting the land and killing countless Fae. The nine kings and queens rallied to the greatest kingdom in the Nine Realms, Gavala, where Queen Calista ruled. Gathering us all under one banner, one kingdom, she drove against the Shadow, and it was a long and terrible war. At last, however, we were flung back, and Calista knew we had to escape. She sent different peoples to different worlds. Those highest in her court, like me, and our most immediate vassals, came to your world just before the gateways were destroyed, sealing Vorkoth in the Fae Lands."

I absorbed this in silence for a moment, feeling my heart beat. "And this castle?"

"Just before we left, Queen Calista cast a spell to summon our castles, most of which were overrun by Vorkoth...and my brother. She knew the thought of them occupied by the enemy was a huge blow to us and that we would do anything to save our family seats from dishonor. I wish Nevos would have been inside the castle when she transported it, but alas, he wasn't. I was only able to kill a few goblins instead. At least I was able to liberate some of the captives they'd been torturing."

"How awful!"

His chest rose and fell as he gave a deep sigh, and I realized I was biting my lip. I made myself stop. *Don't fall for him,* I told myself angrily. *Don't you dare*. But it was hard. I mean, really hard. This noble knight had just opened his soul to me, shared with me his own personal tragedy and disgrace, and not only had he shared *his* own secrets but he'd told me the secrets of the Fae Lords, as well. Now I knew why they'd come to our world, and it was something that I knew very few were aware of. Hell, he'd shared with me something that could even be used *against* his people. The depth of his honesty and trust staggered me.

Could he...? I almost couldn't bear to complete the thought. But there it was, and there was no escaping it—could he be feeling about me the same way I was toward him?

Now it was his turn to squeeze my hand. His flesh was hot, but not with fever, and his grip was firm. I almost melted under his touch. Suddenly, I wished it wasn't just our hands touching.

His blue eyes speared into me. “I want to know about you, Jade. You promised you would tell me. Well, now is the time.”

Slowly, I nodded. He deserved that much. *More* than that much.

“I’m not sure where to begin,” I said.

“Just start at the beginning.”

I hesitated. “Are you sure? It might take a few minutes.”

A small smile touched his lips. “I have time.”

I swallowed. Nodded. “Well, uh, as you know, I’m part dragon shifter. Really, like, a small part. It was my grandmother who was a full dragon shifter. My grandfather was human, and he never Turned. And none of their kids were shifters, either. But one of their kids had me. By that time, the blood was thin, diluted, and I could never shift completely. But I could make wings pop out on my back, and I could…well, I could breathe fire.”

Davril’s expression was fierce, and I had to remember he had some beef against dragons. He still had at least one secret left, it seemed. “What happened?” he said.

“My father and mother were horrified, especially after I set the kitchen on fire one day. I was just trying to toast bread with my breath.” I smiled sheepishly. “It got toasted, all right.”

One side of Davril’s mouth curled up. “Go on.”

“Anyway, I grew up trying to keep it a secret. And trying not to scorch Judith Eans’s hair when she called me Baby No-Breasts. Or sometimes No Bump.”

“Ouch. Well, you showed her eventually.”

I felt my cheeks grow hotter. I was painfully aware my breasts weren’t anything to write home about. But I couldn’t help but be a little pleased that he’d noticed them, anyway. “Well, all the while, my grandmother had a terrible enemy. She loved me more than any of her other grandkids, even Ruby, and she took me deep into her confidence. She told me all about this evil mage named Walsh and how he’d made war upon her and our line for hundreds of years.”

"He's immortal?"

I winced. "Kind of. See, he uses his powers to steal the..." I swallowed. What I was about to say was key. Starting over, I said, "He uses his powers to steal the fire from dragons. When that happens, it's like he takes their souls. He breaks them somehow. In here." I tapped my chest. "They can never shift again. But he can use that fire to lengthen his own life."

"Like a vampire."

"Yes. Something like that. Well, he had a grudge against my grandmother's clan—my clan—because of some battle long ago. I don't know the full story. My grandmother told me all this when I was very young. Growing up, I would always keep my eyes open for some sinister figure with a magic ring lurking around the playgrounds and malls."

Davril swore under his breath, a strange Fae swear. "He was your boogeyman."

"Exactly." I nodded, satisfied that he got it. "Well, when I was about sixteen and just learning to control my powers, Walsh found me. I was coming home from a date—shit, my second-ever date, with Jimmy Gottlieb; he was so cute in that blue blazer; Ruby adored him—to find Walsh waiting for me outside my parents' house. I was coming up the walkway to the front door—alone, Jimmy had gone—when Walsh just sort of...materialized. I don't know if he was hiding behind a bush or using his powers to cloak himself, but he just appeared. Instantly, I knew who he must be. He was dressed elegantly, and his left hand was laden down with fancy rings, all with gleaming jewels in them. It was night, but the outside lights were on—my parents had left them on for me—so I could see everything."

Davril must have been able to see the memory of my fear on my face—I could feel moisture gather at the corners of my eyes—as he reached out and held my hand.

"Go on," he prompted gently. "What happened next?"

I nodded, gathering my strength, and said, "He held up his

hand and spoke a word—a single word. That's all it took. I knew what he was trying to do and started to shift. My wings popped out on my back, totally shredding the cute dress I'd bought just for the date, and I began to gather my fire inside my chest. If I could just reduce him to a cinder before he could cast that spell..." I let out a ragged breath. "But of course he was too fast, too powerful. The air blurred around his hand, and the blur moved forward and grew larger. It folded around me and tightened. Like it was strangling me. At first I thought I couldn't breathe, but then I realized it wasn't my breath he was stealing."

"It was your fire."

I nodded. "Yeah. He drew it out of me, and as he did, one of his rings began to glow—a dark gem in a gold band. I let out a scream and crumpled to the ground. My parents and Ruby burst out of the house and saw Walsh there, all triumphant and evil with me weeping on the ground, my wings gone, my fire gone...*half of me* gone...and my dad went nuts. He leapt at Walsh, fists flying. Walsh could have simply vanished, or he could have frozen my dad in time or something, but he was—is—an utterly evil bastard. He used my own fire, which still glowed in that gem on his finger, to kill my dad. I saw the ring glow bright, and then the brightness came over my dad. Flames consumed him in a heartbeat. Only then did Walsh mutter a spell and flicker out of existence."

Rage boiled inside Davril, the emotion playing on his usually stoic face. In a tight voice, he said, "I'm so sorry that he stole your fire and killed your dad, Jade."

I nodded, feeling my chin trembling, and tears streamed from my eyes despite my best efforts. My hand squeezed Davril's so tight it was painful, but he only gripped mine more firmly in return, letting me know he could take it, that he was there for me.

"My mom, Ruby and I were all devastated," I said. "My mom especially mourned for a long time. We were somehow separated, though. The tragedy should have brought us together, my mom and I, but it only drove us apart. I was in my own little world, a sphere of pain and isolation, and my mom was in her own place, too. It was like the pain built walls around us. Ruby helped, but she was going through her own ordeal, trying to learn the ways of magic even as her body matured and her mom and sister grew remote. I would've turned to my grandmother, but she had set off on a mission of revenge to kill Walsh for slaying her son and stealing my fire. She never did return, and I learned later that he killed her, too."

"Damn."

I sniffed wetly. "I'd had big plans. College. A career. A huge life I'd planned for myself. But after that…I just didn't have the heart for it. I started wearing dark clothes, listening to death metal. I guess I kind of went goth. And all the while, hate festered in me, and I knew I had to give it some release. I had to strike back somehow, if you know what I mean."

"I understand," Davril said.

"I hated Walsh for abusing his magical abilities like he did. So when I learned of a shifter who was using a magic amulet to make himself stronger and using that against others, I made it my business to steal that amulet. Later, I learned about a mage doing nasty things with a seeing stone. And so on. One thing led to another. I learned there were a lot of bad guys in New York, so I went there. Here. There's a whole magical community here, and, of course, where there's enough people, some of them will be assholes. I made it my business to take them down a peg. To take away anything they were using against others, like Walsh used his ring against my dad and me. I turned it into a career of sorts, selling the magical items to fences in the community—under the condition they wouldn't sell them to bad guys. And I made damn sure they didn't. Eventually, Ruby arrived. She said she couldn't let me go through this alone and would help me however I could. It's a shame, because her specialty was always healing magic. For me, though, she learned to use her arts for crime." Old guilt tore at me.

"And Walsh?" Davril said. "What about him?"

I wiped at my eyes impatiently. "He was always my endgame, my ultimate target. All those jobs I pulled before were just practice. Building up my skills to one day break into his lair and steal…it."

Davril snapped his fingers. "The ring!"

"He would feed on a dragon's fire for decades. He could make one dragon's fire last him for half a century. So I knew mine would still be there. Just waiting. Someday, I'll have it, that ring, and then I'll be whole again."

Davril stared at me for so long I thought I had a booger coming out of my nose, but then he wrenched his gaze away, as if with great effort. I knew then he was feeling something for me, something powerful, and he was trying to will himself from feeling that.

Just like I was with him.

Despite our best efforts, we were growing closer.

"So," I said. "What now?"

A long silence stretched. Outside, clouds drifted against the sun, casting strange shadows, and I felt unmoored, unattached to my previous life. I was living a different one now, someone else's, a life of lords and ladies, of Fae magic and terrible enemies.

Davril seemed to think about it. "You mean…about Mistress Angela?"

I hadn't been sure what I'd meant. Part of me wanted to talk about that girliest of all things—*us*—but another part of me knew he was right. It probably made more sense to discuss the more pressing matters at hand. I still had a sister to save and a friend to avenge.

"Sure," I said. "That. Wait!" I held up a hand, just realizing. "Do you think…I mean, do you think she is somehow connected with this Vorkoth—this Shadow from the Fae Lands?"

Davril's brows drew together. "That is Queen Calista's fear, yes. There have been signs, portents, and magical energies detected recently that can only have come from the Dark One's followers. We don't know if he's found a way to cross over into this world or if he was able to send some of his thralls here before the gateways closed, but either way, it presents a dire threat to my kind…and yours."

"What do you mean?" I asked, feeling a stir of dread coil around my gut.

Davril appeared very sober and grim. "The Shadow won't be content just to destroy the Fae, Jade. He'll destroy humanity, too."

CHAPTER 15

I stared at Davril, shock and horror flooding through me. "Destroy *humanity?*"

Davril nodded. "I'm so sorry, Jade. I should have told you earlier."

I pulled my hand away from his, not out of anger with him but because *us* seemed suddenly very small indeed. "Why would he want to destroy humanity?"

"Destroy it…or enslave it. As to why, it's because he serves dark gods and wants to conquer the Fae Lands in their name… and any other world he can gain access to, as well. This is the world that's harbored the Fae Lords, though, and it will especially earn his ire."

I began pacing, suddenly restless. "What do we need to do to stop him? I mean, if it *is* him that's behind all this?"

"I don't know." Davril frowned. "We didn't discover much in our attempts to spy on Mistress Angela, other than her name. Maybe we could track her down."

I shook my head. "She'll have gone to ground. She'll be totally off the radar. Never mind," I said when he raised his eyebrows.

He'd been in our world for ten years, but he didn't seem to know the word *radar*. Priorities. "We need some other thread to unravel," I said. "Like..." I clapped my hands. "The horn!"

"The antler?"

"No, the demon's horn! That's what Angela needed at the cemetery. If we can find out what she needed it for, we'll know what her game is. What her goal is. *Then* we can stop her."

Davril stroked his jaw. "There's a Compendium of magical artifacts and items in Queen Calista's palace. A vast list of magical things and what their various uses are, even if they're just suspected uses. It doesn't have everything, of course, but if Angela knew to retrieve that horn, and if she does have sympathetic compatriots inside the palace, then she might have had access to the Compendium. That's where she found out about the demon's horn."

"At least that's what you're guessing."

"Do you have a better plan?"

"No, but..." I groaned. "Going back into the palace—that's the one thing we were trying to avoid. That's going back into the lion's den."

"I know."

"Someone in that place is a traitor."

"I know."

"They could come after us."

"I *know*."

We looked at each other. At last, I smiled. When I did, he did, too.

"Sounds like a party," I said.

He grinned more widely, then winced. I could tell he was still in pain—physical pain, this time.

"You still need to heal," I said, returning to the bed and sitting down next to him. I was tempted to run my hands across his chest or those tight abs, but I held myself back. It was a struggle.

"I'll be fine by tomorrow," he said. "Then we'll go together into the palace—the lion's den, as you call it. Don't worry, Jade. *This* lion's claws are sharp."

I started to slap my hip, where I normally kept my crossbow, then remembered it was gone. "Mine, too," I said lamely.

An awkward silence stretched as we stared at each other, and I had a powerful urge to bend down and kiss him. One of his hands was opening and closing, slowly, as if he was having a hard time not reaching out and bringing me to him, but he was able to hold himself back—damn it. I was, too, if barely, and the moment eventually passed.

I stood and stretched, liking the way his eyes watched my body when I did.

"I guess I'll go get some rest," I said. "See you in the morning."

"First thing," he said. "I heal fast. We'll have breakfast together —I have an excellent chef—then fly into the palace."

Fly into the palace. It was amazing how easy it was to get used to flying around. Ruby and I had done some flying, but not that much; broomsticks just weren't that comfortable. But Davril's winged car…now that I could get used to.

"Sounds like a plan," I said.

I didn't kiss him, but I did squeeze his hand again. Then, using all my willpower, I left that sexy badass Fae Knight lying half-naked in bed and departed the Tower of Elshe, almost whistling as I did. Could there really be hope for Davril and me? It sounded crazy. I tried to tell myself that he was a stuck-up, self-righteous cop and I had no business with him, but that voice was getting fainter and fainter, replaced by a louder voice that said, *Go for it, Jade! Go for it now!* I smiled widely, listening to that voice, and returned to my rooms in the keep. Fae bowed to me as I went.

Later, Liara invited me to supper, and I went gladly. We supped on a terrace of one of the battlements with a magnificent view of the sun setting over New York. A girl could really get used to this.

Afterward, I returned to my room and tried to get some sleep. I tossed and turned for a long time before dreams finally took me, and I woke up feeling refreshed and optimistic for the first time since this whole mess began. Working together, Davril and I would solve this problem, save Ruby, and the forces of goodness would prevail. And then...who knew? I didn't want to think that far in advance. *Don't count your pepperonis until the pizza is done,* as my father used to say.

Liara had provided me with a toothbrush and other accessories, so I made myself ready, then dressed. The Fae had washed my cat-burglar outfit and mended the tears I'd received during the fight in the cemetery, so I just put that back on. I liked how tight and clingy it was, but it felt weird wearing it here amidst all the knights and Sisters. I felt like my modern-day criminal world was a taint upon the pristine medieval vibe they had going. But whatever, I wasn't going to let that get me down, and in this get-up, Davril could get a much better view of my curves. Such as they were. I never had a lot going on in that department, to be honest, but you work with what you got.

Just as I was putting the finishing touches on my hair, staring into the mirror, the mirror rippled...and the scene reflecting me and the bathroom faded way, replaced by an eerie black background.

A floating yellow skull bobbed in the foreground, eyes alight with fire.

I screamed and jumped back. I'd replaced my crossbow with the knife, and my hand flew to it and lifted it up, blade gleaming. Instantly, I realized how foolish this was. The floating face in the mirror couldn't be hurt by my knife. I wasn't sure what *could* hurt it, if anything.

"Good morning, Jade," Skull-Face said.

I repressed a shudder. I wasn't going to let this bastard see my fear. "Where the hell's Ruby?" I demanded.

The mirror rippled again. The skull disappeared, replaced by an image of Ruby in a stone cell. She looked weary but safe and unharmed. Of course, I had no way of knowing if this depiction of her was real or not. It could have been every bit as fake as the floating skull.

"She's safe and well. But only until I decide I have no more use for her. Or you." With new menace, Skull-Face said, "I need the golden antler. Bring it to the penthouse atop Hartson Tower by tomorrow."

"I'll get you your damned antler," I snarled. "But if you touch my sister, I'll gut you like a fish, you ugly bastard. Just what do you want with the antler, anyway?"

"That's my own affair."

"Are you mixed up in all this? Do you have something going on with Mistress Angela? What the hell does she want with the demon's horn, anyway?"

The fire-eyed skull threw back his head and laughed—long and loud. I wasn't sure if he was amused by my frustration or if he knew something and was just amused he had all the answers I needed, and that the fate of the Queen herself lay in his clawed hands. Or whatever kind of hands he really had. The skull was only his avatar, not the real villain.

I opened my mouth to snap something, but the door burst open and Davril leapt into my apartment. He must have come to escort me to breakfast himself and heard the sinister laughing. The threshold of the apartment was right near the bathroom, and he could see both me and the face in the mirror.

"Jade!" he said.

Belatedly, I realized his sword was out, gleaming with pale fire.

"Davril!" I was horrified. Because I could see from the look on his face that this had come as a shock to him, and not in a good way. He'd just caught the woman he'd come to trust engaged in a secret talk with a floating skull in a mirror.

Skull-Face just laughed louder. "Give me the antler and your sister lives," he said between sinister laughs. "You have until tomorrow."

With that, the mirror rippled again, and Skull-Face vanished, replaced by my reflection.

I stared at Davril, and he glared back. I could see all the trust and positive feelings I'd earned dissolve in an instant. Seeing that, my heart twisted, and I lost the strength in my legs. I staggered back and almost sat down on the toilet, I was so crushed. I just barely kept my feet.

"Jade," Davril said, stepping toward me. He moved like a man in a dream. Completely healed now, he wore his street clothes—a black silk shirt, brown leather jacket, and jeans. As he moved, he thrust his sword back into its sheath, and it became invisible. Good. At least he wasn't going to chop me into pieces. But that look...

"Davril," I said, and raised my hands, palms out, as if trying to calm a spooked horse. Only *I* was the one spooked. My heart was smashing against my ribs like a drum. "This isn't what it looks like. That thing, Skull-Face, it kidnapped Ruby..."

"And you've been working with it to steal back the antler. You were never in this for me or the Queen. You were never in this to save my kingdom from Vorkoth. You just wanted to save your sister. Even if it meant my whole race would be wiped out."

"I...I..." I racked my brain for some explanation, something to tell him that would restore that trust, but at the moment, my mind was horribly, hideously blank. I could only manage to say again, "Davril, it's not what it looks like."

He stepped forward again, anguish in his eyes. Suddenly, he stood straighter. His jaw stuck out. His eyes became flinty.

Oh shit, I thought. What now? Because it was clear Davril had reached a decision, and I didn't think it was going to go well for me.

He reached behind his back and yanked out his set of handcuffs. They sparkled almost prettily, like ice. Like doom.

Swaying on my feet, I stepped back again, nearly falling into the marble bathtub. Feeling it whack my thighs, I realized I could go no further. I could fight Davril…or I could submit.

"Don't do this," I said as he moved closer. "I…I never would have hurt you or the Queen…and I just found out about Vorkoth yesterday!" I could hear the pitiful tone of my voice. I sounded like I was on the edge of tears.

No…I felt the sting in my eyes and the saltiness on my lips. I *was* crying. My chest hitched, and my lips trembled. I just wanted to crawl into a hole and die.

"You betrayed me," he said, and his voice was like stone grating on stone. "You betrayed the Queen. I…" He cleared his throat. "You must come with me, Jade. I must take you back to the dungeon at the palace."

"But…I *never* would have…"

"The Queen will have to make that determination, not me."

He reached me. Grabbing my left arm, he twisted it behind my back, then my right, and I could feel the cold bite of metal as it snapped around my wrists. It didn't physically hurt—he was as gentle as he could have been—but I hurt just the same.

"I can't believe you're doing this," I said as he marched me through the halls. I tried to avoid the eyes of the Fae we passed. "After…" Somehow I couldn't say it.

"After *what?*" Davril said.

Was he really going to make me go there? Damn it, he was. Sucking up my courage, I said, "After yesterday."

"What happened yesterday?"

Rage flooded my veins. *The bastard! We only bared our souls to each other, that's all.* I wanted to snap at him in fury, but I felt defeated by it all. I had come so close to happiness, or at least to the possibility of maybe achieving it someday, after this whole mess was over with. Or at least the *hope*. But now it was all in tatters, ruined because I'd kept the wrong secret.

Because that was the problem. Davril was *correct* to be mad. But...I'd *had* to keep the secret.

Right?

With a sigh, I hung my head as he carefully propelled me into Lady Kay—into the partitioned *backseat* of Lady Kay. A new wave of glum settled over me as I dropped onto the seat. How many criminals had Davril driven to the palace dungeon in this car? How many had sat here, watching the city scroll by just like I was doing?

I studied him as he drove. Jaws bunched like he was chewing steel, he hurled us through the city. Anger boiled off him like a cloud. He was furious. More than furious. *Hurt*. Davril had been wounded by what I'd done.

Damn it all, I thought. I'd really blown it. Like, epically.

Then I realized something.

"Wait! Davril, wait!"

He didn't slow down, but he did turn his head a bit. "Yes?"

"We can't return to the palace! Not like this. We were going into the lion's den, anyway. But that was with two lions that knew the score on the lookout for the bad lions. Okay, this metaphor is starting to break down, but you know what I mean. Now we're going into the lion's den with one lion down and the other with his head totally in the wrong place. No, don't bother to deny it. I can tell. It's really in the wrong place. I'm on your side, you idiot!"

"No. You're on your sister's side."

I growled in frustration. "You say that like it's a bad thing. Of *course* I'm on my sister's side. Why wouldn't I be? She's my sister! But that doesn't mean I'm not on your side. It just..."

"Yes?"

I let out a breath. "It just seemed best not to tell you. If I had, you wouldn't have trusted me."

"Damned right."

I wanted to kick the back of his chair but resisted. I remembered the last time I'd tried it. "Don't you see, you blockhead?" I said. "I couldn't have told you. Otherwise I'd still be in that cell!"

"Apparently that's where you belong."

Now I did kick the back of his chair. Sure enough, a magical blast threw me backward, and I could feel my hair stand on end. *Real smooth, Jade.* Idly I wondered if they'd serve me breakfast in jail. I was starving. And I could sure as hell use some coffee, too. Did Fae drink coffee? I guessed I was about to find out.

The palace came into view ahead. I braced myself. We landed, and Davril escorted me through the high clean halls, bound for the dungeon. Fae stared at me as I walked past, and I wanted to hang my head in shame but made myself keep my head straight. I still couldn't look anyone in the eye, but at least I kept some pride. Then I saw Jessela gaping at me and I had to twist my head as I passed her.

Once again, Davril showed me down to the dungeon, through the dank, squalid passages, and installed me in a cell. It made sense to me now why the dungeon was so eerie and grotesque; it had probably once been underground. This had to be Queen Calista's original palace from her homeworld.

Davril twisted the key, then gazed at me through the crusted iron grate. "It didn't have to be like this," he said quietly.

I watched him. "I know."

He held my gaze for another moment, then looked away. I tried to read his emotions, but he'd clammed up again. Great. How could people communicate if they didn't know where they stood with each other? Of course, I was all too worried that I knew full well where we stood. I was *persona non-grata* to Davril now.

"I am sorry," I told him. "I…really, I never would have betrayed you."

He didn't turn back to me. Still looking away, he said, "I wish I could believe that."

My heart leapt. "You can. You really can."

His chest rose, then fell. Still not looking at me, he said, "I must see the Queen." He moved off through the darkness, leaving me alone.

"Wait!" I called, but he didn't turn back. "Wait! You're in danger, remember! Someone might be after you. Be careful!"

But he was gone.

CHAPTER 16

For hours, I beat my fists against the walls or paced restlessly. A fierce anger had consumed me—anger at myself for allowing this to happen, anger at Davril for overreacting, but most of all, anger at Skull-Face for abducting Ruby in the first place. He was the one who'd caused all this. *Just wait till I get my hands on you*, I thought. Of course, for all I knew, I'd never leave this cell.

Finally, when the sun was setting over the city—which I could just barely see through the tiny, high-set window—someone came to get me. I jerked up from where I was slumped against the wall, my energy finally exhausted, to see none other than Lord Gerwyn Seafoam, the Fae Lord with the brown hair and mustache who I'd met the night of the feast.

"Hello there," he said.

"Er...hello?"

He smiled. I heard the lock click and the door swung open. I rose from the bed and stood before him as he entered. With him in the cell, I was suddenly aware of how small it was. It had been tight before, but now it was claustrophobic. Just why the hell was he coming in here?

"You wanted to see me?" I said. God, had Davril sent Seafoam in his stead because he couldn't stand the sight of me any longer? Had Seafoam come to fetch me to the Queen?

"Yes, I did," Seafoam said. "There is an urgent matter I need to address."

"I hope it's about freeing me, because—"

He yanked a knife from his belt. It glittered like death itself in the dim light streaming in from the window.

"A very urgent matter," he said. For the first time, I heard the menace in his voice.

I stumbled back. Fear filled me. "You," I said. "*You're* the mole!"

He offered a ghastly grin. "Who says there's just one?"

I swallowed, hard.

He stepped forward. I tried to dodge around him, but he was too quick. He interposed himself between me and the door, slashing at me with his blade. Crying out, I danced back.

He stabbed out again. I jumped back. My spine struck the wall. Shit. There was nowhere else for me to go.

"Why?" I asked desperately. "Why are you doing this? Do you serve Vorkoth?"

Instead of answering, he coiled his arm for the killing blow. I was dead, I knew, and there was nothing I could do about it.

Suddenly, a shining sword point stabbed out from Seafoam's chest, spraying blood. His eyes widened, and he gasped. Blood flecked his lips. The sword was yanked back through his chest, leaving a hole, and he fell to his knees. The knife clattered to the floor.

"Why…why…?"

He couldn't complete the sentence but listed sideways, toppling dead to the floor. Panting for breath, I looked up from his corpse to my savior. I expected it to be Davril, but no, it was Jessela, the female Fae Knight.

"Jessela!" I started to step over Seafoam and hug her, but she was still standing there with her sword out. Blood dripped from it to the floor. She looked just as shocked as I felt.

As if sensing my unease, she wiped off her blade and thrust it back through the sheath. Her eyes went once more to Seafoam.

"I...I can't believe it," she said. "He was the traitor!"

I nudged him with my foot, but he didn't move. "One of them," I said. "He hinted that there might be more."

"I heard the last part, when you asked him if he served the Shadow." She sucked on her lower lip. "I wish he'd answered. I want to know what's motivating these bastards."

"You and me both."

Her gaze met mine. "How are you doing, Jade? Did he hurt you?"

"No, and I'd be better out of here, thanks. And so would you, too, I think. And Davril."

"What about Davril?"

I made my voice steady. "He's in danger, especially if there *are* more spies like Seafoam here. We all are—in danger, I mean."

"Explain."

"Davril and I meant to come here to investigate the Compendium, but he got sidetracked by being paranoid, and now we're sitting ducks."

"I just came down to see how you were doing, Jade. I didn't come to break you out. But after what just happened..."

"Yes?"

"That doesn't mean I couldn't."

I beamed. "Really?"

"Really. But first, you have to tell me everything."

Breathlessly, I told her the situation. She interjected a question here or there, but mainly she listened, rapt and obviously believing me. Seafoam's blood hardened on the floor as I spoke. When I had finished, she nodded once, curtly.

"Come with me," she said.

"Just like that? What about the guards?"

"When they see Seafoam's body, they'll understand I need to move you to a more secure location. Besides, I'm not going to let the Queen get hurt, am I? Davril being an ass can't be allowed to have an impact on Her Highness." She paused. "Although, I cannot say his actions were completely in the wrong."

I nodded guiltily. "I know." I stepped out of the cell, and we moved up the hall.

We spoke with the guards, and they swore when they discovered Seafoam's body. Immediately, they agreed to give Jessela custody of me, and we left the dungeon for the brighter halls beyond. Despite the violence, or maybe because of it, my belly rumbled loudly as we moved up through the halls toward what I assumed was the Compendium, and Jessela glanced at me in concern.

"They did feed you, didn't they?"

"Well...a piece of bread and water for lunch. That was it."

"Those cretins. I'll have to speak to their captain about this. While you work in the Compendium, I'll fetch you some food."

"That sounds like a plan and a half."

"You might be needing this." She'd been holding something in her hand. It had been folded up. I hadn't taken a close look at it, but now she held it up and let it dangle.

I squealed in happiness. "My belt!" Davril had confiscated it when he'd arrested me. I hastily cinched it around my waist. If some asshole working for Mistress Angela—or whoever she worked for, if anyone—dared attack me now, I would have some defense. "Thank you so much."

"No problem."

Fae glanced at us curiously as we went, and I had to ask Jessela, "Won't you get in trouble for this?"

She glanced at me sidelong, seriousness in her face. "Not if you find something useful."

Damn, she's putting a lot of faith in me. No pressure, Jade. If I didn't find something, I'd be going back to the cell and *she* might occupy it with me. Or at least one right next door. I wondered if they'd feed her better than they had me.

A question formed in my mind, and I hesitated to ask it. Now wasn't really the time or the place, and we had much bigger things to worry about.

"What is it?" Jessela asked, evidently seeing me chewing my lips in deliberation.

I sighed. "It's just…you and Davril. Were you…together?"

She almost laughed. We turned a corner and kept going, the halls getting higher and brighter around us. Hopefully, she knew where we were going, because I was lost.

"We did, ah, date," she said.

A thousand questions jumbled for prominence in my mind. "For how long? When did you stop? *Did* you stop?"

Now Jessela did laugh. "I can tell someone is interested in him."

There's a lot to be interested in, I thought, remembering him half-naked in the light of the setting sun.

"Anyway, we did date," she went on. "I won't get into all the details—at least not here. But I could sense a restlessness, a sadness, in him."

"I've noticed that, too."

"After awhile of being with him, I realized he wasn't happy—with me, with us. But it wasn't just us. I realized that he could *never* let himself be happy."

"Why?"

Jessela slowed as we approached a certain door of darkly gleaming oak, and I slowed with her. "I think it's because of what happened," she said. "In the Fae Lands. Did he…did he tell you about Vorkoth…and his brother?"

I nodded. "Yes."

She paused outside the door. "Davril feels a terrible guilt about what happened that day. That's what I figured out at last. He never talks about it, about his feelings, but I could tell. He holds *himself* responsible for the downfall of the Fae."

"My God…"

"Of course, it was really his brother. Davril's only mistake was in trusting Nevos, but then, who doesn't trust their siblings?"

I thought of the bond between Ruby and me. I would trust her with my life and then some. "Not me," I said.

Wistfully, Jessela said, "When I realized that he would never let himself be happy because he was punishing himself for the Fae having to leave our homeworld, I knew our relationship was doomed. How could I be with someone who couldn't be happy with me? Who wouldn't *let* himself be happy with me?"

"So you're the one who broke it off?"

She nodded. I could tell the decision still made her sad to think about. "I felt I had to." She paused, and one corner of her mouth quirked up. "However, I would never begrudge another woman her chance at him."

I sniffed. "Never! He's thrown me in jail twice!"

"Then why are you asking about him?"

"Because...because...uh..."

Still wearing that infuriating half-smile, she opened the door and ushered me into a medium-sized, murky room filled with shadows. Fog stirred against the floor, wreathing my feet and lower legs in mist, and in the center of the room squatted a great, moss-covered boulder flecked with age in the middle of a basin of water carved into the stone floor. The boulder came up to my hips. Vaguely, I could hear the flow of water. With the mist and darkness and water noises, it was all strangely relaxing and peaceful.

"I don't get it," I said. "Aren't we going to the Compendium?"

For a wild moment, I thought she'd lured me into a trap. Maybe Jessela was another traitor.

Still looking amused, she moved to the boulder and placed her palm against it. "This is Jade McClaren," she said, and I realized she was speaking to the boulder. What the hell? "Help her with her queries." Lifting her hand, she turned back to me. Hitching her head at the boulder, she said, "That's the Compendium."

"But…I guess I was expecting a library or something."

"Oh, the Queen's library is amazing, but that's not what this is. The Compendium is just a place to store knowledge. Magical knowledge. It had become so vast that sorting through it all started to take more time than we all thought prudent, so it was reconfigured. All the knowledge was channeled into this stone, and a friendly entity put in charge of it. Well, sometimes friendly, anyway. I've just given it permission to help you, so now you're an authorized user of the Compendium. Just put your hand on it. The rest is all mental, or psychic, or whatever you'd like to call it."

"Magic."

"Exactly. I'll go get you some food. Hopefully by the time I get back, you'll have made some progress. We'll go to the Queen, get this sorted out, Davril will understand what an ass he was, we'll go after the parties responsible for all this—"

"Save my sister."

"—save your sister, restore peace to the realm, and all will be made well."

"That's a plan I can get behind." I looked forward to Davril's apology. Not that I expected him to give one, being as proud as he was. But still, he might acknowledge I wasn't an enemy of the Fae. I mean, cripes!

Jessela left, closing the door behind her, and I turned back to the stone. It squatted there in its watery pool, pregnant with magic and possibilities. Being alone with it, I felt a strange sense of serenity about it, almost of sacredness. *This is the hidden knowledge of the Fae,* I thought. Gathered over many years.

I sucked in a breath. Then, slowly, I reached out my hand toward the boulder and placed my palm against it. The stone was somehow both rough and smooth at the same time, and cool under my skin.

As soon as I touched the stone, a new world opened around me. My eyes were still closed, but somehow I could see that I stood in a glade swirling with purple fog. Moonlight glimmered down on me through skeletal branches above, and I could smell grass and loam. It was very natural and very magical at the same time. Magic *was* natural in this place.

"Whoa, toots, get a loada you," said an unmistakably male voice in my ear.

I whirled around.

"Who's there?" I said, my voice quavering.

"Only me, Federico, your humble guide to the Compendium. And you are most welcome here."

"Er…thanks?"

"I mean, you are one tall drink of water. Well, actually, babes, you're kinda a short drink of water, if you follow, but for a short drink, you are pretty tall, if you know what I mean."

"Er, again, thank you, I think." I squinted into the gloom around me. "Where are you and why do you talk like a 1930's gangster from an Al Capone movie?"

"Hold the phone, toots. Who says *they* didn't talk like *me?*"

The voice was right behind me. I turned around again to see a short red demon—almost black by moonlight—with bat-like wings and cloven hooves standing atop a boulder that looked an awful lot like the one I was touching in the real world. Assuming I was still touching it, and I thought I probably was. To an outsider, I probably looked like I was in some sort of trance.

I stared in shock at the demon, and he gave me a lascivious smile. He only wore a loincloth, and it was bulging.

"I'm happy to see ya," he said, and gave me a naughty wink.

"What are you?"

"I'm an imp," he said, affronted. "Haven't you ever seen an imp before?"

"No."

He snorted, then jumped off the rock and approached me. I hadn't noticed before, but in one hand he carried a lit cigar, and he pointed it at me for emphasis. "What sort of person walks into a place like this and has never seen an imp? I mean, just what sorta ignoramus are you, toots?" He stuck the cigar back in his mouth and leaned back, folding his arms across his scrawny chest, as if daring me to answer him.

"The human kind, I guess," I said. I shook myself. This was weird, but was it weirder than anything else I'd seen over the last couple of days? At least Federico wasn't anything like the much scarier Lord Mortock. "But I don't get it. I mean, imps are demons, right?"

"Duh."

"Well...but aren't demons evil? Like, you know, hellspawn?"

He tilted his head, staring at me from beneath his eyebrows. "Whatcher point?"

"Well, I mean, the Fae are good..."

"Ah!" He clapped his hands. "That! Well, see, I ran into 'em in the Fae Lands some years ago. Came to do an honest bit of mischief. All in a day's work for an imp, y'know. Well, Queen Calista didn't exactly appreciate me enchanting her hairbrush to make her hair stand up in devil-horns—although it was pretty funny, I have to tell you—so she bound me in stasis. She decided I was too dangerous to let go, since I could just come and go from her bedchambers at will, and I obviously served what she thought of as the dark powers, but she didn't want to kill me, either."

"That was nice."

"You say so. Anyway, she kinda liked me and wanted to keep me around, and the Fae needed someone to keep track of their newly reorganized Compendium, so here I am. It's not a bad gig, really, and this place keeps me hoppin', I can tell you that. Beats the Sulfur Pits seven days a week!"

"Well...good," I said, not sure how to get back on track. "Um, I came here looking for answers."

Federico smiled and patted his crotch, and I forced myself to keep my eyes on *his* eyes, nowhere else. He looked disappointed. "I've got everything you need, doll," he said. "And then some, believe me."

"I believe you."

He pivoted, strutted back to his stone, as if to give me a good view of his admittedly muscular backside, then hopped up on the boulder and took a seat. Turning back to face me, he gestured with his cigar. It left red tracers in the purple gloom. His eyes reflected the red in eerie little pools, glittering mysteriously.

"Whatcha got for Federico?" he said.

"I need to know what use the horn of a certain demon could be to a powerful witch with ill intentions toward Queen Calista."

His eyes widened. "Queen Calista? Sheesh! That's big, doll, that's real big. Almost as big as me." Once more, he seemed disappointed that I kept my eyes on his. "Well," he said testily. "Show me. Just imagine the item yer talkin' about, and I'll pull it up."

I closed my eyes (again—they were still closed in the real world) and pictured Mortock hovering in the air over his mausoleum, a fireball gathering on his palm. Then I mentally zoomed in and concentrated on his horns, one of which had been cut off, leaving only an obsidian stump.

When I opened my eyes, I could see a curling red horn floating in the air above Federico. The imp had stood up on his boulder and was frowning at the horn, obviously deep in thought. I thought he might be communing with it in some way, trying to divine its nature and possible uses.

At last, he snapped his fingers and the horn blinked out of existence.

"Well?" I said anxiously. "Do you know what it might be used for?"

He leveled his gaze at me, and I could see only grimness there. "You might not think this, but I like Queen Calista. I might not appreciate being bound to her service, but I like her service, and I like the Fae. Good blokes, most of 'em, even if they are a bit stiff, and they're a damn sight better'n most of my fellow 'spawn in the Down Below. So when I tell ya this is bad, toots, you best believe it."

I made myself stand straight. "What is it?"

"That horn can be made into a weapon—one that can penetrate Queen Calista's defensive shields."

I blinked. "You mean…?"

He nodded gravely. "If some powerful magic-user got hold of that thing, they could fashion a weapon that could kill the Queen."

CHAPTER 17

I swallowed down my fear. "I've got to warn Queen Calista," I said. "Even now, Mistress Angela could be coming for her."

"You'd best hurry, hon," Federico said. "With power like that in her corner, I doubt this Angela broad will wait long."

"She'll come herself?"

"She'll need to. Only a powerfully magical person can wield that horn."

I expected him to make some crack about wielding horns, but evidently he took this threat so seriously that it overrode even bad jokes. That told me how dire the situation was.

I nerved myself up, then made myself smile at Federico. He might be a little stinker, but he had really helped me out. Maybe *all* of us out. "Thank you," I told him sincerely.

He touched his cigar to one of his horns, offering me a salute. Then he grinned and said, "Come back anytime, toots. I think an angel and a devil could have a lot of fun together. Just sayin'."

With that, he rippled out of existence, leaving only his smile, just like the Cheshire cat...oh, and his groin. That stayed, too. It faded out of existence just a few seconds after his smile did. *Little stinker.*

The world of the Compendium dissolved, and I found myself once more standing over the stone in the small room of the palace. Just as I took my hand off it, I heard the door open. Turning, I saw Jessela entering with a silver platter bearing food—breakfast, even though it was night: eggs, bread, and some brightly colored fruit I couldn't identify. It was probably grown right here.

She stopped dead in the doorway at seeing my expression. "What is it?"

"No time," I told her. "We have to hurry to see the Queen." I snatched the tray and began wolfing down its contents as I passed her, starting down the halls of the palace once again. For a moment, I was turned around, having forgotten where the Throne Room was, but then I oriented myself and started in that direction. The weird red fruit was awesome, sweet and juicy.

"W-what's going on?" Jessela asked, scurrying at my side.

"It's Mistress Angela," I said. "I think she means to kill Queen Calista."

"Well, we do know that she sent her goons into the palace to—"

"No, no, this time she's coming herself. And she'll have a weapon that can penetrate Calista's protective wards." Briefly I told her what Federico had discovered, and Jessela's face grew pale.

"That's terrible," she said, and I could tell that she believed me one hundred percent. Good. That would save time. She opened her mouth to say something else, but we heard a great commotion—screaming and crashing—and both our heads snapped in that direction.

"Shit," I said. "It's already started."

"What—what—?"

Jessela pressed her lips together, and I could almost see it, her training taking over. She was a Fae Knight, after all, highly disciplined and lethal in battle.

"This way," she said, a new note of command in her voice. She dashed in the direction of the noise, her armor only clinking slightly as she went. She drew her sword with a steely *rrrring*. When I heard that noise, so clean and pure and deadly, I wanted a sword, too.

We burst out into a courtyard. It was probably a lovely place, normally, with tall beautiful trees of a kind I'd never seen before nodding beside a gurgling stream that appeared to flow through the palace itself, with white swans and other majestic but less recognizable animals hanging out in the water or on the tall, soft grass. At the moment, however, two huge trolls were doing battle against half a dozen Fae Knights and a handful of regular Fae.

As I watched, three knights were evading the stamping feet of one troll while their swords hacked at its legs and waist—which was as high as they could reach on the thing. It towered twenty feet overhead, as did its companion. They were both great brutes with thickly muscled arms and bristly hair sticking up all over. Fortunately the hair was thick enough to mask their groins for the most part, because they had ripped their clothes to shreds when they'd transformed. And I completely believed they *had* transformed, that they'd looked just like regular people a few minutes ago.

Becoming a troll evidently shaved a few points off their IQs, though, because they didn't fight with sophisticated weapons or any coordination or strategy. One troll had ripped up a tree and was smashing the ground where the knights stood, forcing them to scatter, while the other simply tried to step on them, receiving many nicks and slashes for its trouble. One knight had already been crushed by its feet, though, and lay embedded in the grass, while blood coated the limbs of the tree the other wielded. Brute strength worked just fine for these assholes.

Jessela lifted an arm, and a beam of light shot out from her palms and struck the tree-wielder in the chest. It was the same sort of magical attack I'd seen Davril do when the vampires ambushed me and abducted Ruby. The beam of light only glanced off the troll's chest. Evidently it had a magical ward protecting it.

Jessela gave a frustrated growl and dashed toward the troll. It was just bringing its tree around in a swing to take out several Fae who were recovering their feet after dodging its last swipe. I almost cried out for Jessela to stop, that she'd be killed, but I didn't. She was doing her duty, and she was brave and righteous to do so. The question was how could I help?

I cast about for answers, momentarily wishing I had my crossbow. Then I realized that a crossbow bolt would probably bounce off these things even quicker than a magical blast would.

I patted my utility belt, trying to determine what spellgredients I had left. Thank God Jessela had thought to bring it back to me. Mm, spider eyes could be mixed with the ginshi root to hurl a green ball of ice, but if the troll's protective wards could repel Fae energy blasts, they could probably handle the magical ball of ice, too. I had to think of something else fast.

Jessela had reached the troll, and she slashed at its wrist as it brought the tree toward the targeted Fae. I thought she'd been aiming for the big vein in the wrist, but her angle was off and her sword only drew a deep line of red. The troll howled in rage, though, and pulled its arm up, breaking off the swing that would have killed those Fae. Jessela shouted something up at it in Faeish that I thought might be something like *Take that, you bastard!* to judge by her tone.

Meanwhile, the Fae that had almost been obliterated were able to stand up and regroup. Some drew weapons or began spells. One rushed toward a Fae who lay crumpled and unmoving on the ground, probably trying to administer aid. By all the blood on the grass near him, I didn't think the helper could do much.

The sword worked, I realized. The enchanted blades of the Fae Knights could cut through the trolls' defenses. Was there some way I could use that?

Yes. There was.

"Jessela!" I shouted and ran toward her. I had to navigate around the other troll that was stomping at people to get to her, though. One of those giant hairy feet hoisted off the ground and hovered right over me. I only just barely leapt to the side as it came crashing down. Mud and grass flew, and I spat dirt from my mouth as I climbed to my feet. Not bothering to look back, I ran toward Jessela. She was busy hacking at the knees of the tree-wielder, but when she saw my expression she drew aside.

"Yes?" she panted. Her face was red and droplets of sweat beaded her auburn hair. Troll blood dripped from her blade.

"Hold your sword out," I said. With a raised eyebrow, she obeyed.

"Whatever you're doing, do it fast," she told me.

We were only about twenty feet from the troll, nearly within range of its tree. Fortunately it was preoccupied with dealing with the knights attacking it. At least for the moment.

I pinched some powder from one pouch and mixed it with some from another, then added in the secretion from a giant gala bird. My fingers shook as I worked, but I was used to managing my digits under stress (I'd be a pretty bad cat burglar if I wasn't) and I was able to keep going. Physically, anyway. Mentally, I was freaking out. Hurriedly mixing it all together in my mixing pool, I thrust my fingers into the bowl, then smeared the poisonous goop along the length of Jessela's blade.

"That should do it," I said, then wiped my fingers on the grass.

Jessela gazed at her poisoned blade for a moment, nodded, then rushed off to battle. She lowered her head as the tree came at her again, this time bearing two thrashing Fae bodies, cleared it, and popped up near the troll's right leg. It saw her and started to draw its leg back for a kick, but it was slow and she was as fast as a hummingbird. Her sword darted out, slashed the troll across the shin, and it bellowed so loudly that the windows lining the courtyard burst inward.

I jumped back, pressing my hands over my ears. Jessela and the other Fae Knights stared up in surprise at the troll. So did the other troll, with its leg raised high in preparation for stomping on more Fae. It recovered and resumed its stomp, but the Fae it had been about to grind into paste had time to roll to the side and escape it. The foot came down hard, sending out a geyser of mud and grass but causing no harm.

The troll Jessela had slashed quit bellowing and resumed trying to knock Fae around with its improvised club, but its movements had slowed and its eyes were turning yellow. I whooped in victory. It had worked! But would the poison be enough?

The answer came seconds later. The troll gave one last groan halfway through a swipe and collapsed to the ground with a tremendous *thud*. The impact almost knocked me off my feet, and it sent Fae scurrying out from under the behemoth.

The Fae stared at the giant corpse—which was already shrinking back to its human size—then at Jessela, knowing she was the one who had delivered the deadly blow. She bowed once to me, then ran over to me as the other Fae turned to the Stomper.

"Can you make more of that stuff?" she asked.

"I think so," I said. "But I only have enough spellgredients for one more."

"That should do it. There's more spellgredients, as you call them, in the palace."

Quickly I made another batch of poison—I had just enough—and she applied it to her sword. Running forward, she evaded the grasping hand of the Stomper—he was trying to squeeze Fae into paste with his hands, having learned another skill, apparently—I would have to call him the Stomper and Squeezer if he lasted much longer—and slashed him on the back of the knee.

Ol' Stompy let loose a terrible roar, then resumed stomping and squeezing. But like before, his movements were slower, and the whites of his eyes began to turn yellow. Within moments he fell to his knees, then toppled headlong to the ground. Fae danced aside, stared at the body, and then cheered.

I felt a smile creep across my face. "We did it!"

"You did it," Jessela said, approaching. Her face was even redder than before, but I could see pride in her eyes. "I'll spread the word," she told me. "Get the Enchanters to mix up that poison en masse. What was in it?"

Briefly I told her how to make the goop, and I could see she was committing it to memory. Even as I relayed it to her, I could hear screams and crashings from other parts of the palace. There were indeed more trolls, and more scenes of violence. Damn it all, this had been far too organized and coordinated.

The surviving Fae Knights approached and gathered around Jessela, some slapping her on the back or cheering her on.

"What shall we do next?" one asked. It was obvious she had become something of a leader to them now. They would follow whatever she said.

"Help me break through to the Hall of Enchantment," she said. "Stick close to me and I think we can reach the Enchanters so that they can whip up more of the poison. Thank our human friend here for the recipe."

They nodded at me guardedly, then turned back to Jessela.

"What about me?" I asked her. "I'm coming, too."

"No, you stay here," she said.

"But—"

She raised a hand, forestalling my objections. "The Queen would have me whipped for bringing someone who's not a knight into the fray."

That hadn't stopped her before. Then again, a few minutes ago, she hadn't been surrounded by other knights who would make her live up to her vows, whatever those were.

"I'm just as much a warrior as you are," I said, but even as I said it, I knew it wasn't true. I was a sneaker, not a fighter, and she may have trained for hundreds of years in the martial arts for all I knew. Hell, thousands.

She gave me a kind look, then turned back to her fellow knights. "Follow me," she said, and ran toward one of the doors leading back inside. I tried to follow, but one of the knights gently restrained me, then rushed off to join the tide of armed soldiers following Jessela back into the palace. I watched them go with a heavy heart. I might be a sneaker, but I wanted payback on these troll bastards. One of them had killed Jason, after all, and whoever was behind them—Mistress Angela, I supposed—was responsible for this whole mess.

Standing in the now-empty courtyard, I watched blood soak the grass and mingle with the water of the brook. Bodies lay all over, some mushed flat, some in pieces. It was a truly grisly scene. *I hope she doesn't intend for me to stay here.*

I could hear roars of trolls and the battle cry of Fae Knights from all quarters of the palace. *Weird that they would be attacking from so many directions,* I thought. *Almost as if...*

Suddenly, I stiffened. Cold dread filled my being.

Almost as if the trolls were trying to draw off the Fae Knights! I thought, completing the horrible notion. *Almost as if the trolls are merely a diversion to leave Queen Calista unprotected!*

CHAPTER 18

"Shit!" I said to the empty courtyard. "I have to get to the Queen!"

I had to hurry, too. Even now Mistress Angela could be stabbing her with the demon horn. Sucking up my courage, I swiveled about, orienting myself, and pictured the layout of the palace in my mind. My cat-burglar instincts served me well. It only took seconds to remember which direction the Throne Room lay.

Hopefully, the Queen would be there, directing the war effort from her seat of office. If she wasn't, I was screwed. We all were.

I shoved through a door and plunged through hallways littered with bodies and torn apart by violent magic. Blood trickled down the walls, pooling at their bases, and severed limbs lay strewn upon the floor. Nausea welled up in me. I tried not to look as I hopped over bodies and edged around pools of blood.

Noise ahead.

Going slower, I turned a curve and neared an intersection. The halls here were high and arched, admitting shafts of sunlight from windows near the curve of the ceiling. In the domed space where the halls met, Fae with winged shoes like that one Greek god made circles in the air, spinning about the head of a terrible troll.

One Fae was gripped in his right hand while the left snatched at the flying Fae. They shot at him with flaming arrows from specially wrought bows all of gold, but the arrows splintered apart in shafts of fire as they struck the troll.

I tried to think of some way to help them but came up blank. The best I could do was save their queen.

Feeling like a coward, I skirted the battle and continued through the halls, desperate to reach the Throne Room before Queen Calista could be killed. I ran past one conflict, then another.

At last I turned a final corner and came in sight of the grand doors leading into the Throne Room. There at the threshold twenty Fae Knights gave battle to three trolls. Unlike the other trolls, these were armored and armed with tall iron lances that must have weighed a ton each. They swung these and stomped at the Fae with their armored feet. The Fae slashed at their legs to no avail.

Shit shit shit. How was I going to get through? Because I could already hear sounds of conflict coming from the other side—there was battle in the Throne Room! I had to hurry.

Shaking, I approached the battle. Again I felt like I was about to throw up, but this time from simple fear. What did I think I was doing? I was a burglar, not a warrior. Not a fricking Fae Knight, for God's sakes. Sheesh! I was really turning into one big idiot. Ruby would've gotten a good laugh at this.

Ruby!

If Queen Calista was being attacked, then it was probably Mistress Angela doing the attacking. She would be leading the assault on Queen Calista, I had no doubt. I still didn't know why she wanted to harm the Queen, but it didn't matter. Angela would probably have the antler of the Golden Hind on her. And if I could get that, I could save Ruby before Skull-Face's deadline tomorrow. I'd never forgotten about that for a moment. A desperate need flamed in me, a need to save my sister.

Sucking it up, I approached the conflict at a faster clip. The Fae Knights, I saw, were so busy dealing with the armored trolls that they were letting opportunities to slip into the Throne Room pass by them. While the rest were engaged, I saw that one or two might be able to sneak by the trolls and into the big chamber.

They won't leave their mates, I realized. The knights had been trained to fight as a unit, not to abandon their comrades. At any rate, I could get by...if I was careful.

I reached the knights and shouted to the tall Fae Knight with the black hair who looked to be in charge. "Hey," I said. "You can't even penetrate their armor! Why are you fighting them?"

"We have to keep them away from the Queen," the commander said, after giving an order to a team of knights. This team raised their hands and blasted one of the trolls with a magical bolt, but as before the blast did nothing. The commander looked grim. "By any means necessary," he added.

They were willing to give up their lives to keep these trolls away from Calista. I didn't think they understood, though, that the trolls were merely to keep *them* away from her. Or if they did know there was nothing they could do about it.

"There's a poison," I said, shouting over the ring of metal and the grunts of trolls and warriors. "It can kill them! It should be coming from the Enchanters' Hall soon. Just stay alive till it gets here, then aim for these trolls' faces." The visors of the troll helms were lifted, and their huge-nosed faces with their overly big teeth and yellow gums were all too plain to see. Hair bristled out from their jaws, noses, and ears.

The commander raised his eyebrow at me, and I could see him think the question, *Who the hell is this girl?* But he didn't argue with me. He seemed to realize I knew what I was talking about. He just gave me one nod, quickly, then turned back to snap another order.

I didn't wait to find out how the rest of the battle went but edged around the side of the room, swinging wide around the three trolls and the Fae Knights that tried to bring them down. One of the trolls reeled backward as two lances drove at him, slamming against the wall near the door and nearly crushing me with its heel. I just barely dove out of the way in time, and even then its other foot came down right at me.

I rolled out of the way. *Boom!* The foot landed, and the ground shook.

Breathless, I glanced up to see the troll, enraged, knocking away the iron lances with the back of its armored arm, then stalk forward, murder in its eyes. The Fae Knights stumbled back while others fired arrows at its head—non-flaming, this time. To the same affect, though.

Hang in there, I thought at the Fae Knights. *Jessela will send the poison soon.* I had faith in her. Huh, at least there was *one* person I could depend on.

The troll was clear of me, so I scrambled to my feet and all but fled through the great door and into the Throne Room. I plunged into the little enchanted forest that grew here, and the sounds of the battle behind began to recede. The forest around me was trampled in spots.

The great mound of a troll body heaped to my left, blood trickling down it. Several knights lay strewn on the ground near it. *I'm too late.*

Sounds of combat ahead. I pumped my legs faster. Sweat stung my eyes, and my breaths came quick and fast. At last I burst from the undergrowth and beheld the magnificent crystal stairs leading up to the throne. An epic last stand was taking place there. Two armored trolls were marching up the stairs swinging metal shafts while a small handful of Fae Knights—shit, just three—mounted a rearguard action as they shepherded Queen Calista up the steps. She and the others blasted the trolls with balls of light and energy, but nothing could penetrate their shields.

Behind the trolls were Mistress Angela, Blackfeather, and several of their goons. All the goons were bare-chested and ritually painted on their arms, necks, and chests. *Damn,* I thought. It was if...

...as if they were sacrifices.

I felt a shudder. These men were prepared to be turned into trolls at a moment's notice, to give their lives if necessary in service to Angela. Or whomever she served, if there *was* someone above her.

One Fae Knight lunged forward and hacked at a troll ankle with his blazing sword, and my heart skipped a beat when I saw it was Davril. His helmet had been ripped off, and his eyes shone with fury and determination beneath sweat-soaked flaxen hair. His teeth were bared in a snarl. He was a wild thing, an animal at bay expending all his rage against an overwhelming enemy.

Grinning savagely, he evaded the thrust of an iron shaft and slashed at the ankle again. A piece of armor tore loose, and I understood. He'd been working at a weak spot, trying to find—or make—a chink in the armor. A wave of pride swept through me, and something else, too. Davril was a fighter, smart and relentless, and a total frickin' badass.

The other troll brought its staff down toward his head.

"Davril! Watch out!" I shouted.

He glanced to me, just for a fraction of a second, then looked up to where I was pointing. Instantly, he sprang aside, and the staff smashed against the stairs, raising a cloud of shattered crystal.

I rushed forward and started up the stairs.

The last of Angela's minions must have heard me coming—no one else seemed to have—and turned to face me. I kicked him in the balls, then punched him in the face when he doubled over. He listed over and toppled down the steps behind me. Another turned and I punched him in the gut. I was faster and stronger than a normal human, and I could handle myself in a fight.

The man kicked at my face. I swerved, grabbed his extended

ankle, and spun him around. He lost his balance and tumbled down the stairs.

By now, the last two goons were turning to face me. Blackfeather turned, too, but Mistress Angela spared me only a glance —fleetingly—before turning back to direct her trolls, shouting orders at them as they went, one grim foot up the stairs after another. They didn't have many left to go. Then the Queen would be cornered on her dais with nowhere to go.

"Shit," I said, my gaze going back to Angela. She carried a red dagger in her hand. A dagger that might well have been carved from a demon's horn.

I didn't have time to worry about that now, though. The last two goons were coming at me. These two, I saw with dismay, were armed with guns. .9mm pistols to be exact. I wished I still had my dragonfire. I would've shown these asshats a thing or two.

"Evicta!" I shouted, hurling a mix of sini seed dust and dryad spittle at them. It didn't turn them to ice, but it slowed their movements just enough for me to get close and kick them both in the kneecaps. Howling, they toppled down the stairs and out of the fight.

Blackfeather opened her mouth, perhaps about to voice the spell that would turn them both into trolls, but by then, I had reached her and rammed her in the solar plexus with my shoulder. I flung her up a few stairs and onto her back.

Cursing at me, she reached into the folds of her cloak and pulled out a dagger. Its blade flashed as it streaked for my throat. I jerked back, struck her outstretched arm with the flat of my hand, then punched her in the nose. Bone crunched and blood spewed.

I caught the dagger as it slipped from her hand.

"Stay down," I told her, mentally cringing at the poor girl with her nose busted and water filling her eyes. What the hell did I think I was doing? I wasn't Dirty Harry. Sure, I could get by in a scrape—I'd had to learn how the hard way—but this wasn't my scene.

Above, between the legs of the two trolls, I could see Davril bravely leading the defense of the Queen. One of the other knights was being crushed beneath the heel of a troll. Enraged, Davril jumped forward, under a flailing fist, and slashed the troll through the hole in its armor that he'd created. It screamed, but that was it.

Just wait till that poison arrives, I thought.

But I knew there wasn't time.

Edging up the stairs behind Mistress Angela, I wondered if I could make her call the trolls off. Or maybe if I just stabbed her with Blackfeather's blade, they would stop. I could feel power pulsing from the dagger and knew it was magical. Hopefully it could slice through any of the protections Angela had gathered about herself. It was my only hope. Maybe Davril and Calista's only hope.

Heart beating so wildly I thought it would punch through my chest, I advanced up the stairs toward Angela. I moved lightly so I wouldn't make too much noise. Above the roars of trolls and the ring of metal on metal, I doubt I could be overheard, but I suspected Angela had enhanced her senses with magic, so it paid to be cautious.

Beyond her, Davril was leaping over the sweeping hand of a troll, then lunging forward again to stab it near the ankle. Blood spurted, high and strong…and kept spurting. Mentally, I cheered. Had Davril hit an artery? Clever knight!

Almost to Angela…

My eyes widened. *At Angela's hip hung the golden antler.* The antler of the Golden Hind! Once I killed her, I could take the antler and Ruby would be that much closer to being saved. *Thank God,* I thought. There was hope for Ruby yet.

I raised the dagger, feeling its balance. One thrust, I told myself. Right between Angela's shoulder blades. Yeah, yeah, I knew stabbing someone in the back was uncool, but with this bitch I'd make an exception.

This is for you, Jason, I thought as I coiled my arm to strike.

Just before I could stab her, Angela spun. Her face had gone rigid and dangerous-looking. Such was the wrath on her face that I paused. I had to fight myself not to recoil.

Behind me, I could hear Blackfeather say, "Kill her!" Of course, with her busted nose, it came out sounding more like *gil er.*

Mistress Angela thrust out a hand, palm vertical and aimed at my face. I could feel a terrible energy gather there. It was about to explode outward, right at my head. I was about to die. I tried to renew my own attack, but she'd somehow paralyzed my muscles. I couldn't move that dagger any closer toward her than I already had. It was as if it were stuck in the air. My arms trembled as they tried to shove it forward, but it was like moving it through petrified molasses.

The energy on her palm built, turning into a purple flame. The flame grew brighter, brighter…it was about to shoot off her palm and engulf my head…

Suddenly, Angela wobbled. She tried to catch her balance but slipped, stumbling on the stairs. The energy on her palm dissipated, as did the feeling of molasses. I could hear Blackfeather huffing to her feet behind me.

What the hell had happened? Then I realized it and almost laughed. The troll Davril had stabbed was bleeding profusely, the wound—it really must have been an artery—jetting a crimson river down the glinting crystal stairs. The thick red flood had washed Angela's feet right out from under her.

I danced aside, not wanting to get mired in the stuff myself.

The troll bellowed, then began to fall over backward. It seemed to move in slow motion, huge and heavy, but I knew in reality it was moving all too fast. Blackfeather cursed as she scrambled out of the way.

I threw myself aside as it slammed down, shaking the crystal beneath my feet. I picked myself up onto my hands and knees to see Angela doing the same thing, spitting out blood from where she'd bitten her tongue. Craning my head, I could see Blackfeather rushing up toward us, her face red.

Above, Davril was jumping back, avoiding a swipe from the final troll. He was the Queen's last defender, and I didn't see how he could defeat this troll. I doubted the same trick would work twice. Calista continued trying to blast the creature magically, but she was looking weary and even she had to know the attacks were pointless. Angela had planned all this out too well.

But she hadn't planned on me.

Still on my hands and knees, I coiled my arm to hurl the dagger right at her black heart. Vaguely I could see Blackfeather laboriously climbing over the side of the troll to my right. Its body had separated us.

"Don't you hurt—" she started.

I threw the blade. It spun end over end.

"—my mother!" she finished even as she leapt through the air. She jumped right between Angela and me. Right in the path of the dagger. The blade pierced her heart, not Angela's.

Blackfeather gasped, blood on her lips, then fell heavily to the stairs.

I stared at the body, horrified. I'd never killed anyone before, at least not a human. Shame welled inside me. Feeling my eyes prickle, I lifted my gaze from Blackfeather's body to Angela. *My mother.*

Stark, living rage filled Angela's eyes.

"You killed my daughter!"

Enraged, she threw back her head and screamed, a wordless cry of anguish and misery. The sound tore at me, and I felt tears roll down my cheeks. I'd just killed a daughter simply trying to save her mother.

Screw that, I told myself. *I was trying to kill the evil bitch who got Jason killed, and a whole bunch of others.*

Wiping the tears away, I stalked forward. I'd rip the dagger free and use it on Angela, too. The same blade could kill both mother and daughter.

Above, at the top of the stairs, I could see Davril placing two of his fingers in his mouth and whistling. With the other hand, he swatted at the troll, but really, I thought he was just trying to keep it busy. What the hell did he think he was doing by whistling?

"GURUM VITAI!" Angela shouted.

Immediately, I heard a strange scream, then a weird grinding, rushing noise behind me. Turning my head, I saw the four goons I'd taken out moments ago suddenly blooming into hugeness. One moment, they were normal, if stupider-than-average, humans. The next, they'd transformed into giant, hairy trolls. Still walking gingerly where I'd hit their knees or balls, the trolls picked themselves up and started up the stairs.

"Damn," I said.

Angela laughed.

I quit worrying about her and turned to face the four trolls. How the hell was I going to get out of this?

Grinning nastily, the huge brutes reached the foot of the stairs, then started climbing up them toward me. Only two could move abreast of each other, they were so big. Great. One minute I'd been about to win; the next, I was about to be a troll snack. And that was if they didn't simply flatten me.

I stepped backward, nearly slipped in troll blood, then moved around it, still going backward. Up toward the crystal dais.

Craning my head periodically, I could see that Angela was moving around the bulk of the troll up there. It had rotated, putting itself between Davril and Calista, keeping him away from her, while Angela approached the Queen. The witch held the red dagger in her hand, the weapon I was sure had been carved from Lord Mortock's horn.

Calista tried to blast her, but Angela simply waved her hand and the magical blast veered to the side, exploding against a wall.

I turned back to the front.

The four trolls were almost to me.

There was nothing I could do to fight them. But maybe there was something I could do for Calista. Swallowing down my fear, I spun about and fled up the stairs, nimbly leaping over the body of Blackfeather.

Panting for breath, I reached the dais. In one corner, Davril was trying to go around the troll's legs, but it was kicking and grasping relentlessly, determined to keep him pinned down long enough for Angela to kill Calista.

Calista blasted Angela again, or tried to. Angela knocked this beam of energy aside, too. She'd backed Calista up against her own crystal throne. The Queen couldn't go anywhere.

"Now comes the rule of Prince Jereth," Angela said. She coiled her arm to stab the Queen with the demon horn—

"Fuck off," I said, and jumped on her back.

Her demon horn rocketed forward, scraping along Calista's side. Blood leaked out. The blade had been aimed right at her heart, but because of my meddling it had only scraped her ribs.

Furious, Calista balled her fist and socked Angela right in the jaw, while I pulled the evil woman's hair.

Angela screamed and thrashed, throwing me to the ground. As I went, I grabbed at the golden antler dangling from her waist and ripped it off. Now *I* had the antler! Blinking sweat out of my eyes, I rose to my feet and stood side by side with Queen Calista. We would face Angela together. Calista nodded to me in appreciation. I nodded back.

Angela smiled, cruelly and triumphantly. "You think you've beaten me?" she said. "I've only just begun." She raised her blade. Blood dripped off it. "The venom of that horn will kill anything—even you, Calista. Not that I'll give you that long."

She advanced a step, meaning to skewer us both, I have no doubt. Behind her, the four new trolls were just reaching the dais.

"It's been nice knowing you," I told the Queen.

She was gracious, even in defeat. "You as well."

Just then, the glass dome above us shattered, at least in one part, and Davril's flying car Lady Kay flew down through the hole right toward us. *That* was why Davril had been whistling—he'd been calling for his car! Davril, having managed to get away from the troll he'd been fighting, jumped into the driver's seat, then shouted at us, "Well, what are you waiting for? Get in!"

CHAPTER 19

Queen Calista and I looked at each other again, then dove into the car. The top had come down, revealing to my surprise that Lady Kay was a convertible. I loved magic. Calista jumped into the back while I took the front, right beside Davril.

"Ra!" Davril said, goosing the pedals, and Lady Kay shot up and away from the dais.

Mistress Angela screamed in rage behind us, and the trolls echoed her cry, lifting their heads and bellowing their fury at the dome. Their volume was so great that several panes of glass cracked and broke off.

Lady Kay blasted right through the hole it had made earlier and rose into the night sky. Wind whipped around me, and I turned to Davril to see his eyes shining and his jaw firmly set. He turned once, to me, and I could see reluctant respect in his eyes. He may not be able to trust me, but I *had* saved his queen.

I glanced back to her, and some of my enthusiasm evaporated. She was holding her side, and blood trickled through her fingers, soaking into the seat.

"Did she get you bad?" I asked.

Calista shook her head tightly. Her color had changed, from flesh tones to a sort of yellow color.

"She said—poison," Calista breathed, and I could tell it took an effort for her to talk. "The red blade—poison."

I nodded. "Mortock's horn, it's deadly, and it can cut through many magical shields. It's why Angela wanted it."

"What's this?" Davril said as he drove.

"Never mind," I said. "Just take us to your castle. To the Order of Elshe. They'll know how to heal the Queen."

I stared at the golden antler. I still had it gripped tightly in my fist.

"Did you get that from Angela?" Davril asked me, and I nodded. Suspicion entered his face once more, and my heart sank. "Is *that* why you helped us?"

"Is—is—?" Anger washed through me, and I had half a mind to sock him in the jaw just like Queen Calista had done Angela. "Did you just say what I think you did, you self-righteous asshole? Do you know what I just *went* through to help you?"

"We all went through a lot, Jade."

I ground my teeth. "I just *killed* someone to help your queen! I've *never* killed anyone before." I turned my face away from him, feeling shame well up in me again. Wind tore at my hair, whipping it away from my face and making my eyes mist.

A long moment of silence passed. At lastI heard Davril sigh.

"Very well," he said, and I could sense a certain guardedness in his tone. "Then I thank you."

"Me as well," said Calista behind us.

Her voice came out trembly. Looking back at her, I could see that she looked even more ill than just a few moments ago. That poison was working fast. In that moment, fear for her drove out all my other thoughts and feelings, even my shame at having killed Blackfeather and my anger at Davril for questioning me.

"Are we being followed?" Davril asked.

I scanned the horizon behind us. Nothing.

"No," I said, "but I see smoke rising from the palace."

Dark trails twisted above the white spires. The sun had set, but its light could still be seen, just faintly, over the horizon, and it painted the city in tones of blood. The palace looked bloody and smoking. I thought of the horror that had taken place inside it—was still taking place inside it—and shuddered. But it wouldn't take long. Even now, Jessela would be distributing the poison from the Hall of Enchantment. The Fae Knights would have the trolls dispatched in no time, I thought. If all went well.

Until then, though, the Queen was our responsibility.

I glanced to Davril and saw him turn to me, then give me a nod, not of trust or respect, but indicating that he felt it, too. That this was all on us. A sacred pact between us to save the Queen.

"Do you think...?" I said, keeping my voice quiet. It came out nearly as trembly as Calista's.

"Yes?" Davril's voice too was low.

I swallowed. "Do you think that was Angela's plan all along—to kill Queen Calista?"

"I..." His jaw bulged as he ground his teeth. His eyes glared straight ahead, and the buildings whipped by to either side. "It makes sense," he said at last. "Angela had her contact at the palace—"

"It was Lord Seafoam."

"Are you sure?"

"Very sure. He tried to kill me in the cell."

Davril stiffened. "He...what?"

I told him what had happened, ending by explaining how Jessela had saved me. "If not for her, I'd be dead," I added when I was done.

He didn't look at me, but I could feel emotion boiling off him like heat off a tarmac. His eyes glared hateful daggers at the world ahead, and he gripped the steering wheel so tight I was surprised Lady Kay didn't complain. I realized what it was, or thought I did.

Davril was mad at himself. He would never say it, but he was furious with himself for endangering me.

My cheeks tingled, and I looked away. Could it be? Could I really be right about that? If so, it meant…

Don't think about that now, Jade. Focus.

I scowled and struggled to get myself under control. "Anyway, so Seafoam tried to kill me," I said. "He must have been Angela's mole on the inside. Or at least one of them. I bet he's the one who has been letting her goons in—the ones who turn into trolls."

"He must have been the one to tell her about the antler of the Golden Hind," Davril said. "And she used *that* to get a horn she knew could be turned into a weapon against Queen Calista."

"That must be it," I said. "Or maybe Seafoam was the one who found out about the horn, too. Maybe *he's* the one who hired *Angela*."

"If he likes to hire people to do his dirty work, then why did he try to kill you himself?"

That was a good question. "So he's not the boss? Does that mean Angela is, or is she taking orders from someone else?"

"I…" Davril held back a swear, I could see it. "I don't know."

"She…mentioned Jereth," Queen Calista said, sounding very weak.

"Are you sure?" Davril said, looking surprised.

"Yes. I heard her. When…she was attacking me…she said, 'Now comes the rule of…Prince Jereth.' That was right before she…stabbed me."

"Who's Jereth?" I asked.

There was steel in Calista's voice. "My son."

"Damn," I said. "I'm so sorry."

She fell silent, and I didn't press her. She obviously needed to conserve her strength. Around us, New York whizzed past. The breeze whipped my hair even more strongly as Davril ground the gas pedal, shooting us faster into space. For one moment, I allowed myself to relish it. My blood sang and the world was laid out before me like a glittering dream, and beside me was a badass Fae Knight. Then the good feeling drained away, replaced by concern for Calista, and I scrambled onto my hands and knees, then slid over the seat into the back.

"What are you doing?" Davril said.

I didn't answer but simply dropped beside the Queen. Reaching out, I grabbed her hand and gave it a gentle squeeze, then continued holding it. She had leaned her head against the headrest, too weak even to prop it up, but she turned and offered me a grateful smile.

I smiled back, but I had to force myself to do it. I choked down sobs and squeezed her hand even tighter.

"Hang in there, Your Majesty," I said. "We'll save you."

I caught Davril's eyes in the rearview mirror. He held my gaze for a moment, then ripped his eyes away. We swung wide around a building and came in sight of his castle ahead. I had never been so relieved to see a building as I was when those pocked gray walls, scarred by war and betrayal, came into view.

"We made it," I told Queen Calista.

She issued a ragged breath. I studied her. She was pale white and so weak her eyes had lost focus and her body all strength.

Davril must have sensed it, too, because I could see him grind his jaw even more.

The knights on watch saw us coming. The castle gates swung open, and Davril flew us right into the courtyard. They closed with a bang behind us as he set the car down on the stone floor. Knights and Sisters of the Order of Elshe gathered to us just like last time. Had Lady Kay sent out a message of distress? Just how did that work, anyway?

There was no time to worry about it now. Knights yanked open the doors, and Davril snapped orders. In moments, the Sisters were bearing Queen Calista to their tower on a stretcher, and Davril and I jogged at their side. We came with them as they entered the tower and took her to what passed for a hospital here.

It was unlike any hospital I'd ever seen. Magical creatures flew through the air or stomped along the floor, some shimmering with bright and exotic colors. I saw what looked like a horse with a mane of flame, a thing like an otter with a zebra-striped coat and that walked upright wearing a pair of spectacles. Many Fae women buzzed about, performing ritual magic, mixing potions and enchanting objects presumably used in healing. They laid Queen Calista out on a bed in a medium-sized room, then ushered Davril and me into a waiting area.

"Stay here until we come for you," said Liara, the white-haired Fae, and left us.

Davril avoided my gaze and stalked to a window, where he stared out over the city. I moved to my own window. Night deepened. Idly my eyes touched upon the golden antler, and I held it up to the light. It shone like fire.

"Is that why you helped?"

Davril's voice snapped like a whip, and I looked up at him, startled. Hastily, I dropped the antler to my side.

"No," I said. *You have until tomorrow,* Skull-Face had told me. *Shit, what am I going to do?*

Davril watched me close, and I knew he didn't trust me. The worst part of it was that he was right. I had betrayed him and the Queen, and I couldn't say I wouldn't do it again. *I'm coming for you, Ruby*. I had what I needed. Now I had to leave this place and see to my sister.

I'd leave when I knew the Queen was well.

I wondered how much Davril saw of this on my face. He said nothing, just turned back to the window. I suppressed a sigh. I hated to deceive him, I really did, hated that I'd caused him pain. But surely he understood on some level, right? I wasn't sure. His own brother had betrayed him, after all. Hell, no wonder he was so sensitive to betrayal. I would be, too. But another side effect of it was that he might not understand the need to help a sibling in trouble. He probably didn't have such lovey-dovey feelings toward Nevos.

We waited for hours, pacing and brooding, while the sounds of the strange animals drifted in from next door. Davril lit a fire in the hearth, and we sat across from each other on fine, old-fashioned couches. Still, we said practically nothing. It got so awkward that I was almost tempted to go into another room. Man, I really missed cigarettes.

I jumped to my feet as Liara entered. Davril stood, too, his face solemn. Liara's face was tight and drawn, her eyes very still. My heart dropped into my stomach. *Please no,* I thought. *Please don't let Calista be dead.* It surprised me how much I cared. I'd been a lone wolf for too long.

Liara approached us and stopped. We waited. I was sure Davril was even more anxious than I was, although I couldn't see it on his face.

"Well?" he said, and his voice was like lead.

Liara blinked, seemed to gather her strength, and said, "Queen Calista is still alive…for now. I…I don't know how long she has."

"But you *have* to save her," I said. "I mean, you have all these charms and animals and…and you have to!"

Liara lowered her eyes. "The demon horn rendered all Fae spells defunct. No Fae magic can cure the Queen, and no human medicine can do it, either."

I staggered back, suddenly feeling weak, and collapsed onto the couch. Davril wore a stricken look. He stared far away and said nothing.

"I'm most sorry," Liara said.

"There…has to be a way," Davril said at last.

Liara wrung her hands. "Well…"

I sat up. "Yes?"

She grimaced. "There is a possibility that some *earthly* magic could cure her. Some magic from *this* world. *Non*-Fae magic."

"Well, can't you just use some?"

"We do not know how. We...we've never needed to learn."

My eyes fell on the antler of the Golden Hind. I spun to Davril and lifted it high so that it shone by firelight. "There's only one thing left to do," I said.

His attention fixed on the antler. "Yes?"

Though I could hear the distrust in his voice, I plowed on. "We have to get Ruby back."

"Excuse me?"

"She's a powerful witch, especially good at healing spells. Remember, I told you?"

"Yes..." After a moment, the doubt in his face began to retreat, at least a little bit. "Go on," he said.

I almost grinned. "We use the antler to free her. She can heal Queen Calista." To Liara, I asked, "How long do we have?"

"As I said, I don't know. However..."

"Yes?"

She seemed to think about it. "I would say by dawn."

My grin faded, and once more I felt weak. Forcing myself, I said to Davril, "Then I'd guess we better work fast." I paused, then mustered my courage. "What do you say?"

Firelight glittered on his eyes. "What are we waiting for?"

CHAPTER 20

My blood hummed as we buzzed back through the streets of Manhattan in Lady Kay. The towers of the city scrolled by to either side, their lit windows leaving tracers as they flashed by. Davril drove so fast I thought the car would come apart or at least elicit a groan of protest, but Lady Kay seemed just as anxious to save the Queen as we were.

Hang in there, I thought, not just to the Queen but to Ruby. *Ruby, I'll finally get to see you again. For* a moment, I was overcome by how much I missed her, and grief and terror welled up and nearly took me over. At the last instant, I wrenched myself out of the gulf of despair. Any longer and it would have consumed me, rendering me incapable of action.

Get it together, Jade, I thought. This was for all the marbles.

We swiftly navigated toward Hartson Tower, the name of the building Skull-Face had told me to meet him at. I told myself I wasn't just doing this for Ruby, but for Queen Calista, too. And it *was* the best thing for her; I wasn't just saying that. Right? *That* was the hard part. I was pretty sure that the answer was yes, but there was still that little tugging doubt that gnawed at me, telling me I was just using Davril and that this wouldn't save the Queen at all.

Can it, I thought at that negative voice. *This IS going to save the Queen.*

"I still don't understand any of this," I said. "Queen Calista mentioned something about Prince Jereth being her son when we were taking her to your place. Why would Angela be serving *him?*"

"I don't think she is."

"But she wants him to rule! She said as much."

"There's…some bitter history there."

"Well? Tell it."

"It's simple. When we came over to your world, we had to leave many people of the Nine Thrones behind us. Jereth raged that they were still in the Shadow's power and would suffer terrible fates because of our cowardice. He said we needed to open the portals once more and return to the Fae Lands to save our people."

"Sounds noble."

"It is," Davril said. "Or it sounds that way, anyway. In reality, if we opened the portals, the Shadow would simply cross over into your world…our world now, too. Vorkoth would bend it to his will just as surely as he's done to the Fae Lands. What Prince Jereth wants sounds righteous, but it would doom us all."

"I…damn. That sucks. So what happened?"

"Prince Jereth tried to convince his mother to reopen the portals. When she refused, he tried to lead an uprising against her."

"Say what?"

"Yes, he was really committed. He felt like we had betrayed our own people. He wasn't willing to face the fact that sometimes we have to make hard choices for the greater good. At any rate, I and the other true knights stood against him. There were more of us, and we drove him and his faction off. Prince Jereth and his followers live in exile now, somewhere…out there." Davril gestured to the skyline, but I could sense he didn't mean New York exactly, but the world.

"Do you have any idea where he is?" I said.

"No, but there are some in the Palace who do."

"Why?"

"He *is* the Heir."

I put a hand over my mouth. "Shit! So if Queen Calista dies..."

"That's right. He would return, install himself on the throne, and open the portals in an attempt to liberate our people still trapped in the Fae Lands."

"And the Shadow would pour through instead."

"Exactly."

"So *that's* what Angela wants!"

"Yes. It would seem like it. She truly is in service to Lord Vorkoth, and if Queen Calista dies, Angela will bring her master a great victory."

Hartson Tower approached, a darkly gleaming skyscraper of black glass thrust up along the coast. It stood like a shadowy thorn in the night. We drew toward the upper reaches, and I nearly whistled at the beautiful penthouse that perched on top—this was one of the few skyscrapers left without a castle on it. Most penthouse owners in New York nowadays had to live with not being the top resident of their particular tower. Instead of going down in value, though, penthouse prices had soared. People *longed* to be close to the Fae Lords, for all sorts of reasons.

But not Skull-Face. Skull-Face operated out of a penthouse that was the uppermost portion of its spire, just like with Hawthorne. I wondered if that meant something.

"This can't be Skull-Face's real address," I said.

"No?"

"He wouldn't give us his real address unless he intended to murder us, anyway. He wouldn't want us to live to spread the word. He'd expect us—or you, or the police—to come after him. He's a kidnapper in league with murderous vampires."

Davril patted the spot where I knew his invisible sword to be. "He won't catch us by surprise, and we're not defenseless."

I had to admire his bravery. He looked so determined hurling us through the air, the lights of the dashboard making his high cheekbones gleam and his eyes spark.

"I guess," I said, but I still had my doubts. "But anyway, I bet he's renting this place. Maybe there will be a paper trail for us to follow afterward."

"Maybe." Now it was Davril who sounded skeptical.

After a moment, I had to agree. "He wouldn't be using his real name, would he? Still, there might be *something*."

"Perhaps."

"I don't want to let him just *get away* with this."

"Neither do I. We need the horn."

We flew up to one of the large jutting balconies of the penthouse and coasted to a stop. Gorgeous plants in huge ornate holders stood all over the balcony, and vines crept up from them and curled along the balustrades. I could see all this from the lights shining from equally ornate fixtures along the exterior wall.

Davril tied Lady Kay to the railing just like hitching a horse, or maybe a boat to a dock, then jumped out. After making sure the place was safe—for the moment—he turned to me and offered his hand. I hesitated, studying his face. Was this a sign of forgiveness? It was dark with him facing away from the lights, and I couldn't tell.

I gave him my hand, and he helped me out of the car. Seemingly unconsciously, his gaze flicked down the length of my body as I settled, then—as he caught himself—hastily jerked up to my face. I stared. His cheeks reddened, which I could see very well as he turned his face to the side in full glare of the lights.

I continued to stare at him, then felt my own cheeks grow warm. *What the hell, Jade? Concentrate.*

I began moving toward the door, but it opened and a man

stepped out. Dressed in fine clothes, he wore a beautiful wool scarf around his neck.

"Won't you come in?" he said.

I reached for the knife at my waist—Davril had given it to me before we left his castle. At least he trusted me with a weapon now. What was more, he knew I could use it, too. Shame at killing Blackfeather rose in me again, and I had to shove it down.

Was this guy Skull-Face?

"Are you the asshat who abducted my sister?" I demanded.

Davril stiffened at my side, one hand going to his hip like an Old West gunfighter.

"His Lordship requests your presence indoors," said the man with the scarf.

"Fuck that," I said. "I'm not going in there. Tell His Lordship—" What the hell was up with that name? "—to get the fuck out here. Right now."

The man blinked at my tone. "I apologize, ma'am, but he is insistent."

I paused, then said to Davril, "I don't want to go in there. It could be a trap like we talked about."

"I'm confident of our ability to spring any trap and come out the victor," he said.

"Jesus, you're a robot. Or a fucking Vulcan. My God, you're a Vulcan!"

"Decide," said the man with the scarf. "Come inside and save your sister. Or stay out here and watch her die."

I glared at the man, feeling heat course through me—sheer, devouring anger. The bastard was lucky I didn't hit him in the belly right there.

"Fine," I said. "Then let's get this stupid thing over with."

The man turned and led the way inside, leaving the door open for us. I stared at the gaping rectangle of darkness, hesitating. Surprisingly, Davril lowered his voice and said gently, "It will be all right."

I swallowed, feeling my eyes sting. Davril looked tense but strangely confident, and I thought I saw something in his face... something warm. Maybe he *wasn't* a Vulcan.

Maybe.

"You think so?" I said.

He nodded, once. "Yes."

Slowly, he reached up and squeezed my shoulder. I leaned into the contact, relishing it. Then together we turned toward the door. Davril went first, and I let him take the lead. He was the knight, after all. I went immediately after, though, one hand on my knife. I was just seconds away, I thought. *Ruby, I'm coming.*

Darkness enclosed us as we entered, but thanks to my shifter senses I could see very well.

"Why'd you turn out the lights?" I asked suspiciously, coiling myself for a fight. I could feel Davril tensing, too.

"My friends don't like a lot of light," our host said. "Now come. This way."

He moved forward down a hallway. Davril and I glanced around, then reluctantly followed. Hairs stood up on the nape of my neck. My legs wanted to run. At the moment, I wished to be anywhere other than there. And yet that was *just* where I had to be.

We passed large open areas and private rooms, and I saw a few people who must live here to judge by their fancy appearances, then some people who had to be servants or staff. All wore scarves.

"I have a bad feeling about this," I said.

Davril said nothing.

Then we began noticing a different group of people, a third group. They stood in the corners dressed in black, their faces pale. They stared at us with hideous dead eyes. One had a trickle of blood leaking down from its lips. He grinned at me with an awful smile, and I shuddered.

"Stay close," Davril said.

I obeyed, almost pressing myself against him.

We continued following the first man with the scarf down the hall. I knew now why he and the other people here wore scarves. Under that swatch of fabric would be puncture wounds. Twin wounds, like the kind fangs would make. Maybe many such wounds.

"The vamps must have put them into some sort of trance," I whispered to Davril. I spoke in such a low voice that I didn't even think the vampires with their preternatural hearing could detect my words. I depended on Davril with his keen hearing to pick them up.

"The vampires' thrall," Davril agreed, pitching his voice at the same volume. "A terrible power to have over anyone."

The man with the scarf showed us into a large study, guarded by two bloodsuckers in black. Their eyes were impossible to see behind their sunglasses. At night. Indoors. With the lights off. *Sheesh,* I thought. *Trying much?* But they were creepy as hell.

Davril and I passed through them and into the study. No fire lit the fireplace, and the furniture had been pushed back along the walls, all except for an expensive armchair facing us. In it sat a figure, a man dressed elegantly and wearing the head of an impala, one of those African deer with the weird horns. An actual fur-covered, horned head. The effect was even creepier than the vamps outside. This must be Skull-Face, I thought, not even willing to show his face to us now. *He wants to remain anonymous.*

That was a good thing. That meant he intended for us to survive.

If all went well. If it didn't, well, he had a lot of vampires to serve him. Did that mean he was a vamp, too? I didn't think so. His skin was too healthy looking, and I thought I heard a pulse.

"Welcome to my home for the moment," he said through the lips of the animal.

"You must release these people," Davril demanded. "You can hold them hostage and feed from them no longer."

"Oh?" Skull-Face's voice sounded amused. I still thought of him as Skull-Face, even though he had an animal head on now. Impala Head just didn't have the same ring.

"Yes," Davril said, and there was iron in his voice. "I won't allow it."

His hand went back to his hip.

I cleared my throat. "Before you two start fighting, I want my sister back." I patted *my* hip, drawing Skull-Face's attention to the golden antler. "I think you want this, right?"

Skull-Face regarded me. "You look…familiar."

"I don't think so, pal. Where's Ruby?"

He paused, and I could sense him thinking, staring at me. I could see his eyes, his real eyes, watching me through the eye holes in his creepy mask. At last he seemed to sigh. He snapped his fingers. A door opened, and two vampires hauled Ruby in. She was wobbly on her feet and seemed drugged, but she looked clean, healthy and not mistreated. Thank God. A huge weight lifted off my shoulders.

I started to take a step toward her.

"Not yet," said Skull-Face. He extended his hand. "A deal's a deal."

I glared at him, then turned to Ruby. She was blinking her eyes and shaking her head, red hair dark by the scant light, and I wasn't sure if she'd seen me yet or was aware enough to know what was going on. She seemed pretty dopey.

"Whatever," I snarled and held up the antler.

"Be careful," Davril told me, and his hand flexed at his hip, as if itching to have at his sword.

"I will," I told him.

I sucked up my courage and started toward the man in the chair. Ruby murmured something and struggled weakly against her guards, but not, I thought, in an effort to get away, but more like someone trying to climb out of a nightmare. My heart wrenched for her.

"I'm right here, sis," I told her, passing very close to her.

She glanced around. Blearily, she said, "...Jade?"

Joy flushed through me. "Yes! It's me!"

Once more, I started to go toward her, but Skull-Face cleared his throat pointedly and, with a sigh, I turned back toward him. Up this close, his impala head was even more eerie and sinister, especially with his real human eyes looking out from it.

I took a step toward him, starting to lift the antler toward him...

He lifted his hand to accept it...

And that's where everything went wrong. Because, as his hand came up, the ring on his middle finger caught the faint light, its black jewel gleaming like obsidian. A chill ran through me, and my body went stiff.

I would know that ring anywhere. It was the ring that had stolen my fire.

My gaze jerked up to Skull-Face. But to me, it was no longer Skull-Face. Seething in rage, I lowered the golden antler and yanked out the knife instead.

"Walsh!" I screamed at Davril. "This is Vincent Walsh!"

CHAPTER 21

I heard Davril give a startled oath behind me, while Ruby stirred in agitation at my side. Before me Skull-Face—now Walsh—was rising to his feet. As he unfolded, I realized just how tall he was. He loomed over me, the horns of his mask arcing up like alien antennae.

With one hand, he ripped his mask away, revealing the handsome but cold features of Vincent Walsh, with his swept-back black hair, straight long nose, and severe jaw. His lips were pouty and cruel. He looked relatively young, but I knew he was ancient. His eyes were as frosty as the Arctic.

"You," he said, and his brows lowered. "I knew I recognized you." He lifted his ring and gave it a quick look, then returned his attention to me. "I think I have something of yours. Well, two things, actually."

I heard Davril unsheathe his sword. Jumping to my side, he said, "This is the mage who stole your fire?"

"Yeah," I said, and it took everything in my power not to leap at Walsh and start hacking. I wasn't sure how many slices I could get before his vamps descended on me, and I strongly suspected he was protected by wards, but I was willing to give it a shot. "He also killed my father and grandmother."

"They were…impertinent," Walsh said.

I wanted to smash something across his pretty face. "I'm going to kill you," I said.

He stared at me. "You know," he said, and I could see him reach a conclusion as he spoke, "I think you're right."

Suddenly, I felt cold. "W-what?"

Walsh looked pitying. "I think you *will* be a problem, and I don't require you to be alive." Raising his voice just slightly, he said, "Kill them!"

The doors burst open and the vampires poured in.

"*AWAY!*" roared Davril and waved his free hand.

A huge wind tore through the room, flipping my hair and ripping at my clothes. The howling wind smashed the wave of vampires back.

"Wow," I said. I hadn't known he could do that.

"Don't thank me yet," he said.

Indeed, it would only hold the vamps at bay for a moment. Worse, I could see that using his magic had tired Davril out, if only a little. He was extremely powerful, but even he had his limits.

Before the vamps could pick themselves up, Walsh, who had not been affected by the sudden windstorm, raised his hand toward me and said, "I think I'll take that, thank you." The golden antler tugged out of my hand, drawing blood, and flew into his palm. His fingers closed around its shaft, and his pouty lips twisted in an icy sort of satisfaction. "Thank you and farewell," he said.

With that, he ducked out through a rear door.

The two vampires holding Ruby had propped themselves up and were still on their feet; maybe by being close to us they'd been in the eye of the storm, so to speak. They each grinned wide, their fangs elongating, and bent toward Ruby's neck. She was so out of it she couldn't even offer up a token resistance.

"Fuck off," I said, and tackled the nearest one to the floor. As I moved, I said a spell under my breath, turning the blade of my knife to wood. The spell would only last for a few minutes.

I'd be lucky if *I* lasted that long.

I stabbed the undead son of a bitch through the heart, then leapt up as he exploded into fiery ash. Sparks whizzed around me. Other vampires had reached us by this point. Davril leapt and slashed with his sword. His enchanted blade apparently worked just as well as wooden stakes, and as he hewed through ribcages and necks the vampires burst into fire, then dissipated in clouds of ash.

Ruby, no longer supported by the vampires, collapsed to the floor. The other vampire that had been holding her flew at me, rage on his face. I must have just killed a buddy of his. Well, too bad.

"You want some, too?" I asked.

I dodged his first pass, then spun to catch him wheeling about for another. Snarling, he hurled himself at me. I ducked under his talons and stabbed him in the heart with my wooden blade. He screamed and burst into flames.

A wave of vampires descended on me, and I hacked and thrust, kicked and punched. At last, I made enough room to bend down and sling Ruby over my shoulder, then stand up again. She wasn't as light as she liked to pretend, or maybe I was just exhausted. I was stronger than a full-blood human but I was no Fae, that was for sure.

"Let's get out of here," I said.

Davril sliced a vampire down the middle of its head, then turned to see me carrying Ruby over my shoulder while fending off a horde of vampires. It wasn't easy. Sweat beaded his face, and his eyes were hard.

"This way," he said and started for the door. He sliced his

sword with every foot, and I hacked and stabbed at his side. I was tempted to ask him to carry Ruby, but we needed him free to move. He must have known that, too, or else he would've volunteered for the task. He was an asshole, but he was a *righteous* asshole.

I kicked a vamp in the balls, then drove my blade through another's skull as we reached the doorway. Davril slammed it behind us and locked it, but it instantly bulged inward. Any second, and it would break.

"Allow me," I said.

Concentrating hard, I laid my fingers against the wood, feeling its grain, and said, "*Havra kuum!*"

I pulled my hand back and the door hardened, became denser, thicker. One moment, it was light and thin as plywood; the next, it was like a sturdy oak. Roots erupted from its sides, digging into the door frame and holding it fast.

Panting, I turned to Davril. "They'll have to go around now."

The look he gave me was downright admiring, and I felt a flush of pride flow through me.

"This way," he said.

He charged through the halls back toward the terrace where Lady Kay waited, and I ran at his side. Vamps, having heard their master's summons, poured out of the rooms. I kicked one back into its room, then stabbed another in the chest. Davril severed one's arm, then sledgehammered another in the jaw with his fist. At last we burst out onto the balcony and ran toward Lady Kay.

I lowered Ruby into the backseat, then scrambled into the passenger seat. Davril jumped behind the wheel and started the engine.

The vampires, the whole damned horde of them, smashed out through not just the door but the walls of the penthouse, too, and streaked at us across the terrace.

"Go go go!" I said.

Davril floored the gas pedal and twisted the wheel. Lady Kay shot up and away from the terrace just as the vampires reached the spot where we'd just been. Raving, they gnashed their fangs and clutched at the air with their talons.

Breathless, I turned to Davril. His face was exultant.

"Good job," I said. "You saved our asses."

"*We* saved...our asses."

I grinned, then turned back to Ruby. She was gasping, too, and blinking her eyes more rapidly.

"Are you starting to come around?" I said.

She blinked a few more times, focused on me, then nodded. "Jade," she breathed, and her eyes filled with tears.

I felt it, too. Strong emotion came over me, and I jumped over the seat top and dropped down beside her. As Davril flew us away from that place of horrors, Ruby and I held each other and cried, in both relief and fear of what might have been. We cried and cried, and at last, I realized I was smiling, too, and laughing. Ruby was, too. In the front seat, Davril said nothing, letting us have our moment.

I pulled back, wiping at my eyes. "I thought I was going to lose you."

Ruby swallowed. "Me, too." A weird look crossed her face. "Jade, it was Walsh! It was Walsh that took me!"

"I know." She must have been so out of it she hadn't even noticed what had transpired back in Walsh's study. Well, his stolen study. I knew it wasn't really his. "I can't believe we ran into him after all this time."

"I hope you didn't give him what he wanted."

I grimaced. "Shit, I think I did. Well, he took it, I didn't exactly hand it over. What does he want with the antler? Do you know?"

She shook her head, red hair flying in the wind. "No, but it can't be good, whatever it is. If a man like Walsh wants it that much, it can only mean dire things for the rest of us, I can tell you that."

I sighed. "We'll have to deal with that another time. For the moment, how do you feel?"

"Crappy. I need a beer or three."

"I'll pretend I didn't hear that...until next month."

"And food. Lots and lots of food." She rubbed her belly, and I could hear it growl. "They didn't feed me at all."

"We'll get you squared away, don't worry." I paused. Now we'd come to the big question. I hated to bring it up because I didn't want Ruby to think we'd rescued her just so we could use her skills, but I didn't see much choice. "Are you up for some healing magic?" I asked lamely.

"Is someone hurt?"

I grabbed Ruby's hand and squeezed it. "I don't want you to exert yourself after all you've been through, but if you can—at all —we need you."

Her face was grave. "What happened?"

"It's Queen Calista—Queen of the Fae. She was stabbed by the horn of a demon named Mortock, and we think she's dying."

"Jeez. That's terrible. Sure, I'll help if I can. Once I've recovered a bit, I think—"

"Aaagh!"

That was me, unfortunately. I wish I could say it was someone else, but nope. Because I had my head half-turned to face Ruby and was able to see behind us...and what I saw was bad. Like really bad. Like really, *really* bad.

A giant red dragon with golden scales along its underside was rising from the top of the skyscraper we'd just left. The one whose penthouse was still swarming with vampires. Well, now above that penthouse was this huge dragon, its great wings pumping, smoke rising in twin trails from its quivering nostrils. Its great amber eyes with their slitted pupils seemed to shine with their own lights, and like searchlights they scoured the skies—and fixed on us.

Ruby, seeing my face go pale, turned in her seat. Then she too let out a strangled gasp.

"Davril," I said, and pointed.

He must have looked in his rearview mirror (I didn't turn to find out; my gaze was fixed firmly on the dragon) because he loosed another Fae swear. Someday, I would have to learn what he was saying. If I lived long enough. Right now that seemed damned unlikely.

"Walsh!" Ruby said. "It must be Walsh."

"But...but...he only absorbs fire, he doesn't become a dragon," I said with some attempt at reasonability.

"Evidently he's absorbed enough of the former that he can become the latter," said Davril from the front seat.

"Thank you, Dr. Spock," I said.

"That's *Mr.* Spock," Ruby corrected me. "Dr. Spock was someone else."

"I really don't think that's important right now."

The dragon—Walsh—was barreling toward us. The few aerial vehicles and magical steeds between the penthouse and Lady Kay hastily found somewhere else to be. I saw a pair of cops riding griffons pop out of an alley where they'd been lurking, waiting to catch some drunken aristos riding their pegasi badly—the cops popped out, took one look at the dragon, glanced at each other, then ducked back into the alley.

Real helpful, guys. They were probably just radioing for backup, but still.

"Um, Davril," I said. "Please go faster?"

He mashed the gas. Lady Kay bucked forward, and Ruby and I braced ourselves against the backseat.

"Shit," she said. She sounded far less bleary now. A huge dose of adrenaline can do wonders.

"Fuck," I corrected her. "This is definitely a 'fuck' situation."

"I bow to your expertise, Sailor Jane."

Behind us, Walsh, smoke trailing out behind him, gained on us.

His wings were so wide he couldn't fly between the buildings but had to go above them. He blotted out the stars overhead. Something cold slithered up my spine.

Ruby and I held hands tightly.

This was it. At any moment dragonfire would consume us, and then it would all be over. Without us, Queen Calista would die and the Shadow would prevail, whatever its true agenda was. Ironic that dragon's fire, that thing I had been trying so damned hard to recover for so long, would be my undoing. At least I would die with Ruby at my side.

Above, fire bloomed in the back of Walsh's mouth; I could see it past his sharp fangs growing brighter and brighter, hotter and hotter. Then it shot out right toward us. In seconds, it would roast us alive.

CHAPTER 22

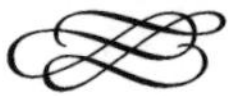

I cried out as I felt the heat of the dragonfire approach and cringed closer to Ruby. She held my hand so tight it was painful.

The car jerked suddenly. Davril swung us around the corner of a building and down a cross-avenue. The plume of fire shot through the space we'd just been, then faded, turning to smoke.

I whooped. So did Ruby beside me.

"We're alive," she said.

I turned back to Davril. "Good driving."

"Thanks," he said, jaw bunched. "We have to get back to my castle. Its walls can protect us."

"Even against dragonfire?"

His eyes briefly met mine, then turned back to the aerial "road". "That's what they were made for," he said.

I didn't have time to wonder what he meant. Ruby gave another cry, and I spun to see Walsh make the turn and sweep through the skies overhead, still on our trail. His nostrils were like chimneys, smoke pouring from them in thick black streams. He must be preparing another blast, I thought.

"Do you have any magic that can be used against him?" I asked Ruby.

"I..." I could see her start to say no, but then she smiled and snapped her fingers. "Lightning!"

I gestured as if seating someone at a table. "Go to it."

Grinning, she cast her hands out and muttered some strange words, too fast for me to understand, all the while making elaborate movements with her hands and fingers. Above, lightning flickered among the clouds, lighting them up from within. Below the dark masses, Walsh slithered through the skies, his amber gaze fixed on us. His maw opened and fire gathered in the back of his throat again, growing brighter with every second.

Ruby made a chopping gesture. A bright tongue of electricity flickered down from the heavens and struck Walsh right in his scaly back. Walsh bellowed. His mouth snapped shut. The fire died.

"You saved us," I said, and gave Ruby a high five.

She nodded shakily. "I-I can't do that anymore. Not if you want me to have strength left to save this queen of yours."

"Save it," Davril said. "I've got this."

I liked the sound of that.

"Hurry," I told him.

Above, Walsh was hunting us again, the pain of the lightning strike evidently having retreated. His wings stretched out, stroking the air, and he moved faster. Fire flickered between his fangs, some spilling out past his lips. It was growing brighter.

Davril swung us around another corner, then another. Walsh couldn't get a clean shot at us. Behind him, from time to time, I could see specks that might have been police officers on griffons, but they were too far away for me to be certain. There was a dozen of them now, but they still didn't attack. Doubtless they were waiting for one of their few warlocks or witches to join them before engaging Walsh. Smart. But not helpful to us at the moment.

Threading our way through the city, we finally broke out into the open space between tall buildings. Ahead reared the gorgeous skyscraper Davril's huge, dark-walled castle stood upon, with all its scarred sides and thick towers.

"That's where you live?" Ruby asked Davril, awe in her voice.

"That's my home," Davril said, his own voice flecked with both pride and sadness.

He mashed the gas pedal again, and Lady Kay shot straight for the castle. I glanced back and up to see Walsh tuck his wings and dive for us. Shit, he was moving fast. No buildings blocked his way, either.

We're toast.

The gates of Davril's castle burst open. Out flooded two dozen Fae Knights on pegasi. The horses' wings flashed under the stars, as did the knights' swords. They flew right up toward us. Some weren't armed with swords but staffs or mirrors or other magical devices, and the Fae turned these on the dragon even as it bore down on us.

Fire licked at Walsh's lips and started to spill over.

The blasts of the magical staffs and mirrors struck the wyrm, and Walsh bellowed in pain but drove on. The fire died back down again, though. I knew that would only last for a moment.

The Fae continued blasting him. Enraged, Walsh veered off and flew wide around. He passed beyond the walls of the castle and kept going.

"He's circling around for another pass," Davril said.

I pointed at the open gates. "Let's get in before he comes back."

Davril stomped on the gas, making right for the gates. I cheered inwardly. The knights on their flying steeds flew around us and escorted us back to the castle in a brilliant cloud. I admired all the handsome and beautiful (some were women) Fae Knights on their equally splendid horses, but only for an instant. My eyes jerked to the right as I saw a huge winged shape burst out from the around the side of the pocked wall.

"He's coming back around," I said, horribly aware of the shrillness of my voice.

"Almost there," said Davril.

Fire gathered again at Walsh's mouth. The riders blasted him once more with their weapons, but this time, he was prepared. He came on, the blasts just glancing off the thick hide of his armor.

Davril flew us through the gate, the other knights with us. Instantly, the doors slammed shut.

I heard a great whoosh of flame, then saw the gates buckle under the heated barrage of Walsh's fire. The gates even glowed orange for a second, or started to, then faded. On the other side, Walsh roared. A moment later, I saw his huge winged form rise over the walls. More Fae were gathered there, a substantial number of them, and they had many weapons with them, some mounted on cannons or catapults. They let loose on him, and a hundred magical bursts exploded all along his length.

He bellowed in rage again, then began circling the castle, but at a distance this time.

Knights surrounded us, along with the Sisters of the Order of Elshe. One checked Ruby while I stood and got my bearings. Things were moving too fast. I could hardly catch my breath.

"Are you all right?" Davril said.

The kindness in his voice shocked me. "You almost sound like you care," I said.

He blinked. I cursed myself for a fool. That hadn't sounded very friendly.

"I only meant..." I fumbled lamely.

He waved it off. "Never mind. But you're fine?"

I nodded, then turned to Ruby. "How are you, sis?"

She smiled weakly while Liara, the white-haired Fae woman, scanned her with a glowing rock atop a scepter. "Ask her," Ruby said.

I did, and Liara said, "She'll be fine. She just needs food and rest."

Outside the walls, Walsh roared loudly. Then, surprisingly, he spoke: "*Stay in there and hide, Jade McClaren. You are now my enemy, and I will have you. You can make me destroy that castle and murder all your friends to get to you, or you can simply present yourself to me.*"

I gasped. Ruby stood and gripped my arm. She looked as stricken as I felt.

"*You have one hour to decide,*" Walsh said. Then his voice turned sinister. "*Or maybe your new friends will decide for you.*"

He laughed, then flew on.

Swallowing, I glanced at the Fae all around me, and I saw them looking back. Hastily, they glanced away. Shit. Would they really do it? Would they kick me out?

And should I let them?

"Don't think about it," Ruby said.

I cleared my throat. "Think about what?"

"Come on."

I had to take a moment. "Maybe...maybe I should. Go out, I mean."

"No."

This came, surprisingly, from Davril.

I turned to him. "How can you say that? I thought you, of all people, would want me to go out there."

He stared at me hard, and I felt my belly do strange things.

"Then you thought wrong," he said, but he didn't say it meanly.

His eyes nearly melted me. They were hotter than Walsh's fire. Gulping, I just nodded, but my gaze never left his.

Ruby cleared her throat to get our attention. Reluctantly, I gave her mine. "Do you want me to heal this queen of yours or what?" she said. "I better do it before I pass out."

"Do you have the strength?" I said. "I don't think we should push you right now. You've been through a lot. Besides, I don't know what good that will do now. Walsh is about to tear through the walls."

Davril was speaking to the knights privately. When he was

done, they scattered, returning to the walls. When he returned his attention to Ruby and me, he looked thoughtful. "Queen Calista can drive off this dragon. She became a master at it during the Dark Times, right before we were driven from our lands."

I didn't ask what he meant by this. I supposed I would find out sooner or later. It must tie into Davril's odd dislike of dragon shifters. "You really think she's strong enough for…him?" I hiked a thumb at the walls.

"Trust me," Davril said.

Frowning, I raised my eyebrows at Ruby. "You think you're up to healing her?"

She bit her lip nervously, then nodded. "I can do it. If it will save us all, I can do." She snorted a laugh. "Hell yeah!"

I grinned. "Then let's get to it."

Surrounded by sisters of the Order of Elshe, we rushed into their tower while behind us Walsh gave another tremendous roar, and I could hear the booms and zizzes of magical attacks. By the continued sound of flapping wings, I guessed they hadn't worked very well.

We passed into the tower and up the stairs at a rush. Liara guided us to the infirmary on the fourth floor where Queen Calista was being kept. Breathless, Ruby examined Calista while Liara, Davril and I eyed each other anxiously. Ruby requested several magical items be brought to her, and Liara went to oversee it. When she came back, Ruby began her work.

"Wait for me outside," she told Davril and me. "I need peace and privacy."

"Can you save her?" Davril asked.

"Yes. But only if you wait outside."

We obeyed and moved to the antechamber, where we paced restlessly and stared out of the high windows. Walsh roared outside, and from time to time I could see him glide past the walls, a huge shadow with flame licking at his lips. The Fae continued to repel him, but I wondered how long they could hold out. I jumped at Walsh's every roar.

Davril and I tried not to look at each other, but we were the only ones there, and there was a lot that hadn't been said between us. I wasn't even sure what there was to say. Maybe we'd said it all. Maybe it was over before it had ever begun. Or maybe whatever *it* was had only been in my head all along.

There it was. It was a horrible thought, but it might be true.

"You know," Davril said suddenly, and I turned to him abruptly. Our eyes met, and I felt a heat course through me. We glanced away from each other. "I..."

"Yes?" I said.

He hesitated, then closed his mouth. "Nothing."

We both turned back to staring out separate windows. On the other side of the wall, the griffon-mounted police were battling the Walsh-dragon. Their mage must have finally showed up. Walsh didn't seem concerned by their attacks, however. Occasionally, he would blast them with his fire, but their mage kept them shielded from the flames. He could do that much, at least.

I turned to Davril. "You know, it doesn't have to be like this."

"Like what?" Wind from the open window ruffled his gorgeous blond hair and misted his eyes.

"Like... Never mind. You really think Queen Calista can drive Walsh off?"

"I'm certain of it. If your sister can save her. Are *you* certain she can?"

"Damn right."

I glared at him for a moment, then softened. I could see his facial muscles relax, just a bit. We were both way too keyed up. I wasn't sure whether to be angrier or more apologetic. I *was* furious with him. He'd acted liked such an ass. But at the same time, I had betrayed him...and his queen.

Finally, Davril said, "What would you have done if I hadn't said yes?"

"Excuse me?"

"When you said you needed to rescue Ruby to save Queen Calista. If I hadn't agreed, would you have gone anyway?"

Would you have deserted me and the Queen? I heard, even though he didn't say so exactly.

I opened my mouth to answer. Outside, Walsh roared so loudly the rafters shook, and I jumped again.

"Well?" said Davril.

I balled my fists at my sides. "I would have saved Ruby—"

"I thought as—"

"—*and* saved the Queen."

He shut his mouth midsentence and stared at me in obvious surprise. He watched me for a long minute, and I tried to get a read on him but couldn't. Damn, but he was tight. At last, he said, with the faintest hint of a smile (which sent a thrill through me), "You know, I believe you."

"You do?"

His smile, or the hint of it, widened, just a bit. My heart sang. "Yes," he said.

Before I could say something else and prolong this amazing moment, the side door opened and three knights entered. The leader saluted Davril and said, "Sir, we received a message from the Palace before your return."

"And some reinforcements," Davril added. "Half those knights belong to the Palace."

"Yes, sir." The troop leader nodded to one of the other knights, who removed his helm and nodded to Davril. I recognized him as Lord Greenleaf, Queen Calista's Grand Vizier. I'd met him briefly the night of the feast.

"The Palace is being put back in order," Greenleaf said, "and the witch and her trolls are gone. But before they left, they accessed the Compendium."

"Damn," Davril said. "What are they up to?"

"I'm not sure, but they've taken something from it. I'll tell you more about that later. For now, you need to know that Prince Jereth has been contacted."

Davril's eyes widened. "What?"

Greenleaf passed a hand across his face. "He is the Heir, Davril, and the Queen was—and might still be—dying. He needed to be contacted. Even now, he's making his way back here, back to the Palace. If the Queen isn't healed, and soon, Prince Jereth will be King Jereth."

"Shit," I said. "I mean, excuse me, but isn't this the same prince that wants to open portals to the Fae Lands? The same prince who would let the Shadow pour into this world, too?"

"I'm afraid so," Greenleaf said.

I shook my head. "You guys really need to look into elections or something. A blood lineage isn't always the way to go."

"It would appear not," Davril said.

"That's treason," Greenleaf said, but he didn't sound as if he disagreed.

In any case, it was clear. If Calista died, so too would the world. *No pressure, Ruby*. I thought of running in and telling her that, but I held myself back. That would probably only make her more nervous.

The doors to the informatory opened. Liara emerged, looking drained. I rushed to her.

"Is it good news?" I said.

CHAPTER 23

Liara smiled and nodded, and I could see tears standing out in her eyes. "My lady lives," she said. "Thanks to your sister."

I hugged her. Though startled, she hugged me back. I then turned to hug Davril, but things got awkward and he just sort of patted me on the back instead. Trying not to sigh, I dashed into the hospital room to behold Ruby bending over Queen Calista, who was sitting up and blinking. Ruby looked pale and sweaty, and I knew she was wiped out. I went to her and embraced her, and I could feel how exhausted she was in her hug.

"Sit down," I told her, and guided her to a chair. Grateful, she sat, and she instantly closed her eyes and began to snore.

Smiling widely, I turned to regard Queen Calista. Color had returned to her cheeks, and her eyes shone brightly. "Your sister saved my life," she told me as Davril and Liara entered. The other knights stayed outside.

"Don't tell her that," I said, "or else her head will grow so big she won't be able to enter a room."

Calista smiled. I rejoiced at how strong that smile was. Davril seemed to see it, too.

"You look well, Your Majesty," he said, taking her hand and bowing to kiss it.

"Thank you. I feel it."

He grimaced, then seemed to hesitate, as if reluctant to ask what he knew he must. "Do you feel well enough to take on a dragon?"

"A *dragon?*"

As if on cue, Walsh roared outside, and the walls shook. Startled, Queen Calista glanced upward.

"What is this?" she said.

"Long story," I said. "But Davril says you're an old hand at fighting dragons."

Walsh roared again. The surprise left Calista's features, replaced by determination. "Give me a staff," she said.

Davril gave an order. In moments, a Fae Knight was pushing a staff into the Queen's hands, bowing as he did so. She looked at it, firmed her chin, and rose from the bed. Davril offered to help her, but she waved him away, and I was amazed at how steady on her feet she was. Ruby had done a hell of a job on her. Casting a glance at my sister, I saw she was still snoring softly. I grabbed a blanket and tucked her in.

"Let's go," Queen Calista said.

She swept from the room, all regal imperiousness, and Davril, Liara, Greenleaf and I were pulled along in her wake. We bustled back through the halls of the Order's tower, then outside. Head held high, Calista moved across the courtyard at a brisk walk as Walsh made another pass outside. He spat out another gob of flame on the wall's defenders, but one Fae raised a staff and the flame dispersed to either side as if having hit an invisible shield, which I suppose it had.

"Hand the woman over or you all die! Your hour is up, Jade," Walsh thundered, hovering in midair before the defenders and leveling his piercing gaze at them. One of the mages blasted him with

another magical attack, and three more joined in. The blue and yellow bolts merely glanced off his armor.

Queen Calista mounted the stairs leading up to the wall's walkway, and everyone scurried after her.

"Begone, wyrm!" she shouted, her voice magically augmented and probably audible for miles around.

Walsh's terrible amber gaze latched onto her. Amusement entered his voice. *"Is this the Queen of the Fae herself, come to do battle with me?"*

"It is I, Queen Calista, and you will begone—now!—or you will suffer my wrath!"

Walsh coughed something that might have been a laugh. *"Look at you, you can barely stand. You couldn't harm a fly."*

He had better senses than I did, I thought, because Calista still looked remarkably strong to me. But then, Walsh *was* far stronger than I was or could ever be. His keener senses shouldn't surprise me. Especially since some of them had probably *come* from me—that is, my fire.

"You had your chance," Calista said.

Without wasting another moment, she leveled her staff at him. A great energy crackled around her, building up inside her. The magic didn't come from the staff, I knew, she was merely using that to channel it through, sort of like a gun firing a bullet. Only *she* was the bullet. Or something like that, anyway.

A bright orange column of energy flooded out from the end of the staff and poured directly into Walsh. The column struck his chest, driving him back, and he roared, this time in pain and fury. The magical blast didn't deflect off his armor like the others had, and it kept on going, just pounding him and pounding him like some sort of magical firefighter water hose.

He opened his mouth to hurl fire at Calista—and the rest of us, since we were all gathered around her—but she simply waved a hand, taking it off the staff for a moment, and Walsh's fire died in his throat, becoming smoke instead. Coughing on the smoke, assaulted by her continuous blasts of energy, Walsh was driven from the walls foot by foot.

"You go, girl!" I told Calista, ignoring Davril's frown. For his part, he had drawn his sword and was holding it firm, as if prepared to leap onto Walsh's head if the dragon-mage should come too close. "Get him!" I added to Calista.

She did. She pushed Walsh back and back, and the Fae along the wall cheered. The magic-users among them joined their weapons with hers, and in seconds two dozen blasts of energy were assaulting Walsh.

"You haven't seen the last of me," he bellowed.

He pumped his wings hard, turned about, and flew away. The Fae along the wall continued to cheer. I pumped my fist and started to pat Calista on the back, then thought better of it. We watched Walsh recede into the night until he was just a speck in the darkness, then not even that.

"You've done it, Your Majesty," Liara told Calista. "You've saved us all."

Calista was breathing hard, and a sheen of sweat had broken out on her brow. She was now leaning on the staff for support, not using it as a weapon. Just the same, she still looked regal and powerful.

She nodded once, accepting the praise. "He is a mighty foe," she said. "Who is he?"

Attention swung to me, and a nervous flutter coursed through me. "I'm sorry, ma'am," I said. "I'm afraid I'm the one who brought him here."

"You?"

Davril stepped in. "To save you, Your Majesty, we had to save a human witch from that monster, who happens to be an old enemy of Jade. He pursued us after we liberated the witch. Fortunately, it worked, and she was able to heal you."

"And you were able to save us all," Liara put in.

I was grateful for Davril's help, but also surprised. I watched his face, but I could get no reading off him.

Fortunately, Calista wasn't so inscrutable. She smiled widely, took one of my hands, and squeezed it, which was as close to a hug as queens probably allowed themselves. Her skin was hot and as smooth and soft as butter. I wondered what hand lotion she used, or if she used any at all. Maybe Fae were like that naturally.

"Then I owe you a debt of gratitude," Calista said.

"Um, well, thanks," I said. "Maybe, you know, you could like not prosecute me?"

"Prosecute you?"

"Well, Davril locked me up and everything, then went to report me to you."

Surprise passed across Calista's face, but then she smiled. "My dear, Lord Stormguard may have done what he felt necessary, but the reason he was with me in the Throne Room when you came upon us during Angela's assault was not to report your misdeeds —well, not exactly; he did have to tell me why he locked you up— but that's not what he was doing. He was *defending* you to me. He was arguing for your *release*."

I gasped. My eyes jerked to Davril. His own eyes looked back for a moment, then, clearly uncomfortable, turned away. I felt a strange heat flutter in my chest.

Ruining the moment, Lord Greenleaf stepped forward. "My lady, Prince Jereth is even now on his way to the Palace. If you do not retake your throne before he arrives, he might well install himself as Lord of the Fae."

Calista blinked, then straightened her spine. She held herself up on her own two feet, no longer using the staff.

"Take me to the Palace," she said.

Ten minutes later saw us all flying in wedge formation over the city toward the Palace. I kept expecting Walsh to come barreling at us out of the darkness, but there was no sign of him. I wondered how long he could maintain his dragon form. Most likely, he was off licking his wounds somewhere. I hoped Calista had hurt him bad. But not too bad. I still wanted to be the one who ended him.

We arrived at the Palace to find it being put back together. Blood was being mopped up, bodies arrayed in lines, halls that had been half-collapsed were being made accessible again. Fae bowed to Queen Calista as she picked her way through the corridors. I was stunned and horrified by the devastation, even though I'd expected it. Angela was a powerful enemy, too, I realized. More powerful than anyone could have guessed.

Breathless, Jessela came rushing up to us just before we entered the Throne Room. "Your Majesty," she cried, and bowed. "You're alive!"

"I am, thank you," said Calista. Lord Greenleaf attempted to shoo Jessela off, but Calista stopped him.

"I just wanted to say, Your Majesty, that we couldn't have defeated the trolls without the help of Jade," Jessela said, and flashed a smile at me. I returned it. "Her quick thinking allowed us to concoct a poison that put them down. Without her, the trolls would have completely overrun us."

"Then it looks like I owe you another debt," Queen Calista told me.

Pride flushed through me, but I just gave a nod.

All together, we entered the Throne Room. Bodies were being carried away, but the marks on the great crystal stairs where the trolls had smashed at them weren't so easily removed. Maybe magic could fix it. But I knew magic could never fix some things. The memory of the battle here would haunt me for a long time.

With amazing dignity, Calista mounted the scarred stairs, paused to survey her gorgeous crystal throne, which was still intact, then turned and gracefully sat down in it. Her crown had rolled aside during the battle, but Davril picked it up and handed it to her, and she put it on her head.

Davril knelt. So did the other Fae, until I was the only one standing. Embarrassed, I knelt, too.

"All hail the Queen!" Davril said, and the others took up the cry—more even than I'd expected. Turning, I could see that all the Fae had entered the Throne Room, or at least what looked like all of them—thousands knelt among the splintered foliage and shattered trees of the main floor, and their voices were thunderous.

"All hail the Queen!" they said, and at their words, something stirred inside me. "All hail the Queen!"

I turned back to the throne to see Calista looking most queenly indeed, even smiling slightly, and at the sight of her sitting there with such pride and power and decency, something moved inside me, and when the next cry came I joined in.

"All hail the Queen!" the Fae roared, and I said it along with them.

"All hail the Queen!"

EPILOGUE

"Look! Isn't that gorgeous?" Ruby said, her eyes lighting up. She reached forward and held aloft a gnarled broomstick etched with ancient runes and banded in gold and copper loops.

"It's nice," I said, "but look at that price tag."

Ruby frowned, looked at the tag, and winced. "Ouch."

"It's worth every penny," the vendor said. We were in one of the magical markets of Gypsy Land close to where we lived, and the vendor looked like a lot of the others here—dressed in layers of black, wearing a lot of necklaces, fetishes, and way too much black makeup around the eyes, even though he was a guy. Gypsies, go figure.

"I'm sure it is, but I don't have it," Ruby said as she put the broomstick back on its rack.

We continued on, pressing deeper into the magical maze. Wonderful displays were all around us, and cool magical items for sale. I saw one woman demonstrating magic wands on a series of unfortunate dummies in one corner, another offering love potions to lonely people in another, and more. One vendor hawked magical beer that—supposedly—I knew better—gave no hangover, while a fellow sporting bristling mustaches with oiled rings in them tried to sign people up for a ride on his pegasus-drawn carriage. The pegasi themselves snorted and stamped if anyone drew too close, but I had to admit their wings were gorgeous.

Ruby paused before one shop, and I felt my cheeks warm to see all the erotic merchandise on display—*magical* erotic merchandise.

"Maybe we should just—" Ruby started, but I dragged her away.

"I don't think so," I said.

"Prude!"

"Ha! I just don't think I want to shop there with my *sister*."

"Oh, so you'll come back as soon as you drop me off at home, huh?"

I grinned. "Well, you *are* only twenty."

"Twenty-one!"

"In two weeks."

Her expression fell, and we paused a moment. I knew she must be thinking about Jason—the last time we'd been discussing her upcoming birthday had been around him. It had been a huge blow to Ruby to learn of his death, but in the last few days she'd been slowly coming out of it. We were just lucky to be alive ourselves, and she knew it.

I wrapped my arm around her shoulders and we forged on.

"You know, it is good to have you back," I said softly.

She leaned her head against me. "Yeah. It is. I'm awesome."

I blew air past my lips, making a raspberry noise.

"Well, I *am*," she pressed.

"I guess. When you're not acting like a brat. Which is most of the time."

"I did save the Queen of the Fae."

"Yeah, but who saved you?"

A throat cleared behind us, and we spun.

Davril was standing there, his arms folded across his chest, looking most handsome. He wore his street clothes, a tight shirt stretched across his abs and deep chest with a brown leather jacket on top and jeans encasing his muscular legs below. He also wore a small smile.

"You did have a little help," he said.

Suddenly, I couldn't speak. "Er," I tried.

Ruby looked from Davril to me, then back. She beamed wickedly. "Hey, Davril," she said in her most sultry voice.

I resisted the urge to strangle her.

Davril had eyes only for me, though. "The Queen would like a word with you."

Was that disappointment I felt? *Jeez, girl, get a grip*. "The Queen, huh?" I said.

He unfolded his arms and gestured behind him. I saw Lady Kay parked along the curb, white wings folded at her side.

"May I take you to her?" he said.

"I don't know," I said. "Ruby and I were just shopping."

"You go on ahead," Ruby said. "I'll just go back to the sex shop."

"Sex shop?" Davril said.

"Don't you dare," I told Ruby. "You go straight home."

"Do I *have* to?" she pouted.

"Yes!"

"Allll right."

We hugged again and she sauntered off through the crowd, oohing and ahhing over every little thing. *She better not go back to the sex shop*, I thought, but I had to admit to the possibility that she would. Slut.

I turned back to Davril, and we regarded each other in silence for a moment. Well, not *silence*. There was plenty of noise all around us, firecrackers going off, salesmen and -women hawking their wares, the sound of meat frying. My mouth watered at the smell. The sight of Davril didn't hurt, either.

"Well, shall we?" He nodded his head at the car.

Suck it up, Jade. "Let's go."

He opened the passenger door for me and I slid in, loving the feel of the smooth leather under my fingers.

"Glad to be up front this time," I said as he dropped behind the wheel.

"Yeah, sorry about that." He mashed buttons, flipped a switch, and we rose into the air, Lady Kay's wings unfolding beside us. People turned to stare as we went up. Several pointed and snapped selfies.

"Wait, did you just *apologize* to me?" I said.

"Well, I was wrong. Kind of."

He twisted the wheel and guided us through the air between towers of steel and glass and stone. It was nighttime, and the city was laid out like a collection of glittering jewels all around us.

"You *were* going to betray us," he added. Before I could protest, he said, "But I understand. Walsh had your sister. You were only doing what you had to do. Or at least that's how you saw it."

"How *I* saw it? Wouldn't you have done the same thing?"

Wryly, Davril said, "If it had been *my* brother?"

"Okay, bad example."

We drove on. I fidgeted.

"What's this about, anyway?" I said. "What does the Queen want from me?"

"I'll let her tell you that." He paused, seeming to debate something, then said, "What do you intend to do now?"

"*Do* now? I don't get you."

"Well...after all this...you're not going back to your old life, are you?"

And Ruby called *me* the prude. "I'll have you know, Ruby and I were just about to plot our next burglary, actually. Against a very bad guy who deserves to get taken down a peg. Why, is that beneath you, all high and mighty up in your castle?"

"Yes, and it should be beneath you, too."

A flash of anger rose in me. "Why, you sanctimonious sack of—"

"Whoa, whoa."

For a moment, I wasn't sure if he was talking to me or Lady Kay. Then I realized he must mean me. I crossed my arms across my chest and waited.

"Yes?" I prodded.

"I just meant..." He frowned. "I would want better for you. I would want better *of* you."

"Well, too bad, Mr. Fae Knight. I steal stuff from bad guys. One day, I'll get good enough to steal my fire back from Walsh, if I can find him. That's it. The end. I don't have any greater calling or purpose, other than to be a good sister and to try to make this world a little better by what I do. If that's not good enough for you, then screw you. Also, what am I doing here?"

"You're here because the Queen requests your presence, not me."

I started to say something, then clamped my mouth shut. I didn't want to say something I'd regret, and I was already afraid I might have. Besides, my emotions were so stirred up I didn't even know *what* I wanted to say, or what I really did think. I felt so many different things, and so many of them conflicted with each other. Why couldn't things go back to being simple again? Before all of this had started, things had been a lot more clear.

But also, and I had to admit this, kind of crappier. Before being exposed to the world of the Fae...before Davril...I'd been, well, lonely and depressed, really. Trapped in a sad cycle of crime and revenge that might never come, and if it did come it might consume me. But now...now I knew a different world existed. A world of righteousness, of good against evil. Of nobility and purity and magic. And a dashing, tortured Fae Knight who obviously felt *something* for me, though just what that was I wasn't sure, and I wasn't sure I wanted to know, either. Sometimes, the fantasy was better than the reality.

Ahead of us, the skyscrapers opened out, and there in their midst was the greatest one of all, the glorious spires of the Palace rising from its tip like the most beautiful flower in the world. The moonlight stroked its white towers with loving, ghostly fingers.

Davril set Lady Kay down in one of the hangars. Lord Greenleaf, the Grand Vizier, met us along with a contingent of knights. For a moment, I feared they'd come to arrest me and tensed, but Greenleaf only smiled and said, "Welcome back to the Palace, Mistress McClaren."

"Mistress?"

"It is that or Lady, and, well..." Lord Greenleaf swallowed. "At any rate, may I take you both to the Queen?"

"Please," Davril said quickly, as if to forestall any more awkwardness. I was grateful.

"I could be a lady," I snarked to him as we walked through the halls.

"I'm sure," was all he said.

I'd show him how a lady can be, I thought.

"By the way, whatever happened to the people at that penthouse?" I asked. "The ones the vamps had put in their thrall?"

"I returned to Hartson Tower to find the vampires gone and the residents confused and weak, drained of blood," Davril said. "We restored them and helped them put their home back in order. They're fine now, or at least as good as they can be."

That was something, at least.

On the way to the Throne Room, I noted how much work the Fae had done restoring the place. Walls that had been collapsed and columns that had been smashed were back to normal, and there was no sign of any bodies or bloodstains, thank goodness. I could see many of the Fae dressed in gray, however, their color of mourning, and knew that the dead rested heavily on their hearts. Davril and Greenleaf looked somber now, too, as if passing through these corridors reminded them of the Fae lost here during the attack.

Soon, we came to the grand doors the trolls had guarded that terrible day and we passed into the Throne Room. Many of the trees and other foliage that had grown here were gone, simply removed, but I saw a whole bunch of new plants shooting up, some still the bright green of young plants everywhere. It smelled heavenly as we cut through the forest to approach the stairs leading up to the throne, and I noticed a whole riot of red and purple flowers, each one as big as my face and framed by curls of bright green leaves. As if in a dream, I almost floated up the stairs, and in moments I—and Davril, too; Lord Greenleaf was hanging back—stood before the throne.

Queen Calista smiled down at us. Her throne was raised, and she was just above our eye level. But not much. She was no cold and lofty ruler, but warm and personable. But still a ruler and very respected. It was clear she had the love of her people.

"Thank you for gracing us with your presence, my dear," Queen Calista told me.

"I wouldn't call it *gracing*," I said. "More *debasing*, really." Hadn't Davril just told me I was a no-good criminal?

One corner of Davril's mouth quirked. "I think that was for me, not you, Your Majesty," he told his queen.

"I don't understand," she said.

"It's okay," I said. "Look, I'm sorry. It was a stupid thing to say. I'm really glad to be back. You've really done a lot to fix the place back up." I realized I was sounding like a jerk but wasn't sure how to *not* sound like a jerk. It was either be overly impressed and look like a dweeb or act aloof and above-it-all. I tried to find a third option, but it just wasn't working for me.

"Why, thank you," Calista said, as if I hadn't been so classless. "We have you to thank for it."

"Oh. Um, it was nothing. The least I could do." I mentally kicked myself. Was I *trying* to piss her off? My foot was like magnetically compelled to insert itself in my mouth.

"You did us a great service, and we treated you abysmally," Calista said, still as graceful as anyone could be. "Isn't that right, Lord Stormguard?"

I could see him grinding his teeth. Sometimes, he wasn't very stoic at all. Had *I* done that to him? If so, that somehow made me happy. I was getting to him.

"It is, Your Majesty," he said. "I…was wrong to distrust her." He swallowed a deep breath, then turned to me in a strangely formal way. "Mistress Jade of the House McClaren, I beg your apology for mistrusting you."

"Didn't we already do this?" I said.

"I…want the Queen to witness. I do apologize, Jade."

I narrowed my eyes. "Why?"

He started to narrow his own eyes, and I could almost see the thought *Are you really going to make me say it?* flash across his face.

I planted my hands on my hips. *I am.*

He steeled himself, then said, "Locking you up nearly cost you your life, Jade. What's more, it nearly cost Her Majesty her life. If I'd just trusted you to begin with, none of that would have happened. Do you accept my apology?"

I made him wait a moment, then said, "I do." Then I added, "I guess."

"Very well," Queen Calista said. "I'm glad. Now, Jade, if I may call you that, I have something to discuss with you."

I started to say *Yeah?*, but then made myself take my hands off my hips, lower them to my side, and say, "Yes, ma'am?"

She folded her hands in her lap and her face grew serious. "We have prevailed over our enemies, thanks to you, Jade, but they are still out there, are they not? Mistress Angela was foiled in murdering me and installing my son on this throne, but she did succeed in accessing the Compendium."

I remembered Greenleaf mentioning that. "What for?"

"We don't know," Davril said. The thought clearly bothered him. He didn't try to hide it.

"She took something," Calista said. "Some piece of knowledge that might help her cause."

"Which is?" I said.

"The Shadow. I could feel its mark upon her when we fought."

"Damn."

"Yes. She was hoping to replace me with Jereth so that he would open the portals back to the Fae Lands. Obviously her master can't do it from his side. I'm afraid that whatever information she stole from the Compendium will further that end."

"Can't Federico tell you?"

Calista's lips thinned. "Unfortunately, when I say she took information, what I mean is she took Federico."

I put a hand over my mouth. "My God! Poor Federico. Is he okay?"

"I don't believe he's in danger. She'll need him to succeed… with whatever her agenda is. And it's not just her we must contend with now, but this Vincent Walsh as well."

"I'm sorry about bringing him to your doorstep."

"Don't be. I'm glad you revealed him to us. He would have shown himself to us sooner or later. He has not hidden from us since our arrival because he's a friend, after all."

I snapped my fingers. "*That's* why I haven't been able to find him. He's been hiding from you guys. But why?"

"Again, we don't know."

"We also don't know what he wants with the antler," Davril said.

I nodded. "We got Ruby back, but he got something, too, didn't he? And if he's no friend of yours, that could be something to use against you someday, right?"

"That is what we'd been thinking, yes," Calista said. She drew herself up and fixed me with a stern yet warm gaze. "Jade McClaren, because of all these reasons, we have concluded that we need an ally. A human ally. And I don't mean the police or the politicians. We have plenty of them. We need a smart, capable person aware of the magical world, but also with a toehold in the criminal underworld, as that seems to be where our enemies operate from. We need you, Jade McClaren."

"*Me?*"

"Tell her, Lord Stormguard."

Davril switched his gaze from his queen to me. I could see the urgency in his eyes, the sincerity. But also, annoyingly, the reluctance. He didn't want to ask for my help, but he knew that's what his queen wanted. Maybe even that that's what the situation demanded.

"We...need your services, Jade."

"My *services?*"

"That's not—I mean that we need you to help us. Only..."

"Yes?"

He grimaced. "We don't deal with spies or assassins, Jade. Our agents are Knights of the Enchanted Realm. Knights of the Nine Thrones. Noble and above reproach."

"Well, that leaves me out."

"Not necessarily," Calista said. "You...could join us."

"Become a Fae?"

"Well...an honorary one, anyway. An honorary citizen of the Nine Thrones who can be granted titles and offices."

"Will that mean giving up my U.S. citizenship? Because that ain't happening."

"We both allow dual citizenship, Jade."

"Well...good." I wondered what Ruby would say. "Then that's one thing." I could sense there was another shoe waiting to drop.

"You would need a sponsor," Calista said. "A trainer. Also, we will need you, as our first human field agent, if you like, to have a liaison with us. An intermediary between this Court and your, well, agenting. It makes sense that this should be the same individual. In other words, you'll need a partner."

Davril looked sharply at Calista. "You can't mean...?"

I almost laughed at his shock. Obviously they hadn't rehearsed this part.

"I'm afraid I do," Calista said.

"Jessela," Davril said. "Make it Jessela!"

"Now now," Calista said. "Jade needs to partner with someone she already has a working relationship with. That person can only be you, Lord Stormguard."

He gnashed his teeth and clenched his fists at his side, for once completely uncaring of how he was seen. Or maybe he *wanted* me to know how annoyed he was at being saddled with me. That was more likely, I thought. And it might even mean something. Because if he was putting on a show, then maybe...well, maybe he wasn't so annoyed, after all.

It wasn't much to cling to, but I would take it.

"Well?" Calista asked me graciously. "Will you accept, Jade? The duty will be dangerous, I know it, but it is vitally important, to your people and mine. And it may help put you on the trail of this Vincent Walsh."

"So you know about that?"

"Indeed I do, and you should know the Fae believe in blood feuds strongly, and in righteous vengeance. We will help you if we can. Or give you the tools to help yourself."

"But only if I join up."

"Only a Fae Knight would have access to those resources." She paused. "Like I said, it will be dangerous. Maybe even deadly. I won't lie to you about that, Jade. If you join with us, you might not live to an old age. But, as a reward, you will be made a knight... and a lady."

"Me...a lady?"

"That's right. A knight must be a lord or lady."

I grinned at Davril, then flashed a thumbs up to Greenleaf behind us. He'd gone rigid.

"Then that seals it," I told Calista.

"Think about this," Davril said.

I looked him right in the face. Oh yeah, I would do this to nettle him if nothing else. And there was a lot more else. Hell, the entire world could be at stake, maybe even two worlds. I would do all I could to stop Walsh, Angela and the Shadow, whatever the heck that really was.

And I did like the sound of Lady Jade.

"Is it really so bad?" I asked Davril. I wanted to know. I mean, if it was a torture for him to be around me, maybe this was a bad idea, after all.

He was silent for a long moment. His anger had drained away, and there was something different in his eyes now when they looked on me. But it wasn't sadness. I remembered Jessela saying that he was always sad, always tortured, and I remembered him being like that in the beginning of our, for lack of a better word, relationship. But he wasn't like that now. Maybe it was me annoying it out of him, but one way or another, I'd had an impact on him. An impact, I thought, for the better.

"No," he said at last, and his voice was a rasp. A thrill ran through me. He added, "It wouldn't be so bad at all."

I turned back to the Queen and bowed. Standing up, I beamed, and I could feel my eyes burning.

"I'm in," I said.

The End

Made in the USA
San Bernardino, CA
30 March 2018